LISTEN TO THE SHADOWS

When artist Katie Summers emerged from a four-day coma, she remembered vividly the horror of that night — the terrifying dead eyes that stared back at her in the rear view mirror, causing her to crash her car. But no one believed her. Released from the hospital, Katie took a taxi to her remote farmhouse on Black Lake. Darkness had already fallen. There was only the wind in the trees to greet her — and the cold, empty house. But the house was not quite empty. Something awaited her, upstairs in her bedroom. Something with cold, dead eyes . . .

JOAN HALL HOVEY

LISTEN TO THE SHADOWS

Complete and Unabridged

ULVERSCROFT
Leicester

First published in
the United States of America in 1991

First Large Print Edition
published 2001

British Library CIP Data

Hovey, Joan Hall
    Listen to the shadows.—Large print ed.—
    Ulverscroft large print series: mystery
    1. Detective and mystery stories
    2. Large type books
    I. Title
    823.9′14 [F]

    ISBN 0–7089–4359–4

Published by
F. A. Thorpe (Publishing)
Anstey, Leicestershire

Set by Words & Graphics Ltd.
Anstey, Leicestershire
Printed and bound in Great Britain by
T. J. International Ltd., Padstow, Cornwall

This book is printed on acid-free paper

For Mel

Prologue

Beneath his attic room, the house slept.

Stealthily, he made his way along the darkened hallway, stopping at a door with peeling green paint. He fitted his key into the lock, turned it, and heard the familiar scraping of wood on linoleum as the door opened inward. His calloused, blunt fingers then groped along the inside wall to his left, found the switch and flicked it on. Instantly, the cramped space was washed in harsh light from a single bulb hanging from the ceiling, revealing a few pieces of scarred, make-do furniture, including a single cot covered by a worn-thin, grey army blanket, drawn so smooth and taut he could have bounced a quarter from its center.

Though shabby, the room was painstakingly neat.

Wearing an air of contained excitement, he strode across the room to where the calendar hung from the wall like a window-blind and advertised A & R Realty in black lettering. He peeled back the months of September and October. Then, taking the pen clipped to his shirt pocket, he drew a red circle around the '5' in the month of November. He saw that the fifth fell on a Sunday. Not that it mattered. He regarded the carefully drawn circle for a few seconds, then dropped the pages, letting them whisper back into place. He moved to the table with its rickety legs that managed to support his double hotplate and serve as his dining table. He opened the table's single drawer, and from beneath a red plastic flatware tray that held only a steak-knife, fork, spoon, can-opener and a butcher-knife, he withdrew a soiled and yellowing envelope. As he shook the photograph from the envelope, his hand trembled.

As he had for many months now, with almost religious dedication, he studied her features, let his gaze travel over her long, shapely body. She was wearing shorts and a halter-top. Her long brown hair blew in the breeze. She smiled out at him in open invitation, her almond-shaped eyes crinkling a little at the corners. Her feet were bare.

The wait was over. Finally. Triumph raced through him, settled like molten lava in his loins. He welcomed the almost painful arousal.

Katie Summers. His patience would be rewarded at last. The debt would be collected.

On November fifth. The day he would kill her.

His eyes lowered to the butcher-knife in the drawer, and he reached in and picked it up. He gripped the black wooden handle, liking the feel — the heft of it. Slowly, thoughtfully, he ran the thumb and forefinger of his left hand over the flat of the blade. Up and down, up and down. Stroking, stroking, until gradually a dull film began to slip over his eyes. Abruptly, the rhythmic movement of his hand stopped. His eyes cleared. He tossed the knife back into the drawer where it clattered to silence.

No. That was not the way he would do it. It felt wrong. And everything must be exactly right. He'd waited a long time.

As his gaze returned to the girl in the photograph, inspiration flashed in his mind. Yes, there was a much better way. A perfect way. A slow smile spread across his features — one that entirely missed his pale, cold eyes.

Ah, yes, Katie Summers, he thought. You will most definitely be worth the wait.

1

Katie Summers breathed in the tangy salt-sea air wafting in through the screened windows of the Surfside Restaurant, blending with the aroma of freshly brewed coffee. Through the glass upper section of her window, she could see the white gulls dipping and soaring, now gliding on a swift current of air, their free spirits causing Katie a moment of envy. On the horizon, the setting October sun was a great orange disc sliding slowly into the sea, streaking the blue sky with spectacular mauves, pinks and gold, cutting a red-bronze path across the water. The scene took Katie's breath; she almost wished she'd brought her paints and easel. She would come here by herself sometime before winter set in, find a perfect vantage point, and paint to her heart's content.

'I take it you approve,' Drake Devlin said, across from her.

It both surprised and touched Katie to see the anxious expression on Drake's boyishly handsome face. 'Approve?' she said, keeping her tone deliberately light. 'A woman would have to be totally without romance in her soul not to appreciate all this.' Keeping her tone teasing, she added, 'The view — the champagne . . . ' She grinned and sipped her wine. The bubbles tickled her nose. Looking at Drake over the rim of her glass, she decided she rather liked the smattering of freckles across his tanned cheeks. Maybe partly because she knew they came not from lounging on a sandy beach somewhere, but from long, hot days of toiling on his father's farm.

'For someone who's got his heart set on becoming a lawyer, Drake Devlin, you are an incredibly romantic man.'

'Someone tell you lawyers aren't romantic?' Katie smiled.

Drake drew forward in his chair, his eyes holding Katie's with an intensity that made her uncomfortable. 'You inspire me, lady,' he said softly, and clinked his glass against hers. 'Here's to inspiration.'

An innocent enough toast, and Katie drank to it. Yet she felt as if the air in the room had thinned slightly; she had the uneasy sensation of going too fast, and in a direction she wasn't at all sure she wanted to travel. Her hand moved to the frilly collar of her gold crepe blouse. She found herself wishing for a cigarette; it would give her something to do with her hands. But she'd given up that increasingly unpopular habit, after numerous failed tries, more than two years ago. Returning her attention to the view outside her window, Katie began to get second thoughts about the wisdom of finally agreeing to a dinner date with Drake. Had she made a mistake?

Drake had been looking at her in that I-mean-to-possess-you way for over a month now. She could count on his coming into The Coffee Shop at some point each day, taking the opportunity between customers to tell her of his dreams and aspirations, refusing absolutely to take no as a serious response to his repeated requests for a date. Katie was the only one surprised when he'd finally worn her down.

That determination and persistence were revealed in the square, slightly jutting jaw, and Katie had to admit to a certain admiration for those qualities; you didn't get too far in this world without them. She liked to think she also possessed her own fair share of determination and persistence, particularly when it came to her work, but she sensed in Drake a drive far more powerful than her own. She had to admit, it frightened her a little — made her feel threatened. Katie tended to shy away from serious, intense men. And Drake certainly was that.

7

Thinking about it now, Katie realized with some surprise that it had been months since she'd accepted a date with anyone, shy or otherwise. Not that she didn't get a respectable number of offers, but somehow they rarely seemed worth the effort. Katie suspected she was fast becoming your stereotypical 'old maid' — set in her ways, jealously guarding her 'space' — needing only her work to sustain her. Yet it was directly the result of that work which led to her high mood, and ultimately to her being here with Drake tonight.

Despite Katie's insistence that she wasn't even close to being ready yet, Mr. Jackson, her art teacher, had gone ahead and submitted several of her paintings to the local art gallery for showing, all of which were now garnering high marks from patrons and critics alike. Two of her paintings had even sold. While it was true that Belleville was a small town, there was a strong appreciation for and awareness of the arts here. The praise had done much for Katie's often flagging confidence which her friend and mentor, Jason, put down to a lack of encouragement and support while growing up. Not that her parents didn't care about her; it was just that they'd been so busy ripping each other apart, there wasn't much room for anything else.

Not so surprising perhaps that at thirty-six years old, reading favorable comments about her work in the local paper was having a deliciously heady effect. She'd, of course, made a point of telling Mr. Jackson how grateful she was for his continued belief in her abilities, but now she wondered if she'd managed to convey the depth of the gratitude she felt. She would find the perfect card, she thought, and send it to him.

'Where did you go, Katie?'

'I'm sorry, Drake,' she said, turning to him and flushing guiltily. 'Did you say something?'

He raised an eyebrow at his drink, then smiled a mildly accusing smile at Katie. 'We were drinking a toast to inspiration,' he said. 'Or at least I was.' He smoothed his sandy, slightly receding hair across his broad forehead. 'What were you so deep in thought about, Katie? Or is that an intrusion?'

'Not at all. Actually, it's sort of in keeping with your toast. I was thinking about my exhibit at the gallery.' Said aloud, it sounded terribly immodest and self-absorbed, and was, she supposed, insensitive. But she felt a kid's excitement at the success of her showing, and wanted to share it.

'Your painting means a lot to you, doesn't it?'

She admitted that it did. To herself she thought, My painting is everything to me. It's my life, my purpose. Unconsciously, she reached for a strand of her long, beige-blond hair, a habit since childhood when she grew thoughtful about anything, and began to wind it about her finger.

'I think it's great you have a hobby you enjoy,' Drake said, and Katie's finger froze in mid-curl. Her hand dropped from her hair; the curl sprung loose. But before she could launch a verbal attack, a smiling young woman wearing a pink crocheted mini-dress, and with a basket of matching roses draped about her neck, approached their table.

'Half a dozen,' Drake said at once, already reaching into his back pocket for his wallet.

'No, please, Drake. I really don't want . . . '

He bought them over her protests. She would have had to make a royal scene to stop him. Feeling a confusing blend of pleasure and annoyance, Katie arranged the roses in her glass of water. She couldn't resist sniffing their sweet, heady fragrance.

About the room, conversation was lively if subdued; cutlery tinkled against china, while at the far end of the room on a raised platform, a tall, thin man was playing forties music on the piano, a tune she recognized but couldn't at the moment put a name to. For some reason, it made her think of her mother, who was now living in Florida with her new husband. She decided not to let Drake's overtly sexist and condescending remark spoil the evening. She doubted it had been deliberate, and he was, after all, knocking himself out to please her.

'The flowers are lovely, Drake,' she said, moving the makeshift vase to the center of the snowy table-cloth. 'Thank you.' As she was about to withdraw her hand, Drake caught it in his own. His hand felt warm and strong over hers. 'They're not half as lovely as you are, Katie,' he said, his eyes gazing so dolefully into Katie's that she had to look away. There was a brief, panicky moment when she almost laughed. Allowing her hand to linger in his only a moment, she then, as casually as she could manage, withdrew it and placed both hands primly in her lap, as though for safe keeping.

A sheepish grin crossed Drake's face. 'You're right. I do come on a little strong, don't I? I guess it's just that I've always had to work so damned hard for anything I wanted, Katie, I never learned there was any other way.'

She, of all people, should have understood that. Katie wished she could say something that would erase the look of hurt from his

11

face, but could think of nothing Drake wouldn't take as further encouragement, so she remained silent, her hands quietly in her lap.

'I don't mean to rush you, Katie.'

After a pause, she said, 'I know that. But — just friends for now — okay, Drake?'

'You got it.' He looked relieved at the hint of promise in her words. Then, abruptly, he raised his glass to her. 'In any event,' he said heartily, 'champagne is for celebrating, and I believe a celebration is in order.'

More than receptive to having things on a lighter note, Katie lifted her own glass, saying brightly, 'Oh? What's the occasion? Your birthday?'

'Oh, much, much better than that. At least I think so, and I hope you'll agree.' He was keeping his tone deliberately mysterious, but it suddenly occurred to Katie what Drake's news might be and a rush of excitement coursed through her, replacing her discomfort of a moment ago. But she wouldn't guess aloud and ruin his surprise.

'Well, tell me, for heaven's sake,' she said. 'Don't keep me in suspense.'

Drake's entire face was lit in a wide, pleased grin. 'Okay, I won't. Aside from the incredible fact of your sitting here across from me, no mean feat in itself, I might add,'

12

he said, the grin wider, 'I think it's safe to tell you you might just be dining out with Belleville's own Perry Mason.'

'Oh, Drake, you've done it. You've passed your bar exams,' Katie said, impulsively leaning across the table to kiss his cheek. 'Congratulations!' His boast had been made lightly, but you didn't have to be clairvoyant to see the pride of achievement written all over him. 'And you're damned right it's something to drink to. So let's.' After she set her glass down, Katie allowed her voice to take on a more warm and intimate quality. 'I couldn't possibly be more pleased for you, Drake. And I am truly honored that you chose to share your special moment with me.'

For a brief moment, Drake surprised Katie by dropping his eyes, seeming almost shy. It was a side of him she had never seen before. 'Your saying that means a lot to me, Katie. You can't know how much.'

The waiter came then and took their orders for dinner — the house specialty — seafood platters with baked potato and sour cream, steamed broccoli in cheese sauce. When he left, Katie, feeling relaxed for the first time since they'd arrived, asked Drake why he'd waited so long to go to university. He must have been near her own age, and maybe closer to forty. 'Why not — well, when you finished high school?' She had her own reasons for not having pursued her art career in the usual way, but she wanted to hear his.

'The Vietnam war came along,' he said, a bitter note creeping into his voice. 'That stopped me.'

She nodded in understanding. 'Yes. The war stopped a lot of people.' Some permanently, she thought.

'But I have no real regrets,' Drake said, reaching for the carafe to refill both their glasses. 'I believe if a man wants to live in a free country, he should be willing to fight for that freedom. I get a little sick of all the bleeding-hearts.'

Katie was taken aback by the venom she'd heard in his voice. 'A patriotic man?' she said tightly. 'Commendable.'

'That didn't sound as if you meant it.'

'I'm sorry, Drake,' she said, managing a thin smile. 'Of course I mean it. It's just that like a lot of people — bleeding-hearts as you call them, I can't help thinking there must be a better way of settling our differences than killing one another. We're all supposed to be so civilized . . . '

Drake folded his arms across his broad chest, leaned back in his chair. 'And what do

14

you think the answer is, Katie?' he asked, a question that was clearly meant to challenge her. Katie felt the evening beginning to sour. 'I don't pretend to have the answers, Drake. I'm not smart enough. But I do care enough to question.'

He looked at her in what seemed to Katie begrudged admiration. 'Well said. And, of course, you're absolutely right, and let's not talk about it anymore.' As though on cue the waiter came with their dinner.

Having set their dinner before them, the waiter then removed the globe from the candle holder and lit the candle with a match from the card of matches in the ash tray. The tiny flame sent shadows to play on the white tablecloth, shadows that vanished as the globe was returned.

'Enjoy your meal,' he said, flashing a young, toothy smile.

Outside the window, the sun had gone down, leaving only a fading smear of color on the horizon. There were only a few gulls still circling.

Katie concentrated on her food. 'This looks delicious,' she said, picking up her fork.

The conversation moved on pleasantly enough, and Katie was relieved to have the strained moment behind them. Shortly into

15

the meal, Drake asked her to accompany him to a dinner party being held in his honor on Saturday night. 'Professor Walters' generous nature,' he said. 'Ordinarily, of course, I would have graduated with my class, but since spring means planting time to a farmer, and Dad isn't as young or as fit as he used to be, that wasn't possible. But I'm not complaining. I was grateful for summer extension classes.' Drake heaped sour cream onto his baked potato.

'It must have been terribly disappointing, Drake, after all your hard work, not to have been able to graduate with your classmates.'

He shrugged and grinned. 'Oh, I probably would have felt like the senior citizen of the crowd, anyway. Too, I wouldn't have had the opportunity to ask you to be my guest at dinner.'

Katie had to marvel at Drake's special knack of always being able to find the silver lining in every cloud.

* * *

At Belleville General Hospital Dr. Jonathan Shea, head of psychiatry, sat behind his desk staring blankly at the wall in front of him, his phone off the hook. It had been off the hook since he'd received the phone call informing

16

him that one of his patients, Jodie Williams, had o.d.'d on heroin, and was now lying on a slab in the morgue, her toe tagged for I.D. Sixteen, for Christ's sake. Sixteen and dead. Why hadn't he been able to reach her? He'd thought it was going well. He'd thought there was progress. He glanced in disdain at the degrees and diplomas hanging on the wall like so many framed obscene jokes. What the hell good were they? What did they mean?

Sighing heavily, he replaced the receiver and remembered to put out a fresh box of tissues.

He had a patient waiting.

A middle-aged man who would spend most of the session in tears. He was being eased out of his position as sales manager in a company he'd given faithful service to for over thirty years, as well as a piece of his soul. His whole identity was tied up in his job. He reminded Jonathan of Willie Loman in Arthur Miller's 'Death of a Salesman.' He even looked a little like Dustin Hoffman.

2

What was keeping Drake? For at least the tenth time, Katie glanced at her watch. Nearly eight-thirty. He was supposed to meet her here at eight. The storm must be holding him up. But surely he could have found a phone. With eyes narrowed, Katie peered through the plate glass window of The Coffee Shop for a glimpse of Drake's blue Pinto station wagon, but with the sky so black and the rain coming down with a vengeance, it was impossible to see anything.

Katie had accepted Drake's invitation almost without hesitation. Knowing what tonight meant to him, she could hardly have done otherwise. Actually, she found she was really looking forward to the dinner. It had been some time since she'd enjoyed herself in a social gathering, and too, it would do her heart good to see Drake finally getting some reward for all his hard work and determination.

So where was he? She was beginning to feel slightly wilted in her new dress, and her feet hurt.

About to move from the window, she

18

spotted Mrs. Cameron, her employer, coming out from behind the cash register, purposefully threading her way through the small tables toward Katie. Katie groaned inwardly, then, resigned to her fate, she smiled.

'Yes, much nicer,' Mrs. Cameron said, approaching her. 'You mustn't frown so, Katie, dear, you'll make wrinkles.' She patted the fat, white braids that encircled a broad, rather flat, Germanic face. 'Don't worry. I'm sure your young man will be along shortly.' Shorter than Katie, Mrs. Cameron had to look up to speak to her, but that didn't stop her from being a formidable presence.

'I wasn't really worr . . . '

'Oh, of course you were,' she cut in, dismissing Katie's denial with a wave of her plump hand. 'It's perfectly understandable. Courtesy doesn't keep one waiting. Promptness, as we know, is the virtue of kings. And forgiveness the virtue of Christians. I expect it's the storm that's keeping him.'

Katie couldn't help smiling. Mrs. Cameron had a seemingly endless supply of adages for every occasion, some of which Katie suspected she made up, and liked nothing better than the opportunity to quote them. Not that Katie didn't appreciate — well, at least the more amusing of them. As she appreciated the woman herself. Mrs.

Cameron was a no-nonsense person who, after the sudden death of her husband six years ago, had taken her life into her own hands and built a thriving little business in The Coffee Shop. Unfortunately, the early struggles and constant driving were clear in a chronically flushed complexion, the result of high-blood pressure, and the reason she'd given over much of the daily running of the business to Katie. She was here every night, though, and Katie suspected she'd be lost without The Coffee Shop to come to. It had become a second home to her. Too, Mrs. Cameron liked to keep an eye on things.

As she was doing now. Her sharp, black eyes on Katie were reminiscent of a mother bird's. 'My, aren't you looking pretty tonight. That lovely green dress matches your eyes perfectly. Real silk, is it?'

Katie said it was, and felt a pang of guilt thinking of the price tag. But she'd wanted to look especially nice tonight.

'You know, Katie, you could be a model. One of those high-paid ones, too.'

'Thank you.'

'But what did you do to your hair, dear?' she questioned, beginning to circle Katie, frowning. 'It looks — different.'

A few heads turned to look. Katie touched a self-conscious hand to her new hairdo.

The hairdresser had assured her the feathery, textured style softened the strong angles of Katie's face, and was becoming. Katie had liked it, too. 'Just a new cut,' she said.

'Yes, of course. Well, I suppose it's not so bad. I'm glad you've left the back long, though it's not as long as it was, is it?' This last was said almost in accusation. 'Makes you look younger, Katie — like a schoolgirl.'

Katie thought she liked 'model' better. She wasn't sure that at her age, she wanted to look like a schoolgirl. But she knew it had been meant as a compliment. At least she hoped so. With Mrs. Cameron, you could never be sure.

To Katie's enormous relief, a woman approached the cash register, bill in hand, and Mrs. Cameron had no choice but to hurry off to attend to business.

Katie turned back to the window, but aside from the darkness and rain, there was only her own ghostly reflection in the glass. A half hour later Drake still had not arrived, and Katie began to worry that he might have had a serious accident. Surely if it was something minor, like a flat tire, he would have tracked down a phone by now. There had to be an awfully good reason why he would miss a dinner party being given in his honor.

Was it possible that Professor Walters, unaware that Drake had invited a female guest, had already arranged for a dinner partner for Drake, and Drake was too embarrassed to face her with it? No, she was being ridiculous.

Then why wasn't he here? He'd seemed so pleased when she'd agreed to go with him. Katie shifted her feet in their two inch heels, slipped a throbbing foot out of her shoe.

The rain, sounding like thunderous applause, was coming down harder than ever, though Katie hadn't thought that that was possible. Behind her, dishes clattered, the cash register rang. Across the room, a woman laughed, and Katie darted a look behind her. You're being paranoid, she told herself, finding no one paying her the slightest attention. She'd been doing that a lot lately. Getting the feeling that she was being watched; feeling eyes on the back of her neck, turning to look and finding herself quite alone. It gave her a creepy feeling.

The crowd had thinned to a few stragglers, but she knew that in an hour from now the place would be jammed with university students from B.U. The Coffee Shop, with its knotty pine walls and high-beamed ceiling, was a favorite Saturday night haunt. They came bringing with them their ideals, their

22

poetry, much of it dark and angry, a running commentary of man's inhumanity to man, and focussing on acid rain, oil spills, the nuclear arms race. They were young men and women on the threshold of uncertain futures. And they were frightened.

Katie thought they had good reason to be. She knew something about war. And thoughts of it brought, as always, memories of Todd Raynes her young and perfect love, and a long ago letter telling her that he was missing in action — lost somewhere in the steamy jungles of Vietnam.

'Missing' — a terrible word. Was he being held prisoner in some war camp enduring atrocities she didn't even dare let herself think about? Was he lying wounded in some far off makeshift hospital? Did he cry out for her in dreams of a different life? Or maybe he was the victim of amnesia. And on and on it went. Never knowing for sure — that was the worst. She came to long as much for proof of Todd's death as she did for his return, which, even after all this time, filled her with a terrible guilt.

'TWO BLTs with fries,' Francine called out in her shrill, nasal voice, pulling Katie up from her painful reverie. She again checked the time, then began buttoning her beige all-weather coat. Drake wasn't coming.

She'd suggested they meet here because she figured it would be easier for him than having to drive all the way out to Black Lake. Had he misunderstood? Was he perhaps at her front door now wondering why she didn't answer his knock? Well, not a whole lot she could do about it now, was there? She drew the hood carelessly up over her new hairdo. Imagining the pitying glances of the waitresses and Mrs. Cameron — maybe even Joey and Frank (Poor Katie, she'd been stood up), Katie told herself 'to hell with it' and pushed open the plate glass door.

Earlier, out in the parking lot, the door of Katie's blue Comet had opened and closed softly, the sound swallowed up in the roar of wind and rain.

A gust of wind caught The Coffee Shop's door with force, nearly whipping it from Katie's grasp. Head bent against the driving rain, she raced to the parking lot at the side of the building, her shoes slapping on the wet pavement as she made her way to the sanctuary of her car.

3

Unlocking the car door, Katie practically flung herself inside, then groaned aloud to find the seat wet beneath her. Damn! The window on her side had been left open a crack. Katie quickly rolled it shut. Getting careless in your old age, girl, she thought.

She turned the key in the ignition, said a silent 'thank you' when the engine fired at first try. Often, when the wires got wet, the eight year old Ford sputtered and whined as if in pain, and refused to start. Katie put the car into drive and eased out of the parking lot, stopping at the edge of the driveway, looking both ways, having to briefly roll down the fogged side window again to see. Satisfied the way was clear, Katie pulled out onto University Avenue, and turned left toward the highway.

Hunched behind the wheel, shoulders drawn forward, muscles tensed as rain lashed the windshield and drummed on the metal roof above her head, Katie turned the wipers up full. It made no appreciable difference, and she had to strain hard to see the white line on the road through the wavering wall of water.

There were few cars on the road. A couple of taxis passed her. An occasional tractor-trailer swished past her going in the opposite direction, a blast of air buffeting the car as if it were merely a toy, the sway causing Katie's stomach to clench, her hands to tighten on the wheel.

Once or twice, she considered pulling off to the side of the road and waiting out the storm, but there was no guarantee it wouldn't continue for hours, so, though damp and miserable in her wet clothes, she decided to push on.

The trees along the avenue were bent low to the wind. A branch had broken off one of them and lay in the road. Katie maneuvered carefully around it, watching for oncoming car lights. She was taking her time, consoling herself with thoughts of a long, hot soak in the tub. The rain had been bone-chillingly cold, going right to the marrow, and Katie shuddered at the thought of coming winter, suspecting they'd enjoyed the last of Belleville's warm, unseasonable temperatures.

She switched on the radio for company and found herself beginning to relax as soft guitar music floated into the small space with her, blending with the monotonous hiss of wheels on wet pavement. Music never failed to make the twelve mile drive home seem less long, and tonight, for some reason, a little less lonely.

The strain of a day of pacifying distraught customers and refereeing squabbles that erupted all too frequently between the waitresses and the hot-headed cook, Frank Cramer, had been all but forgotten in thoughts of a pleasant night out celebrating Drake's good fortune. But now tiredness seeped into Katie's bones, overshadowing her initial disappointment and mild humiliation at being stood up. An unkept date, after all, was hardly a major tragedy. And she was sure Drake had a perfectly legitimate reason for not showing up. If not an accident, then perhaps his father had taken a bad turn. Katie hoped neither was the case. Drake had had more than his share of suffering.

She liked Drake Devlin — liked him a lot. Given time, maybe . . . if only Drake wouldn't push so hard.

Katie saw that the rain had stopped, just a light drizzle now, for which she was grateful. She slowed the wipers and minutes later turned right off University Avenue onto the main highway, never noticing the car lights that had followed her all the way

27

from The Coffee Shop parking lot, keeping a safe distance behind.

Was she ready for a new relationship? Katie wondered to herself. Did she even want one? There'd been a couple of men in her life in the years since Todd, but nothing serious, at least on Katie's part. They'd wanted more of her than she could give. It was as if with Todd's dying, something vital in Katie had died as well.

With the ugly crumbling of her last affair, Katie had thrown herself into her work with renewed commitment. And painting had saved her sanity. As it often had. Work demanded of you. But it gave back, too. Work didn't abandon you. Abandon? Todd didn't abandon you, a small voice said. Todd died. He was killed in the war.

Was he? Was he really?

Todd Raynes' face — until the dream, or rather the nightmare from which she'd woken last night, bathed in perspiration, heart pounding, had grown hazy in her memory over the years, a face remembered mostly from the photograph on the dresser. She saw clearly now the shy grin, the warm brown eyes with their sweet blend of mischief and sensitivity. In the dream, however, Todd had not been smiling. What was the expression on his face? Rage? Fear? Try as she might,

Katie could not recall, as she could not recall one detail of the dream. She could only feel the uneasy sensations it had left her with.

After she'd received the telegram telling her that Todd was 'Missing in action', she'd been consumed with her loss, and swore to be true to his memory, always. Their love was meant to last even after death into all eternity. For her, there would be no other. And she supposed that in any way that really mattered, there hadn't been. But it was, of course, a vow made not by a woman, but by a grief-stricken child, destined to be broken. Let go, she told herself now. Maybe that's what's wrong inside of you, why you can't sustain an intimate relationship, maybe even the reason for the nightmare. You've never let go.

'Good-bye, Todd,' she whispered in the dark confines of the car.

Metallic rock music blasted out suddenly from the radio, seeming to mock her silly attempt at exorcism, and Katie reached angrily to switch it off. With the slight movement of her head, she found herself looking directly into the rearview mirror. Her eyes locked there. A scream bubbled up from the depths of her, wedged mutely in her throat.

As sightless, unblinking eyes stared into hers.

Brakes screamed as the car swerved wildly out of control, as if other hands were at the wheel, gripping it, wrenching it away from her. A great, dark wall rushed at Katie, and deep down in some functioning part of her brain where terror did not reach, she understood that the moment when she might have done something to prevent what was about to happen, was gone. There was an explosion of glass. Just before the swirling blackness swept her up into the crushing center of itself, Katie knew a terrible sadness.

And then she knew nothing.

Nothing at all.

Within mere seconds of the crash, a truck pulled slowly up behind the wreckage that was Katie's blue Comet. The man got out and strode to the spot where the driver's door had been flung open on impact. The front end had crumpled like tinfoil. The hood had flown up. Clouds of steam hissed from the radiator. One surviving headlight lit a pale yellow path along the black, shiny pavement.

She lay unmoving, head lolling to one side, blood streaming down her face. She looked dead. For a moment he was only incredulous. Gradually, rage replaced the initial surprise, and he felt himself trembling. Letting out an animal cry, he drew back and struck her across the face with the back of his hand. The sound echoed in the stillness. Her head lolled to the other side. But no sound issued from her. No complaint. No! He would not be denied. He would not! Again, he struck her, harder this time, and again, tears of black fury welling in his eyes. Wake up! Wake up, bitch! Goddamn bitch cheated him. The sound of a car approaching forced him to get control of himself. Even so, he'd barely had time to take care of business and make it back to the truck, backing a safe distance away, before they came in droves. Cars stopping. Doors closing. A crowd swiftly gathering, seeming to come out of nowhere. Scavengers to the kill, he thought.

A woman's shocked voice, 'Oh, my God, is she dead?' Frightened whispers, craning necks. Now a man's voice — urgent — a voice accustomed to giving orders, having them obeyed. The man in the truck hated him at once, a quick, seething hatred, not unfamiliar. 'Someone call an ambulance. Who has a phone in their car?'

'I do,' said another, and there was the sound of running footsteps.

31

Slumped down behind the wheel, head-lights off, the man watched the goings on in dulled rage and frustration. He hadn't meant to kill her, goddamn it! Not like this. Only to shake her up a little, have some fun, get things moving. He'd waited so long, so patiently, given such close attention to each detail of his plan, going over it and over it in his mind. And now she was dead. Depriving him. Depriving him of his just revenge, damn her! He brought his fist down full force on the steering wheel, almost enjoying the leap of pain from his hand to his arm. Then a voice spoke to him, a soothing voice, wiser than his own. Maybe she isn't dead, after all, it said. Maybe she only looked dead. You couldn't really be sure. There was so much blood. He felt the stickiness of it now on the back of his hand. Maybe she was just unconscious.

Sirens sounded in the distance, rising in volume as the ambulance raced nearer. Get the hell out of here! the voice commanded, and at once he slipped the car into gear, ready to obey, but at the last second he changed his mind. He had to know. He had to know for sure. Switching on the lights, he drew up closer to the scene. No one paid him any attention as, for the second time in ten minutes, he climbed out of his truck. Fixing his face with a mimicked expression of solemn concern, the man in the khaki slicker joined the throng of onlookers.

In the distance, a siren screamed.

4

Monday morning dawned cold and grey, which seemed to Dr. Jonathan Shea fitting as he sat warily behind his recently cleared desk, drawn and unshaven, shirt-sleeves rolled to his elbows, dictating a letter of resignation to Jeannie Craig, his secretary of five years.

He stared past her as he dictated, and when he finished he laced his hands behind his head and tilted back in the swivel chair and contemplated the square white ceiling tiles. He sighed heavily, and with a bitter note of satisfaction said, 'Well, that's it.'

The blonde young woman peered at him with moist hazel eyes through round granny glasses. When she spoke, her voice shook, sending vibrations to the yellow pencil in her hand.

'Are you really not going to be working here anymore, Dr. Shea?'

'I'm really not, Jeannie.'

'Well — what will I — I mean who will I be working for? Or will I — ?'

Hearing the anxiousness in her voice, his hands came from behind his head. He straightened in the chair. Her face was merely questioning, but he saw the tension in her thin shoulders — tension he hadn't seen for a long time. Of course she would be worried. Why hadn't it occurred to him? She was a single mother with a five year old son to support. Damn! Why was it everything he did (or didn't do, a small voice taunted) seemed to affect someone else?

He raked his thick, straight black hair and tried for a reassuring smile. 'Don't worry about your job, Jeannie. I'll recommend you. There'll be no problem.' Surely he was not without a little influence.

Jeannie had come to him as a patient five years ago following the birth of her child. She'd been raised in an unloving foster home by strict, fanatically religious people, and ran away at seventeen. Not so surprising that she would be easy prey to the first man who offered her a kind word and a little affection. He remembered how she would suddenly burst into tears, wring her hands, often quoting self-damning scripture — fire and brimstone stuff. They'd done a good job on her. Her self-esteem was practically nil. After six months in analysis, he'd known she had basic secretarial skills acquired in high school, and on impulse, since his own secretary was leaving to get married, he'd hired Jeannie. He'd never been sorry.

'What will you do?' she asked, breaking into his thoughts. She sounded stronger. The tension had left her shoulders. Jeannie would be okay. She'd come a long way.

He gave her a wry grin. 'Maybe I'll just be typical and write a book.'

'That sounds exciting,' she said, smiling at him. 'What will it be about?'

'I don't know. Maybe you can come up with some ideas for me.'

She just looked at him.

'Or maybe I'll find work as a mechanic. I used to be pretty good with cars when I was a kid.'

Her smile twitched. 'Oh, Dr. Shea, you're joking, aren't you?'

He managed a laugh, admitted he was. The idea, however, was not without appeal. Cars didn't feel.

'I've loved working for you, Dr. Shea,' Jeannie was saying. 'Working for someone else — well, it won't be the same.'

'No, I guess not. Maybe it'll be better.'

Hurt leapt into her eyes, and he silently cursed himself for his insensitivity. 'I'm sorry, Jeannie. That was sweet of you to say. I'm just — well, I'm not . . . '

'I know. It's Jodie, isn't it? You think it's your fault. It isn't, you know.'

He was touched at her loyalty, however

misplaced. Anyway, Jodie was only part of the reason he was leaving Belleville General Hospital. Impulsively, he stood up and came around from behind his desk and took Jeannie's hand in his. 'I've enjoyed working with you, too, Jeannie. You're a special lady, and don't you ever forget that. You're also one hell of a secretary and whoever gets you will be very, very lucky. I'm going to miss you.'

Her fair skin reddened, and he saw her eyes behind the glasses brim over with tears. 'Thank you,' she said, her voice breaking.

Jonathan crossed the room and stood looking out the window at the greyness outside, without really seeing it. 'Well, if you'll just type that up, Jeannie, I see no reason you can't take the rest of the day off. You've cancelled all my appointments.' He would likely have to stay on a couple of weeks, clear things up. But not today. He couldn't see patients today. He would also have to go see Milton Evans, the administrator; he couldn't avoid that, as much as he would like to. 'You have cancelled my appointments, Jeannie?'

'Yes, Doctor.'

'Good. So get out of here. Go get that great kid of yours and take him to the beach.'

'Dr. Shea, it's October,' she giggled. 'Anyway, the sun isn't shining.'

He turned to see her looking at him oddly. Burying his hands in his pockets, he grinned at her. 'You know, you're absolutely right. Well, how about a shopping spree, then — write yourself a check; I'll sign it. Call it a bonus. You deserve it. Buy yourself a Halloween costume. Go trick or treating.'

She giggled again, a nervous giggle. 'The hospital pays my salary.'

'Oh. Of course. Then I'll write you a personal check.'

Her smile wavered as she stared at him. 'Dr. Shea, are you all right?'

'Fine, Jeannie. Just fine.'

Clutching her notepad and pencil to her chest, the girl moved toward the door, hesitated. Casting one last worried backward glance at her employer who had turned back to the window, she then slipped out the door, closing it softly behind her.

'Code ninety-nine, code ninety-nine,' came the female voice over the sound system. 'Dr. Miller to emergency. Dr. Miller please report to emergency at once.'

Poor Dr. Shea, Jeannie thought, wishing she could do something to help. Something to repay him for all that he had done for her.

It was during her second month in analysis that she fell madly in love with Dr. Shea. She'd begun dressing for their sessions, trying desperately to make him notice her as a woman, to love her back. She'd been totally out of control, buoyed by her fantasies, soaring to exquisite heights one minute, plummeting into black despair and self-hatred the next. It was a bad time for her. The worst. It couldn't have been too great for Dr. Shea, either, she thought, flushing a little, remembering. Especially when she began making those middle of the night phone calls to his house when she couldn't get to sleep for thinking of him.

Not once did he make her feel a fool for her feelings. His voice ever calm and caring, he explained again and again about transference and dependency, until gradually she was able to put their relationship into perspective. Dr. Shea was a good man. He was moody was all.

Funny, though he'd often told her to call him Jonathan, she could never quite bring herself to. Calling him by his first name — well, that would be showing a lack of respect. She heard herself on the telephone to him, saying, 'I love you, Dr. Shea,' and smiled to herself. It really was quite funny when you thought about it.

5

The woman's voice seemed to come from far off, faintly, as though carried on ocean waves. Once, Todd had called her from Vietnam, and his voice over the telephone lines had sounded like that.

'Katherine Summers — Miss Summers? Wake up, now. The doctor is here to see you.'

Someone calling out to Aunt Katherine. But Aunt Katherine was dead. The voice grew louder, insistent, grating along Katie's nerves, making her aware of the throbbing pain in her head. She longed to tell whoever it was to go away, but the effort to speak was too great.

'Miss Summers. Wake up now. Open your eyes. That's a good girl.'

'No, go away,' Katie managed through parched, swollen lips, aggravated at the bright cheerfulness of the woman's voice that seemed like mockery when Katie felt so horrible. Why didn't she just let her alone. Let her sleep. She was so tired — so very tired . . . The next voice she heard was a man's. It was a gentler, more soothing

40

voice. They weren't going to let her sleep. Katie tried to open her eyes. They felt as if there were weights attached to them. Through slitted eyes, she could make out the blurred white figures bending over her. The figures wavered, seeming to have no substance, like pale ghosts. Gradually they drew into focus, and then more sharply, as did the stark white room Katie was in. The smell of anesthetic was strong in her nostrils. She could almost taste it.

'My head hurts,' she whispered.

'I'm not surprised,' the doctor said, bending over her and peering into each of her eyes with a tiny light. His scalp showed through the thinning grey hair. 'You have a nasty concussion. But we can give you something for the pain.' He straightened and smiled at her, looking, Katie thought, pleased with himself for some reason. 'I'm Dr. Miller, by the way. This is Nurse Ring.'

'Ring, if you need anything,' the nurse sang, and Katie groaned.

Dr. Miller laughed. 'You must be on the mend, my dear, if you can recognize a warped sense of humor.'

'Really, Doctor,' the nurse said in mock indignation.

'But even if she doesn't make it to *The Tonight Show*,' he went on, 'she's an excellent nurse. You're in good hands.'

Looking into the two pairs of eyes that were watching her intently for a response, Katie understood that the lighthearted act was meant to reassure her, to keep her from feeling afraid. She wished she could feel more appreciative. She wished she could feel anything other than this sick, throbbing pain in her head.

'Could you tell us your name, where you live, that sort of thing?' the doctor asked. 'Routine, but necessary, I'm afraid.'

Her voice when she spoke came out weak and raspy. She felt as if she were trying it out for the first time. 'My name is — Katherine Summers.' Of course. They hadn't been calling to her aunt at all, but to her. It was just that no one had called her Katherine since she was a child, and even then, only her mother. 'Katherine Anne Summers,' she said, 'but everyone calls me Katie. I live in a house at Black Lake. It belonged to my aunt when she was alive.' This last was said as much to clear it for herself as for anyone. To make her own existence real.

'Yes,' the doctor said, smiling again. 'I've heard of her. I knew the name rang a bell. She was a writer, wasn't she? Well, that's good, Katie. Do you remember what happened? What brought you here?'

'Yes.' She didn't want to remember. Remembering made her head hurt worse. She licked dry lips. 'May I have some water, please?'

A gentle hand supported the back of her head while the cup was placed to her lips. 'Just a little now,' the nurse said. 'Sip it.'

Her head again resting on the pillow, Katie closed her eyes. She shivered inwardly as the image flashed back to her. 'Something in the rearview mirror. A man.'

Frowning, the doctor bent lower. 'I'm sorry, Katie. I didn't hear you. Can you speak up a little, dear.'

'Eyes — dead eyes. In the rearview mirror.' The effort of speaking was taking its toll. She felt her heart racing, her cotton hospital shirt growing damp. She caught the questioning look that passed between the two.

'Are you telling me,' Dr. Miller said, making his words slow and deliberate, 'that there was a — a dead man in the back seat of your car?'

At his look of incredulity, Katie struggled to sit up, but the doctor eased her back down on the bed. 'Just lie still, please. You mustn't upset yourself.'

'But they must have found the body.'

'Perhaps they have,' Dr. Miller said too

43

quickly, 'and they're just not making it public yet.'

The nurse's smile was strained.

'I'm not crazy,' Katie said.

'No one thinks you are, Katie,' the doctor replied kindly. 'But perhaps it's possible that . . .'

'I didn't imagine it,' she cut in, fighting to keep her voice controlled and even, knowing that hysteria wouldn't help her cause. 'There was a man in the back seat of my car, and he was dead. I swear it. My God, I saw his eyes. I'll never forget them. It's what made me lose control of the car.' She stopped, sighing. 'But I can see you don't believe me.'

'Of course I believe you. At least I believe that's what you think you saw. Certainly something must have happened to make you slam into a telephone pole on the wrong side of the road.'

A telephone pole. The dark wall that had rushed at her. 'Yes,' she said wearily, 'and I've told you what it was.'

After a moment of contemplation, Dr. Miller asked, 'Was the man you — saw — someone you knew?' Katie could see through the new approach; he was afraid of upsetting her further, afraid of pushing her over the edge. The thought frightened

44

her as much as anything. She wasn't used to being treated with kid gloves.

There was no choice but to answer. 'No, at — at least I don't think so. But I can't be sure.' Those eyes staring at her — it had all happened so fast. Katie closed her eyes against the mounting pain in her head, like repeated stabs of a knife inside her skull. She began to feel nauseous.

'Are you experiencing more discomfort?' Dr. Miller asked.

She could only nod, imagining her fingers moving upward to gently massage her throbbing temples, but she did not have the strength to raise her arms.

'Try to put the incident out of your mind for now, Katie,' he said. 'I've kept you talking for much too long. There'll be time for further talk later when you're feeling up to it. And you will be, I promise. You're coming along nicely. I expect that's hard for you to believe just now, feeling as you do. I'll have the nurse bring you something for the pain.'

The whole session had left Katie drained, and when Nurse Ring returned with the small white pill in its plastic cup, Katie swallowed it eagerly, only too glad to let it work its miracle. Which indeed it did. Within minutes, the pain receded to a dull echo of itself. Through half-closed eyes, Katie followed Nurse Ring's movements about the room. She walked on silent feet, busying herself, smoothing this, plumping that, now and then a hand going to the short, dark hair beneath her crisp nurse's cap. She transferred folded linen from the chair by the door to the closet shelves facing Katie's bed. This completed, she moved to the window and opened it a couple of inches, adjusted the drapes to let in some air. Sensing herself being watched, the nurse turned, a faint expression of wariness in her eyes. 'Is there something I can get you?'

'No, I'm fine, thank you,' Katie half-whispered. Then she blurted out the question that had begun to prod at her. 'What day is this?' Outside her window, the day was sunny, the sky a clear, unbroken blue as far as she could see. The last she remembered, it had been dark and raining.

The nurse didn't answer right away. Then, her bright, practiced smile switched on, she said, 'Wednesday. You've had a long sleep, Miss Summers.' She pretended to study something on her chart.

Katie's mind did a fast computation. Wednesday. The accident happened on Saturday. A feeling of uncanniness, cool as ice-crystals, swept through her. Four days gone from her life. Just as if they had never been.

'Is — is there anything else I should know?' The question brought a puzzled look from the nurse. 'No, I don't think so. There'll be further tests, I expect — those that couldn't be performed while you were comatose — but you heard what Dr. Miller said. He feels you're out of any immediate danger.' She hesitated, and Katie sensed there was something else.

'I really should wait for Dr . . . '

'No, please. You tell me. It'll stay between us, I promise.'

'Well — uh — you did give us quite a scare on Monday morning.'

'Why? What happened?'

'You just decided to stop breathing. A little bout of respiratory failure. The shock; it happens sometimes. It got pretty tense there for a while. We had to hook you up to the respirator for a few hours. But you rallied nicely, thank the Lord.'

Yes, thank the Lord. She could simply have died right there on the table, just slipped away, and not been aware of anything that was happening. In one way, it had nothing at all to do with her. Today, instead of waking, she might have been buried. Katie gave herself a mental shake to expel the morbid thoughts. The nurse approached the bed and helped by slipping a thermometer under Katie's tongue, feeling for a pulse, talking. Her hand on Katie's wrist felt cool and light. 'By the way,' she said, 'you've had friends calling to ask about you. Maybe tomorrow, if you're a very good girl, you can have visitors. I'll see what Dr. Miller has to say about it. Oh, and there's an absolutely spectacular bouquet of red roses out in the corridor with your name on it. Someone special, maybe?' she added with a conspiratorial wink. 'Would you like me to bring them in?'

Katie managed a 'yes' around the thermometer.

'I didn't bring them in right away because some patients are allergic.' Removing the thermometer, she shook it, read it, then jotted something down on the chart which Katie tried to catch, and couldn't. 'Besides, flowers use up precious oxygen, and you did have that episode.'

Surely there was enough oxygen for herself and one lone bouquet of flowers, Katie thought, and said so. She wished the nurse would stop treating her as if she, Katie, were a child. Or mentally deranged, which is probably what she did think, and who could blame her. Katie was beginning to doubt her own sanity.

Alone now, she puzzled over the fact of the police finding only her at the scene of the accident. Why? Surely there was some logical explanation. There had to be. She was just too exhausted to think of one. Her last thought before drifting off were of the flowers out in the corridor. Jason must have sent them. Dear Jason — such a dear, good friend. The nurse had been right about one thing — it was 'special' to have someone in your camp who asked nothing of you but your friendship. She smiled drowsily, and by the time the nurse returned with the roses, so many they obscured her face, Katie was fast asleep.

Hours later, she awoke to the clatter of supper trays being wheeled down the corridor on noisy carts, and someone across the hall calling out in a voice for the deaf, 'Wake up, Mrs. Patterson, your supper's here.' The food smells blended with the heady, sweet fragrance of roses, two dozen in all, arranged perfectly in a milky-white vase on Katie's night table, their crimson velvet petals in full bloom.

As Katie read the card which had been tucked in among the roses, a faint smile of surprise crossed her face.

Katie,
I'll see you soon, my darling. Please get well.

Love forever,
Drake

'Good evening,' Nurse Ring sang out, bursting into the room, toting a supper tray. Katie returned the card to the bouquet. 'And how are we feeling, Miss Summers?' she asked, setting the tray down on Katie's bed table, and sliding it toward her. 'Hungry?' Why did everything the woman uttered sound like lines from a bad play?

'No, not really,' Katie said, struggling to sit up, wincing at the raw spot on her elbow, caused, she guessed, by harshly laundered sheets. 'But I don't want to speak for you.' The instant the sarcastic words were said, Katie wished she could pull them out of the air.

At first Nurse Ring just looked at her, then she colored a little, and then she laughed. A real laugh — infectious — for which Katie was enormously grateful. 'We do get into a rut around here, don't we? But some of the patients like the 'we' thing. Makes them feel pampered.'

Katie just smiled.

'But not you, huh?' She grinned sheepishly.

'Okay, point taken. Now it's my turn.' Her dark eyes met Katie's squarely. No sheepishness now. 'Hungry or not, you must try to eat. You've been on I.V. for four days, and you're a lot weaker than you might imagine, lying in that bed. Just wait until the first time you put your feet on the floor. You'll see.'

Gingerly, Katie removed the metal cover from the dinner plate — one half scoop of cottage cheese, two prunes swimming in brown juice. She quickly buried them under the cover, raised a smaller one, revealing a clear, dark soup smelling faintly of beef. She thought she might manage that. Picking up her spoon, she asked the nurse if there was an evening paper, and was told the boy who brought them around had already come and gone while Katie slept.

'I don't think there's anything in tonight's paper about the accident, though,' the nurse said kindly, surprising Katie with her perceptiveness. 'There was a short bit in Monday's. Just that you were rushed in here after your car struck a telephone pole. The weather was mentioned as probable cause.' She lowered her eyes. 'It also said you were the lone occupant of the car.'

Well, what did you expect? She'd driven her car into a telephone pole; she didn't die. Small news. Yesterday's news. Eyes in a rearview mirror indeed. That was the sort of stuff of which grade B movies were made, destined to be repeated endlessly on late night television. And yet they'd seemed so real — so horribly, vividly real. But she must have imagined them, mustn't she? What other explanation could there possibly be?

'The flowers are beautiful, aren't they?' the nurse commented, admiring the roses. Agreeing that they certainly were that, Katie had to smile at the subtle change of subject. To herself she thought Drake's declaration of eternal love a bit premature, to say the least, if not downright presumptuous. Still, she was touched and pleased at his thoughtfulness, while at the same time she could not ignore the slight unease his note had stirred within her.

With Nurse Ring looking on like a watchful schoolmarm, Katie tentatively spooned the warm, salty broth into her mouth. It tasted strongly of bullion cubes. She broke off a small piece of dinner roll and ate it unbuttered. Apparently satisfied, the nurse left the room, and after a couple more spoonfuls of the broth, Katie abandoned it in favor of the tea, which, although weak, was at least hot. As she raised the cup to her lips, the dead eyes rushed unbidden to the front of her mind like a close-up on a movie screen. The tea shivered in her cup, some of it spilling onto the faded peach bedspread. The cup rattled in its saucer as she returned both to the tray.

She *had* seen the eyes. She had. Wide, ice-blue, staring. The squeal of brakes, the explosion of glass, all of it echoed now in her memory.

Katie rolled the bed table from her, pushing it all the way to the foot of the bed, rattling the dishes on the tray. Her headache was threatening to come back in full force. Automatically, her hands rose to her head, and for the first time, her fingers felt the thick wad of bandage above her right eye. She brought her hand away.

Don't think about the accident anymore, she told herself. You were lucky to come away with your life. Answers she supposed, would come eventually. She turned her attention to the window on her left, framed with beige drapes that stirred lightly in the breeze. Up so high, she could see the top part of the radio tower, and a hawk in the distance, so far away it seemed no more than a scrap of charred paper floating against the blue sky.

Lying there, Katie found herself thinking about the last time she was in the hospital. She was just six years old, and she'd come in to have her tonsils removed. That was when her mother and father were still together, and they were all living in Lennoxville, just outside of Portland. But the fighting that kept her awake nights, that made her pull the covers up over her head to keep out the ugly, scary sounds, had already begun. How abandoned she'd felt lying in that hospital bed, in that dim, shadowy room so very much like this one, her throat raw and sore, the metal sides of the bed drawn up around her, trapping her there like a small, frightened animal.

As she was afraid now. Afraid, forced to acknowledge how often in the weeks before the accident she'd felt the unnerving sensation of someone watching her. Especially at night after work as she made her way across the darkened parking lot to her car, spurred on by the lone sound of her own hurried footsteps on the pavement. And then, later, amidst the shadow-steeped trees surrounding her house at Black Lake — whispers, movement — causing her to race up the steps, not daring a look over her shoulder, frantically fitting the key into the lock and letting herself inside, out of breath with fear and running. Later, she would laugh at herself. There hadn't really been a menacing whisper in the soughing of the trees, in the soft lapping of the lake against the shore. No. Of course there hadn't. She was being silly, paranoid, letting her imagination get the better of her, reacting to the darkness as if she were still that little girl of six.

You've had an unfortunate accident, she told herself firmly. You survived. Let that be the end of it. She wanted to. More than anything she wanted to let that be the end of it. But deep down, where wisdom is greatest, she knew it wasn't. You could only credit so much to imagination.

Sighing, Katie reached above her head to turn out the light.

* * *

Down below, in the crowded parking lot, a man stood in the gathering dusk peering up at the windows on the sixth floor. He knew her room number. He also knew she'd come out of the coma and was recovering nicely. They'd told him that when he phoned. 'May I tell her who called,' the woman asked. 'Just a concerned friend,' he had answered, and hung up. He could have told her his name. It wouldn't have mattered.

She would be his, just as he'd planned. He wasn't going to be deprived, after all. Oh, you'll like it, Katie. You will. For awhile.

His lips stretched slowly over his teeth in a
death mask grin.

★ ★ ★

The elevator doors slid soundlessly open
and Dr. Jonathan Shea stepped out, strode
purposefully down the wide, polished corridor,
oblivious to the interested glances of the two
nurses on station. He had a patient to see
— one of Jim Miller's. He strongly suspected
Jim was just trying to take his mind off
Jodie Williams. When Jim had walked in
on him on Monday he'd been standing at
the window, staring out at nothing, had
been for an hour, ever since Jeannie had left
his office to type up his resignation. Evans
refused to accept it, insisting Jonathan take
a sabbatical instead — a year if he needed
it. Well, resignation or sabbatical; it didn't
really matter a damn to him.

Jodie would be buried tomorrow. At the
thought, the blackness he carried within him
deepened sharply. He should be there, offer
his condolences to her parents, pay his
respects. He knew he should. He also knew
he wouldn't be.

'You did what you could, Jon,' Jim had
told him, standing at the window with him,
laying a compassionate hand on his shoulder.

'It happens sometimes. You know that. My God, you know that. You lose one. You go on. You have to.'

Why? he thought fiercely, approaching room 623. Why in hell do you have to go on? What's the point? As he tentatively pushed open the door, a pale, feminine arm reaching for the light switch above her head paused in midair as the patient turned to look at him.

Standing there in her doorway, he suddenly felt ridiculous. A fraud. 'Miss Summers,' he heard himself say. 'Miss Katherine Summers?'

'Yes, I'm Katie Summers,' she said, dropping her hand, eyeing him curiously.

'You were just about to turn off the light, weren't you? I'm sorry. I'll drop by later.' Or perhaps not at all, he thought bitterly. Let someone else pick up the pieces of shattered psyches. He, like all the king's horses and all the king's men, was obviously not that good at it. His thoughts rang loudly with self-pity; he knew it and didn't care.

'No, it's all right,' Katie said to the man filling her doorway, a fierce expression on his face. 'Come in, please.'

He did so reluctantly. 'Dr. Miller asked me to look in on you, Miss Summers. I'm Dr. Shea.' He crossed the room to her bedside and pulled up a chair. For such a tall man, he moved with fluid grace, his wide shoulders straining against the soft camel wool of his blazer. His cheekbones were sharply defined, and Katie guessed him to be of American Indian ancestry. Donning dark-rimmed glasses, he scanned the chart in his hand. His eyes were not brown at all as Katie would have imagined, but blue, a deep, astonishing blue.

'So, how are you feeling after your ordeal?' he asked, not looking up from the chart.

'Confused,' she said, the word coming out automatically.

He looked up at her, nodded, his face unreadable. Why was he here? she wondered. Surely a concussion was a relatively normal case for a neurologist, which was Dr. Miller's field. Admittedly, she'd been in a four day coma, but she was fine now. Wasn't she? And then she knew. 'You're a psychiatrist,' she said flatly.

He laughed, as if she had said something hilarious, a rich, vibrant laugh, but Katie didn't miss the note of bitterness. Strange man, she thought, feeling slightly annoyed, watching him run a hand through his longish black hair.

'Perhaps you'll share the joke,' she said coolly.

'I'm sorry. It's just that that sounded suspiciously like an accusation — as if I'd just confessed to being a witch doctor.'

Katie colored. 'Then it's I who should apologize. I certainly didn't mean to suggest . . . '

'No, it's okay,' he said, raising a hand to shush her. 'And probably closer to the mark than either of us realizes. Now that I think of it, practicing psychiatry isn't all that far removed from witch doctoring. And maybe not even as effective.' Anger flashed in his eyes, then flickered out so quickly there was no time for Katie to discern if it was directed at her, at himself, or if she had merely imagined it. Unexpectedly, he laid a hand on her face, and an electric warmth flooded through her.

'Not too scientific, but I'm afraid I didn't bring my thermometer,' he said by way of explanation. 'And I can't very well feel for fever through all that bandage, can I?' Amusement came into his eyes. 'It's all right. I practiced legitimate medicine before I went into witch doctoring.'

'I wasn't questioning your qualifications, Doctor. But I'm quite sure my temperature is recorded on that chart in your lap.'

'Your color isn't good,' he said, as though she hadn't spoken. When he removed his

59

hand from her cheek, her skin felt oddly naked where he had touched it. 'Are you having any discomfort?'

'Just a headache,' she answered, feeling more than a little flustered at her physical reaction to his touch, but satisfied he hadn't noticed.

'I can order you something. I see Dr. Miller has it okayed here.'

'Thanks. But I'd like to try and do without pain killers if I can.'

'Sensible. But there's a fine line between courage and martyrdom. You don't want that line I see etched between those lovely eyes to become permanent.' His smile seemed to mock her, and Katie decided right there and then that she didn't much care for Dr. Shea. She didn't like his arrogance, his condescending manner, or his weirdness. 'I've been ill, Doctor. It's why I'm here. This is a hospital, after all, in case you haven't noticed. It doesn't trouble me in the least if I've gained a few lines on my face.' This, of course, was a lie but she'd be damned if she'd admit it to him.

'A woman without vanity. Remarkable.'

What was his problem? Why was he goading her? Before Katie could respond to the uncalled-for remark, he changed direction. 'Dr. Miller tells me you're called

Katie, but that your true name is Katherine. A lovely old Irish name, Katherine. My father was Irish.'

Was this some new form of bedside manner? If so, it very definitely wasn't working. Irish? His father was Irish.

'My mother, however,' he said, breaking into a grin at Katie's puzzled expression, 'was a full-blood Indian. Navajo.'

Katie would not be drawn into this foolishness further. 'Why are you here, Dr. Shea? Is it, by any chance, because of what Dr. Miller said about my accident? About what I said — caused it?'

He removed his glasses, slipped them into his breast pocket. 'Yes, actually it is.' Leaning back in the chair and crossing his arms over his broad chest, he reminded Katie in that instant of Indian chiefs she'd seen in numerous old Westerns when she was a kid. 'If indeed you saw what you say you did,' he said, 'then the hospital has a legal obligation to report it to the police.'

Alarm flared in Katie. 'The police?'

'Of course. If, on the other hand — well, it won't do much to speed your recovery if you're hounded by the press — interrogated by the police. They might ask questions like: if there really was a body, what was it doing in your car? Did you kill the man and, on your way to dispose of the body, have an accident?'

She stared at him. 'You're crazy.'

'That possibility, I can assure you, has occurred to me on more than one occasion.' A smile played about the corners of his mouth. 'But we were talking about you, Miss Summers.'

A surprising, perverse fascination took hold of Katie at the bizarre twist of conversation, as if she was caught up in some macabre parlor game of 'who-done-it?' 'Then what happened to the body? A minor detail you seem to have overlooked in your gruesome theory is that I was unconscious.'

'I haven't overlooked it. But then you could have had an accomplice following in another car, and he managed to get to you before the ambulance and the police arrived.'

'And removed the body.'

'Exactly. Mind you, this is all theoretical.'

'Well, thank you for that much, at least.' Why had she allowed herself to become a willing, yes, even eager player in this ridiculous game? Why? 'If you knew me even slightly, Doctor,' she said, 'you would know I'm not capable of such a violent act.'

'We're all capable of violence, Miss Summers — of murder,' he said calmly.

62

'Given the right set of circumstances.'

The theory was not unfamiliar to Katie. She'd heard it spouted on more than one occasion. And she didn't buy it, not for a minute. 'Could it be, Doctor,' she said with saccharine sweetness, 'that because, in your line of work, you so often deal with madness, your perception has become a bit narrowed?'

He gave her just the trace of a smile. 'We're all a bit mad, Miss Summers. It's all a matter of degree.' He leaned forward in the chair, his dark blue eyes penetrating hers, seeming to challenge her. 'Another question that might be raised during an interrogation is why you didn't see the corpse propped up in the back seat of your car when you got in.'

The word 'corpse' raised gooseflesh on Katie's arms beneath the hospital shirt. 'There was a downpour and it was dark,' she said, beginning to lose patience. 'And I was running to keep from getting thoroughly soaked.' Anger erupted in her. 'You're the one conducting the interrogation, Doctor. If this is an example of how you help patients, I'd be surprised if any of your patients get well.'

He reacted visibly to her words, actually blinking, as if she'd slapped him, and Katie at once regretted them, even though she did feel at least partly justified. He rose quickly to his feet, the chair legs scraping the tile floor. Standing there, he seemed to Katie suddenly vulnerable, lost. There was clearly something at work here she didn't understand. He was starting for the door. 'I'm sorry,' he said. 'I just thought you should know what you might be in for if the police are called in.'

'Since it's obvious neither you nor Dr. Miller believe a word I've said,' she answered quietly to his retreating back, 'I don't think it's likely they will. Although I can't imagine why you think I would lie about it. What could I have to gain?'

He turned in the doorway, thrusting one hand in his pocket. The chart dangled from the other. He shrugged lightly. 'It's not entirely unheard of for a lonely woman to fabricate such a story — perhaps to gain attention. Maybe she'd been doing it since childhood. It works. I have to admit, though, this particular story is not without a certain — flare.'

Barely trusting herself to speak, her face burning, Katie finally managed through tight lips, 'I'm not lonely, and I don't need attention that badly.'

'No,' he said, his eyes falling on the

bouquet of roses on her night table. 'I don't suppose you do. I'm sorry if I offended you, but you did ask. Could it possibly have been the trick of the car lights reflected in the rain?' he offered. 'Or perhaps an animal on the road. Some freak illusion.'

'Anything's possible, I suppose,' Katie conceded, suddenly exhausted from all the questions, the speculations, the ridiculous sparring with this very strange and disturbing doctor. She looked away from him, stared at the hairline crack snaking out from the light fixture in the ceiling and waited for him to leave, thinking over what she'd heard about the majority of psychiatrists being crazier than their patients.

'Do you mind if I ask . . . ?'

'The roses are from a friend,' she snapped. 'His name is Drake Devlin, and he's a lawyer. In fact, he just recently passed his bar exam. Anything else?'

'Not about your social life. Unless there's something you wish to tell me. And I had no intention of asking you who the sender of the flowers was, I assure you.'

'Oh.' Katie found herself blushing again. 'Then what?'

'It says on your chart that you live at Black Lake. I'm familiar with that area. I was just thinking that it seems a rather isolated spot for a woman alone, that's all.'

'I can take care of myself.'

He studied her for a long moment as if trying to decide something about her, then, 'Yes, I'm sure you can. Oh, by the way, we did do a bit of checking. Just a couple of discreet phone calls. The morgue, missing persons, that sort of thing.'

'But no bodies unaccounted for.'

'Not a one, I'm afraid.'

Both heads turned toward the middle-aged, heavyset nurse who stopped in the doorway and was beaming a million dollar smile at Dr. Shea, yellow curls bobbing appreciatively beneath her cap.

'It's all right, Nurse,' he said, quickly stepping to one side. 'I was just leaving.' To Katie, he said, 'I'm afraid a hospital isn't always the best place to find rest. We'll talk again. Perhaps when your test results come back. We'll know more then.'

Psychoanalysis time, Katie thought wearily. Well, why not if it would help her get at the truth?

'Won't take but a minute, dear,' the nurse said, seeing Katie eye the blood pressure apparatus dangling from her hand. 'Well, what did you think of him?' she whispered conspiratorially, wrapping Katie's arm snugly with the wide rubber band. 'Dr. Shea is the resident heart-throb around here, you know,' she went on, pumping air that hissed from the little ball until Katie's fingers began to tingle. 'You just wouldn't believe how otherwise mature and competent nurses can turn into simpering teenagers when he's around.' She made a little sniffing sound. 'It's positively disgusting.'

Katie grinned.

6

The tantalizing aroma of coffee wafted from the corridor, where breakfasts were being wheeled and distributed to the rooms on either side. Since Katie was being taken for tests, there would be no tray for her this morning. Feeling mildly deprived, she turned away from the corridor to look out the window, and was consoled to see that another perfect day dawned, the sky a bright enamel blue, broken only occasionally by a wispy cloud or two. How exquisite the trees at Black Lake would be just about now in their profusion of golds and scarlets. Oh, how she did love the autumn. Though the longing for a cup of coffee did not leave her, she longed now to have it in her studio in front of the fire. She would throw open the drapes and gaze out upon the trees in their show-offy colors, and her beautiful lake, a view of which, no matter what the season, Katie never grew bored. Perhaps, she continued to fancy, if it was warm enough, she would just take her coffee out onto her little balcony. Feeling a pang of homesickness, Katie wondered when she would get out of there.

'Ready?' Nurse Ring asked brightly, coming into the room, toting a rich burgundy overnight case which Katie had never seen before.

'Ready as I'll ever be,' she answered, and slid her legs out from beneath the sheet, then stared at them as if they belonged to someone else. They were thin and nearly as white as the sheet, her skin almost translucent, showing a fine tracery of veins beneath. True, between working at The Coffee Shop and her painting, there wasn't a lot of time left for sunbathing, but Katie couldn't remember her legs ever being so pale before, or so thin. Hoping they would support her, she placed her bare feet on the cool tile floor and stood up.

Instantly, the room began to spin around her, and Katie had to clutch the edge of the mattress to keep from falling. In a single stride the nurse was there, her arm around Katie's waist. 'Easy now. Just sit quietly for a few minutes. You moved too quickly is all. Do you feel faint?'

With her blood thrumming in her ears, and her entire body enveloped in a cold sweat, Katie could only nod. She felt as if the strength were slowly being sapped from her body by some unseen force.

'Place your head between your knees and take nice deep breaths,' the nurse advised. Katie obeyed, and gradually the spinning room slowed, her heartbeat returned to normal. A long shudder of breath escaped her.

'Okay?' Nurse Ring asked.

'I — I think so. Can't say I wasn't forewarned, can I?' She slid her damp palms down the sides of her nightshirt. 'Whew. That was awful. I've never fainted before. It's not anything like in the movies, is it?'

The nurse smiled. 'Hardly. But then few things ever are, right?' After a couple of minutes, she said, 'Do you think you can make it over to the chair now? Do you feel up to it?'

Katie listened closely to her body, then said yes, and began to ease herself off the bed to place her feet again on the floor.

'Take your time. Just lean on me.'

Katie didn't need to be coaxed. Wary now after her sickening experience, she stood slowly. And felt relieved when the room didn't move. Taking small, careful steps, and with the nurse's support, at last she was across the mile of floor and being settled into the big chair. The vinyl upholstery was cool on her skin, and Katie had to laugh as she tucked the two ends of her nightshirt beneath her bottom as best she could. 'I feel absolutely naked. You know, it just occurred to me I don't have a darned thing to wear other than this God-awful hospital gown.'

The nurse grinned slyly and knelt to the overnight case at her feet. 'Oh, I think you do,' she said, beginning to undo the small, gold-plated buckle. 'He said everything you need should be in here.' She glanced up at a puzzled Katie. 'Shall I open it?'

'Are you sure it's for me?'

'Absolutely. The gentleman was quite anxious that it be delivered to you right away.'

Pleasantly surprised, assuming that this was her friend Jason's doing, Katie gestured to the nurse to go ahead and open the case. Jason, knowing where Katie kept an extra key, must have driven out to the house and picked up some of her things. Odd. It wasn't like Jason to be so practical on his own. Thoughtful, yes. Sweet, yes. But practical . . . ? Well, she mustn't underestimate him in the future. The bag must be his. It certainly wasn't hers. 'Did my friend leave a name?' Katie asked, fully expecting to hear the name 'Jason Belding.'

Linda (which Nurse Ring had insisted Katie call her) unzipped the case and opened it, releasing the scent of new leather which wafted up to Katie. 'Drake Devlin,' she said, as she removed a pair of gold brocade slippers from the case and fit them over Katie's feet. And then she was holding up a creamy luxurious robe for Katie's viewing, oblivious to the stunned expression on her patient's face. 'Isn't this absolutely the most gorgeous thing you've ever seen in your entire life?' she breathed, struggling with the yards of skirt.

There was nothing here of Katie's. Everything was brand new, and far more expensive than anything Katie could ever have afforded. 'It is beautiful,' she agreed, watching in astonishment as the nurse dove back into the case and with all the enthusiasm of a child on Christmas morning, held up, one after the other, three peignoir sets, all satin and lace in delicate shades of pastel. Eyes glittering, she handled each with the reverence of a pirate finding treasure. When these were sufficiently admired she returned them and withdrew a teal-blue suede drawstring bag from the case. 'Wow!' she said, peering inside. 'French perfume, makeup . . . he wouldn't happen to have a brother, by any chance.'

Katie gave a nervous laugh. 'No, I don't think so. Anyway, I certainly can't keep any of this.'

The nurse raised dark, bewildered eyes. 'Why not?'

Despite her amazement, which was gradually turning to anger, Katie had to laugh. 'Because this stuff must have cost a mint, and I hardly know Drake Devlin. I only dated him one time, for Heaven's sake.'

The nurse remained kneeling at the case, staring up at Katie. 'You're kidding. Well, you must have made one hell of an impression because he sure wants to make sure he gets a second date.' She grinned and caressed the velvety robe. 'I think I'd be willing to give him a chance.'

'Whoever would have thought you were so materialistic, Linda,' Katie teased. After a shaky start, she and Linda Ring were becoming more like friends rather than just patient and nurse.

'Neither did I,' Linda replied wistfully, letting the satiny fabric of an ice-blue negligee slide sensuously through her fingers and back into the case. Standing abruptly, she held up the robe, her chin tilted in decision. 'Well, you'll have to wear this at least, and the slippers. You've nothing else and this is an emergency. You can always return the rest, if you're sure you really want to.'

'Linda, you're not hearing me. I can't wear any of this,' Katie protested, but the nurse had turned a deaf ear and was already deftly sliding Katie's arms into the flowing sleeves of the robe, now tying the sash.

Katie sighed in resignation. 'You're taking advantage of my weakened state, you know,' she said. She supposed it wouldn't hurt to wear the robe just this once, and pray she didn't soil it. Glancing down at her feet clad in gold brocade, she guessed it would be appropriate to keep the slippers as a gift.

'There,' the nurse said, stepping back so Katie could view herself in the full-length mirror hanging on the inside of the closet door. 'You look like you just stepped out of a dream.'

Katie stifled a gasp at seeing herself. A dream, all right. More like a nightmare. Her eyes were dull and hollowed beneath the bandage, and there was an ugly bruise on her left cheek that was fast turning a ghastly yellow, still tender to the touch. She looked like the victim of a beating. Her new hairdo hung limp and lifeless, some of it matted — with her blood? 'The robe looks great,' she said dryly. 'I look like I died and came back to life — almost.'

'Well, you haven't exactly been vacationing in Acapulco, have you? Not to worry. When you get back I'll give you a shampoo. That'll pick you up.' She knelt to sift again through the case. 'Shampoo, soap, toothbrush, let's see — comb, brush . . . just like he said;

everything you need. A shampoo and a little makeup from this lovely case, and you won't know yourself.'

'I'll hold you to your offer, but I've got makeup in my purse and that'll do just fine.' Despite her resolve, Katie couldn't resist stroking the luxurious velvet that fell in soft, rich folds to the floor. Maybe, she thought, as Linda Ring helped her into the waiting wheelchair, it would be okay to keep a few of the smaller items. It really was very thoughtful of Drake. Thoughtful? No, Katie. The flowers were thoughtful. This robe and what's in that overnight case looks more like a carefully planned trousseau for a bride.

7

Other than the photograph of Katie Summers, which was now thumb-tacked to the A & R Realty calendar just above the red-circled '5' in the month of November, there were no other pictures in the man's room — nothing to suggest family or friends — to indicate past. He'd had parents, of course, just like everyone else, but he rarely thought of them and when he did it was with the indifference one afforded to strangers, or, on occasion, contempt. Particularly for his mother, which was ironic since she was the one person in the world who absolutely adored him, for whom he could do no wrong.

He recalled her hugs, the way her soft, cushiony breasts would mash against him, and felt the same revulsion he'd felt then. A silly, simpering woman, his mother. Not that he wasn't always very careful about hiding his feelings; he wasn't a fool, after all. She had her uses. He could, for instance, always manage to persuade her to open her purse and fork over a dollar or two from her house money, meagre fruits borne from his father's bookkeeping job in a department store. 'Love you, Mommy . . . beautiful Mommy . . . love you,' and her face would go all soft with love for him, and he knew he was her 'sweet, precious boy,' and that she would deny him nothing.

His father, on the other hand, was a different story. Almost from the beginning he'd sensed in his son, an only child who'd come to them late in life, something not quite so sunny, so innocent. In fact, sensed something dark — something that frightened him, over time causing the small, grey man to withdraw into himself, becoming a silent phantom in the house.

Until his death when the boy was thirteen. A tragic accident, everyone said. A horrible accident. The small orange plastic radio his father liked to listen to when he was having his bath had fallen into the tub with him (must have caught the cord with his hand, they said) and electrocuted him. He saw the boy in the bathroom doorway — saw the radio perched on the edge of the sink — and knew. Perhaps he'd always known. His scream was short. All the lights in the house had gone out, but the boy managed easily to slip back to his room before he heard his mother's panicked footsteps bounding up the stairs.

'Call an ambulance,' she'd cried hysterically,

as he came running to join her. 'My God, call an ambulance.'

His father's face wavered just beneath a skin of cloudy bathwater, his mouth open in a silent scream, his eyes on the boy wide, staring, accusing.

Tears streaming down the boy's face, he ran to obey.

In the beginning, it was his father's interference in his life that got to him, his trying to tell him what to do. He couldn't stand people telling him what to do. After a while the old man gave up and let him be. But it was his eyes that drove him nuts — those eyes following him around, watching him — knowing things.

Winding a length of rope about his hand, the man smiled, remembering the time his father had walked in on him and the little girl next door. What was her name? He couldn't remember. It didn't matter. They were in his bedroom, and he was holding a pillow over the girl's face, taking it away, listening to her gasp air back into her lungs, begin to cry and plead with him, bringing it down again, holding it firm with his strong, thin arms, using all his strength, giggling at her helpless, flailing hands, sitting on her legs so she couldn't kick. It was fun. A game. Until his father had rushed in and whipped the pillow away, barely able to speak his rage and shame, backhanding him so hard that he practically flew off the bed.

Well, he'd never hit him again. He'd fixed him.

For good.

The man jammed the brand new coil of one-quarter inch white nylon rope into his pocket, gave a rare thought to his mother, with whom he lived for the three years following the 'demise' of his father, until she, herself, fell dead on the kitchen floor of a massive stroke.

He was sure his mother guessed things about him toward the end. He really didn't mind her knowing. From time to time, he would catch a fleeting horror in her eyes as certain thoughts took shape, another piece of the puzzle slipped into place — once when a neighbor came to the house wailing and complaining that her cat, 'poor, dear Fritz,' was found hanging by his neck from a tree behind the school, sweet pink tongue lolling. She pointed her finger straight at him, who stood behind his mother, grinning his mocking grin at the old hag, quickly wiping it off when his mother turned questioning eyes on him. Then there was the time that new boy on the block suffered a fractured skull delivered by a wielded baseball bat. The cops had come to the house that time. He was fourteen, then, his accuser seven. He denied it, of course. Must have been someone who looked like him. Why would he do it? He didn't even know the kid. He denied all of it. There were never any witnesses. He was always very careful about that. In the end, as he knew he would be, he was again his mother's 'sweet, precious boy.'

In the end, she believed what she wanted to believe.

The knife lay on the cot with the flashlight. He picked it up, fondled it. Nice and new like the rope. Never used. Virginal. He picked up the flashlight. Everything he would need to accomplish his feat, he had. A crucial part of his plan, of course, waited behind his closet door. He glanced there now, and grinned. He would drive out to her house tonight, get a feel for the place while she was still in the hospital. Things had worked out sweetly for him, after all. Better than he could have imagined, given the forced change in plan. Fate was on his side.

He believed in fate.

8

It was after one o'clock when Katie arrived back in her room, just in time, as Linda Ring had predicted, to miss lunch. Despite feeling shaky and weak from her ordeal of being tested, probed and prodded, Katie was undoing the robe practically before the wheelchair was through the door, and a moment later, returning it to the case, perfectly folded. She would phone Jason and ask him to drive out to the house and bring her a few needed items. She would make a list.

As promised, Linda shampooed her hair, blow-drying it with a dryer borrowed from a kindly patient. A little lipstick, blush and mascara, and Katie had to admit, she both looked and felt a lot more human. The nurse then thoughtfully brought her tea and toast before going off duty. Now, having finished it, Katie lay back on the bed and closed her eyes. It had been a long day, and it was only half over. Still, she knew she was getting stronger all the time.

Lying there, listening to the blaring television set across the hall, Katie guessed her neighbor, Mrs. Patterson, was indeed a little on the deaf side. A man was passionately raking someone over the coals . . . probably a woman . . . a soap. Katie tuned it out. Eyes closed, she drifted.

The scene rode to the front of her mind as if it were being captured by a movie camera on a trolley, a single frame, starting small, becoming swiftly larger in closeup. She saw a boy dressed in ragged clothing running in a field, waving his arms about as if in greeting. In the act of running, the boy's body suddenly froze in midair; then it spun, arms and legs flailing in grotesque pantomime. Blood spattered the blades of grass like red rain, dripped from a leaf just above Katie's head. Behind where the boy lay dead, a chorus of anguished voices rose up in terrible mourning, and it reached into Katie's very soul.

Her eyes shot open, while behind her eyelids the picture continued to play. It was several seconds before it finally faded to let the room shimmer whitely back into focus.

Across the hall, the television set grew louder.

A nurse poked her head in the door. 'Anything wrong in here?'

'No, nothing. I didn't ring.'

'One of the patients thought she heard

someone cry out in here.'

Katie smiled thinly. 'Sorry. Wrong room.'

Sitting up in the bed, Katie rubbed her eyes, as if to rub away any residue of the scene. My God, what was that all about? A dream? Yes, she must have been dreaming. Yet she was sure she'd only closed her eyes for a moment, sure she hadn't been asleep. She put a hand to her cup on the night table; the remaining tea was still hot.

Frowning, Katie lay back on the pillow to think. It had, in a way, been like seeing in her mind's eye the eyes in the rearview mirror. And yet it hadn't — not exactly. The 'eyes,' she was certain now, were a memory. Her memory. The boy had seemed more a vision. And there had been no sound except at the end when that awful cry, like some primal wail, went up in chorus, leaving Katie with a heavy sadness. Had she had a psychic experience? A premonition of some kind? A vision from the past? Katie believed in such things, as had her aunt before her. Not that either were fanatic about it, and Katie knew there were plenty of frauds around only too willing and able to con the gullible and the lonely, but there was also no doubt in her mind that there were some things human beings had no answers for — some things that defied scientific explanation.

Who was the boy? she wondered. She had had no sense of recognition, although admittedly she hadn't seen his face clearly. Just as she hadn't seen with any clarity the surroundings, only that there'd been grass and trees. Was it Black Lake? It hadn't felt like Black Lake. And yet she'd been part of the scene. She'd been there.

'Everything okay?' Nurse Ring said, coming into the room, wearing her coat and carrying her purse over her arm. Clearly, the other nurse must have related to her that her patient had cried out, just as Linda was about to leave for the day.

'Everything's just fine,' Katie said cheerfully. 'The tea and toast really hit the spot. I hope you're not neglecting your other patients, what with all this fussing over me.'

'I enjoy fussing over good patients. Besides, I'm a fast nurse.' She started away, and turned back. 'And don't take that the wrong way.'

Maybe she was making too much of the 'vision' or whatever it was she'd experienced. One thing was sure: she had no intention of telling anyone else about it. Dr. Shea had already suggested she'd concocted the story of seeing the eyes in her rearview mirror. Adding to it might just end her up in a rubber room somewhere, instead of on her way home.

Katie started at the feel of warm lips on hers. The sight of Drake drawing back from her, smiling down at her as a mother might smile at a sleeping child, was dreamlike. Lost in thought, she'd neither seen nor heard him enter the room.

'I think that's called taking unfair advantage,' she said tightly, struggling to a sitting position and drawing the sheet up as far as it would go to cover her hospital shirt.

'You're right and I apologize,' he said, looking immediately sheepish. 'It's just that you looked so like a little girl lying there, I couldn't resist.' His grey eyes were innocent of ulterior motive as he lay a hand on her shoulder. 'I was so worried about you, Katie; I've hardly slept a wink since you've been in here.'

At once, Katie's initial annoyance faded, and she gave him a forgiving smile. The kiss had been kind of sweet, now that she thought about it. Remembering to thank him for the roses, she followed by telling him how handsome he looked in his charcoal grey suit, white shirt and silk striped tie in soft shades of grey, white and coral. 'You look very much the prosperous lawyer,' she said, while in the back of her mind she wondered how to broach the subject of the expensive gifts she had no intention of keeping.

'All for show,' he replied, grinning. He went to the foot of her bed to raise her up. His movements were quick and precise, like pencil strokes. 'Enough?'

'Perfect.' He had nice, square teeth. His mouth was a little on the thin side, but sensuous. Drake really was quite nice looking. She watched him smooth already neatly combed hair across his forehead — a familiar gesture. A nervous habit, she thought. Drake drew the chair to her bedside — the same chair Dr. Shea had sat in yesterday; it appeared to fit Drake better. Drake was shorter than Dr. Shea, but more stockily built. She wondered why she was making the comparison. She also noticed that Drake's fingernails were dirty, and felt crummy for noticing.

'I hope everything fit,' he said, glancing down at the overnight case which stood unopened against the wall beside the closet. 'I guessed at the sizes.' His smile was tentative.

Understanding his nervousness now, knowing he'd expected her to be wearing something from the case, Katie braced herself. 'That's something I need to talk to you about,

Drake,' she said, relieved he'd raised the subject himself.

The anxious, intense expression she'd seen Drake wearing so often now spread across his features. Even his tan seemed to have paled, leaving his freckles naked. 'You didn't like my choices?'

He wasn't going to make this easy. 'Your choices are perfect, Drake. The clothes — everything is exquisite. And I'm genuinely flattered by your generosity. But I — I can't accept these things.'

He frowned. 'I don't understand.'

Knowing that she was hurting him and wishing he hadn't made it necessary, Katie explained as if speaking to a not-so-bright child that these were gifts a man might give to his wife, or perhaps his wife-to-be. 'I'm sorry if you can't accept my feelings about this, Drake,' she finished lamely.

After a lengthy pause, Drake surprised her by smiling. 'But I do, Katie,' he said. 'I do understand. I see I've put you in an awkward position, and I respect you all the more for your principles. I just wanted to do something — special for you, that's all. It's because of me, after all, that you're here, that you had that terrible accident.' He lowered his gaze. 'It's because of my not showing up to take you to that damned dinner that you

87

were out driving in that storm,' he ended hoarsely.

Until this very instant, Katie had completely forgotten about the unkept dinner date. Poor Drake. He was miserable with self-reproach. She felt something melt within her.

'You're blaming yourself for something you had nothing to do with,' she said softly. 'And that's silly. The accident was just something that — happened.' Fleetingly, dead eyes flashed in her mind. She blocked them out. 'It wasn't your fault.'

'Maybe not directly, but I still feel responsible. There's a good reason I didn't show up, Katie. It was unavoidable. I did try to call you, but the lines were down.'

'I knew there had to be an awfully good reason for you to miss such an important occasion, Drake. And believe me, there's no need to explain.'

'But I want to, please. Katie, I hope you don't think I'm trying to buy your affections.' His hand went to his hair.

'No, of course not,' she said, and hoped she sounded more convincing than she felt.

'Good,' he said, the color returning to his face. He seemed to relax. 'Because I wouldn't do that. Do you know when you'll be going home?'

Glad for the change of subject, Katie told

him that if the tests came out okay, Dr. Miller had promised her that she wouldn't have to remain in the hospital more than another week or so.

'I'll come and get you,' he said flatly, leaving no room for argument. 'Now that you're allowed visitors, I'll be here as often as I can. You just be sure and let me know when you're being discharged, okay?'

As he smiled at her, Katie was suddenly struck with the sensation of the room growing hotter, of the flowers on her night table smelling sweeter. 'Drake, I . . . '

He reached for her hand. 'No strings, Katie,' he said gently. 'No pressure. I promise. I just want to be your friend. Will you let me?'

Despite not quite believing him, Katie was relieved. 'Of course I will. Thank you, Drake.'

In the middle of explaining to her what had happened to prevent him from meeting her at The Coffee Shop and taking her to dinner, (the reason Katie had suspected and feared), a tall, slim gentleman with snowy white hair, Mr. Jackson, Katie's art teacher, appeared in the doorway carrying a small bouquet of violets.

9

Aside from his mother's photograph, the only other item on Jonathan Shea's desk was Katherine Summer's chart. Jim had scrawled 'for your information' across the top. Jonathan had read it, admittedly reluctantly, but he had. All her tests had come back negative and that, at least, was good news. He supposed he should have followed up with a second visit as he'd promised, but there seemed little point. His one visit had done little more than to upset and exhaust her. He'd been angry with her. Why in hell had he reacted that way? He didn't even know the woman. He'd been unfair. She'd been right to accuse him of a lousy bedside manner, which, of course, had been a gross understatement. He hadn't wanted to leave. He was the one looking for therapy, for Christ's sake. He'd wanted to lose himself in the green pools of her eyes. Despite the confusion he'd seen there, even the fear, her eyes were alive, filled with spirit. They challenged him. Maybe he'd hoped some of her passion would rub off on him, for he was, without doubt, feeling more dead and empty in his soul than he had ever felt in his life.

Correct that. Since he was twelve years old.

Since his mother.

Sagging deeper into his chair, Jonathan rubbed a hand over his unshaven face.

Dead and empty. Like Jodie. Jodie lay under the ground now. He hadn't attended her funeral. He knew he wouldn't — couldn't. It was not easy to face one's failures. Obviously, impossible for him. Thrusting the girl's memory from him, he let his gaze wander to the photo on his desk which he'd left until last to pack. His mother smiled wistfully out at him, her black hair falling softly to her shoulders, framing her small, oval face. She looked so young in the photo. Her eyes seemed almost too large for her face. They were gentle eyes, never accusing, yet he felt their accusation deep inside of him like a heavy stone in his heart.

'I couldn't even help you, could I, Momma?' he whispered.

Only the soft ticking of the wall clock answered him.

Jeannie looked up from her typewriter as Dr. Shea strode almost angrily past her desk, bursting through the swinging double doors and out into the corridor heading straight for

91

the elevator. The door swung to and he was gone from her vision.

She turned the diamond ring on her finger. Jeffrey had given it to her on Saturday night. She'd been dying to tell Dr. Shea her exciting news, but the time didn't seem right. She'd hoped he might notice the ring, even though it wasn't real big, but she guessed he just had too much on his mind.

The doors swung open and Constance Sewell was suddenly standing at her desk. 'Is Jonathan in his office, Jeannie?'

Jeannie cringed at the familiar, demanding voice, at the sight of the woman looking as always, in a royal blue cape and with her hair piled on her head like a flaming bush, as if she'd just stepped out of *Vogue*.

'He just went out, Miss Sewell,' Jeannie said pleasantly. 'You just missed him. Would you like some coffee? He should be back any . . . '

'Page him!'

Jeannie's face warmed. 'Miss Sewell, I don't think . . . '

The woman let out a long-suffering sigh. 'Please don't aggravate me, Jeannie. I'm not in the mood. Please do as I ask. Please.' She favored Jeannie with a cold smile.

'Very well.' Without another word, Jeannie did as she was told, knowing Dr. Shea wouldn't be too thrilled about being paged since it wasn't an emergency. But she didn't think he would be mad at her. He hadn't taken his coat, so she knew he was still in the building. As she paged him, Constance Sewell, cape flaring out behind her like a mad bullfighter's, flounced into Dr. Shea's office as though she owned it, and shut the door behind her.

* * *

Several miles away, the man stood alongside his blue, badly rusting half-ton, leaning on his shovel, his eyes raised to the swollen purple clouds moving swiftly across the grey sky out of the west. A storm was brewing. Damn! He hoped to hell that didn't mean snow. Snow would make his work a lot harder. It would leave tracks, too. Naw, he argued with himself, too early for snow. More rain, probably. At the sound of childish giggling, he turned to see two kids coming up the path toward him. Tossing the shovel onto the back of the truck where it thumped and rocked to silence, he straightened his shoulders in the faded army jacket, and waited.

As they came closer, their steps suddenly faltered, and the man grinned to himself.

93

They sensed he was a man to be reckoned with. He liked that. You couldn't too often fool kids — although there'd been a couple who hadn't been too sharp, and they'd paid the price. He thought of that boy's home they'd stuck him in after his mother died, and then those foster homes he'd been in and out of like they had revolving doors. Some of the kids in those places thought, just because he was an orphan, they could lord it over him. Well, they found out different soon enough. No one ever told on him, either. They knew better. Anyway, they probably wouldn't have been believed. Most grownups liked him. Most told him what a 'lovely, sweet boy' he was.

Oh, yes. It was the grownups who were easy. You just had to tell them what they wanted to hear, that was all.

The dirt path leading up to the house was fairly long, maybe two hundred feet, and he watched, unmoving, as they drew nearer. The taller of the two kids was peering uneasily at him through holes in the sheet he wore, while the little one, a girl, he figured, about six or seven, adjusted her black witch's nose. Fine, blonde curls escaped the pointed hat. They stopped a few feet from where he stood.

'Trick or treat?' came the thin, timid voice from behind the sheet. A boy's voice.

The man made no reply, only continued to look down at the two of them, enjoying his effect on them. Instinctively, the boy reached out to take the girl's hand in his. His feet shifted in their dirty, scuffed Nikes. 'Is — is Mrs. Nickerson home?'

'No. No one's home.' The man's voice was barely audible, yet filled with menace. His lips stretched in a slow, cruel smile. 'Only me. Now you two move to hell out of here, or I'll give you a treat you won't like.'

For a moment the two stood frozen, caught like a pair of rabbits in the man's pale, icy stare. Then, as he took a threatening step toward them, they were suddenly off and running, feet flying over the dirt path, back the way they had come, the sound of the man's chilling laughter ringing in their ears.

He was still chuckling low in his throat long after the two had disappeared from sight. They'd probably squawk to their parents, he thought, but to hell with them. To hell with all of them. He would be moving on in a few days, anyway, once he took care of things.

Taking the knife from his pocket, he tested its sharpness against his thumb. Just a slight touch of the blade and a bead of blood leapt to the surface of his skin.

It was called simply a 'hunting knife.' Gripping the bone handle hard, he smiled at the appropriateness of the name.

The knife felt good in his hand, better than the butcher knife. More authority. He didn't really want to use it, though; that would spoil things. Unless, of course, she gave him too much trouble. He would use it, then.

Thoughts of her, as they always did, began the blood throbbing hotly through his veins. Slowly, he turned the knife over in his hand, observing how, even in the last light of day, it gleamed like polished silver. Head bent in admiration, it suddenly shot up at the sound of a car coming up the road, and he quickly returned the knife to the front pocket of his army jacket, patting down the flap. Fear coiled and stretched and coiled again, cool as a serpent in his bowels as the full implication of what had just happened struck him. What he had said to those kids was stupid, he now knew. Careless. People knew him around here; they could mess things up. In spite of the cool temperatures, sweat trickled down his sides.

He was getting impatient, that was all. But he mustn't. Had to keep it together. He'd waited too long to blow it now, and November fifth was only five days away. Then, he would be rewarded for his patience, for his careful attention to detail.

A frown worked itself between his brows

96

as again the voice reminded him that he had put the plan in jeopardy — had in fact nearly caused the entire plan to backfire.

But 'nearly' was the key word here. It hadn't backfired. What happened had actually allowed him to complete much of the work without fear of discovery. What happened was, in fact, an improvement on the plan, so it didn't matter. He figured it was an omen — a kind of sign that the plan was taking on a force of its own. The thought calmed him.

As did the sight of the brown Chevy moving on down the road, now slowing, the driver taking no notice of him.

But he must be careful from now on. Very, very careful.

Tossing the coil of rope jammed in his pocket into the truck's cab, locking the doors, he then turned and headed for the house, only vaguely aware of the sound of distant thunder. He would sit awhile and look at Katie's picture. That always helped to bring the moment closer.

That sweet moment when he would be with her.

She would be so beautiful.

Trapped there beneath him, soft and naked and helpless, writhing and moaning in pain and ecstasy — for there could be no real ecstasy without pain. He could feel her body against him now, moist and slippery, feel himself thrusting hard into her, again and again — he heard her cries inside his head, and his legs trembled as he climbed the stairs to his room.

Once inside, he closed the door behind him and sagged against it. Shutting his eyes, he let his mind savor what would be the best part of all.

Her death. An exquisitely slow death — one chosen with great care.

Just for her.

10

Rachael and Billy Martin ran the half mile home without stopping, like the breath of the devil was at their backs. Now they bounded up the porch steps, raced past the two jack-o-lanterns with their glowing eyes, propped on either side of the railing, and burst into the house. Their costumes were gone, their treat bags dropped somewhere along the way.

Their mother was in the kitchen, a sweet-faced woman in a flowered dress, up to her elbows in sudsy dishwater. At the sight of her, Rachael began to cry.

Alarmed, Mrs. Martin quickly dried her hands and came forward. 'Billy, honey, what happened?' She smoothed his hair, then knelt to put her arms around her little girl. Both children were trembling and out of breath.

'Bad man, Mommy,' Rachael sobbed between gasps of air. 'The man scared us.'

'It was that man up at the Nickerson's house, Momma,' the boy said, panting for breath. 'He told us he was going to do something bad to us if we didn't get the hell out of there.'

'Don't swear, Billy.'

'Mom, I didn't say it. He did. He said he was going to give us a treat we wouldn't like. Rachael's not kidding, Mom. He really was scary — just like — like — Freddy Kruger.'

'Must have been someone dressed up in a costume,' his mother reasoned. 'Someone teasing.'

Billy made a move with his knees that looked like he was going to jump up and down. He didn't. 'No, it wasn't, Mom,' he yelled in frustration. 'I told you, it was that man at the Nickerson's. It was.'

'Okay, honey, okay. Calm down.' She'd seen the man up at the Nickerson's, and he certainly bore no resemblance to the infamous Freddy Kruger. Kids had such lively imaginations. Then again, you never knew what was out there. Halloween wasn't like it used to be when she was a kid — soaping windows, being invited inside the houses of warm, friendly neighbors, while they pretended to try to guess who you were beneath the mask. Halloween had been fun, exciting. Now it was poison and razor blades. Even though she didn't think there was anything like that around here, she thought maybe this was going to be Billy and Rachael's last year for trick or treating. Next year she would suggest a little party, invite some of their school friends.

'Well, some people just don't like kids,' she explained, though the notion was totally inconceivable to her. 'Some people just aren't very nice at all.' To herself she said, And some people are creeps, getting their jollies frightening little kids.

When she had Billy and Rachael calmed and into their p.j.'s, sitting in front of the TV with their cups of hot chocolate topped with tiny marshmallows, and a plate of freshly baked chocolate-chip cookies, she began to think a little more seriously about the man up at the Nickerson's.

Those kids had been a lot more than just a little frightened. They'd been terrified.

Maybe tomorrow, she thought, putting the last of the dishes in the cupboard, she would just take a little walk up there and have a friendly chat with Rose Nickerson.

11

Katie was perched on the side of the bed anxiously waiting for Linda Ring, who was to escort her downstairs in a wheelchair, (hospital policy) and then Katie would take a cab home. She knew full well Drake would be hurt she hadn't let him know she was being discharged today, but she felt an almost urgent need to be alone on her first day home, and Drake would have insisted on coming to get her.

She glanced down at the overnight case at her feet and sighed. It, like the proverbial bad penny, was still with her. Well, she had tried to give it back. Dismissing for the moment Drake's gifts to her, Katie stood to check her appearance in the mirror. Her legs were shaky now that she'd exchanged slippers for heels. Her navy and white dress hung on her. She tilted her head in the mirror, lifted her hair to examine the fresh bandage above her eye. At least the bruise on her cheek had faded and was now scarcely noticeable under makeup.

'So, you're leaving us, Miss Summers.'

Katie turned at the remembered voice.

102

The sight of Dr. Jonathan Shea standing in her doorway brought an unexpected rush of pleasure, shot with alarm. She realized with some surprise she'd been half hoping she would see him again before she went home, though she hadn't expected to see him looking so tired and drawn, as if he hadn't slept in days. His clothes were rumpled, and he was badly in need of a shave. She tried not to let these observations show in her face as she said hello.

'Not exactly The Ritz in here, is it?'

'It's not so bad,' Katie replied. 'But I can't say I'm sorry to be leaving. It'll be good to get home.'

'Is someone coming to pick you up?'

She hesitated, afraid he might give her an argument, but ready for him. She would sign herself out if she had to. Anyway, he didn't look like he would be much of a match for her today. 'I'm waiting for the nurse to take me downstairs. Then I'll take a cab home.'

His dark brows drew together. 'But surely there'll be someone there to meet you when you arrive.'

Katie laughed. Clearly, he had a little fight left in him. 'I sincerely hope not. Really, Dr. Shea, I'm perfectly fine. Though I do appreciate your concern.' She could see he was about to pursue the matter, then, defeat

103

clouding his face, he appeared to change his mind. Katie felt a slight disappointment to have won so easily, and found herself growing more and more curious about this man standing before her.

'Well, I'll just bid you goodbye, then,' he said, 'which is all I really came to do. Take care of yourself, Miss Summers.'

'I will. And thank you.' Gathering up her all-weather coat from the bed, Katie turned to see Dr. Shea still in her doorway. Neither said a word. Then, seemingly on impulse, he whipped a pen and notepad from his breast pocket and proceeded to scribble something down. He tore off the sheet of paper and handed it to her, saying, 'My home number. Just in case . . . in case you need . . . to talk. I'm not sure how effective I'd be in dealing with any real problems, but I've been told I'm a pretty good listener.' With that he turned on his heel and was gone, leaving Katie feeling at once pleased and bewildered. Why had he spoken in such self-deprecating terms? And why hadn't he suggested she call him at the hospital?

She folded the piece of paper and was putting it in her purse when Linda Ring entered the room, preceded by a wheelchair. 'Your limo awaits, m'lady,' she announced brightly.

Once settled in the wheelchair, the basket of fruit sent by the staff from The Coffee Shop, the overnight case, and Jason's beautiful arrangement of dried fall flowers on her lap, Katie's irrational fear of maybe being held here against her will began to disappear. Irrational fears brought her thoughts back to Jason. He had dropped the flowers off at the desk, which was as far as he'd let himself come. She understood. He had an aversion to hospitals and funeral parlors.

'I just saw Dr. Shea coming out of your room,' Linda said, releasing the brake and carefully maneuvering the wheelchair over the threshold so as not to jar her patient. 'How did he seem to you?'

'Pleasant,' Katie said, glancing over her shoulder at the nurse. 'He dropped in to say goodbye. Why?'

She shrugged. 'Just wondered.' They stopped to allow a little fair-haired boy on crutches, wearing a full-leg cast, to hobble past. He stared at Katie. She winked at him. He grinned. Nurse Ring went on, her voice dropping a notch as a clutch of doctors in animated discussion hurried past. 'He's been taking everyone's head off around here the past few days,' Linda said, while over the intercom a female voice was paging a Dr. White. An orderly wheeled a noisy gurney past them, on which lay an old woman either asleep or unconscious, the sheet drawn up to her neck. Katie could see pink, freckled scalp through the grey, thin hair. Soft whistling noises emitted from the woman's nose, stripping her of her dignity. Katie looked away. 'He lost a patient last week. Suicide. Tragic. She was just a kid.'

They went down in the service elevator. As the elevator came to a stop, the wheelchair rolled smoothly out through the open doors, down the wide corridor, turning onto a cement ramp, and finally out into the bleak, grey day where several cabs waited at the curb for fares. Linda Ring kept up a steady stream of monologue, mostly centered around Dr. Jonathan Shea. How he kept to himself, rarely attending any of the social functions, though rumor had it he was seriously dating some society woman — a woman of 'means.' A couple of the nurses had seen her, and reported back that she was a knockout.

Katie felt a little uncomfortable being privy to such personal information about the doctor, who was obviously a favorite topic of conversation among the nurses. God, how women loved to solve the mystery of a man. And wasn't she just a little curious herself?

The patient's suicide explained a lot. It saddened her to think of a young girl who found life so painful that death was preferable.

As the cab wheeled around the circular drive where fallen leaves skittered along the gutters and sidewalks, Katie waved goodbye to the slim, white figure who stood waving at her, finally disappearing inside the cavernous stone building.

Soon they were speeding along the highway, and a wave of weakness washed over Katie. She sank back against the maroon cushiony upholstery, hoping she hadn't been reckless in insisting to Dr. Miller against his arguments that she be allowed to go home. She would rest better there, she said. In truth, she had had her job to think about. She couldn't afford to be out of work indefinitely. She hoped she still had a job to go to.

Through the car window, the sky hung low and threatening. Soon, the highway ended, and they were on the narrowing road, where tall trees blew darkly in the rising wind. Katie shivered inwardly, knowing a cold house would greet her, and dreading it. Why hadn't she thought to ask Charlie Black to lay fires in the fireplaces? Well, it was too late to think of that now.

The cabbie was a much faster driver than Katie, and after a long stretch of bumpy, winding road, at last they were there. The driver got out and came around to open her door for her. 'Better have hubby batten up the old hatches tonight,' he said cheerfully, holding onto his cap. His nylon windbreaker billowed in the wind. His pants flapped around his legs.

'Yes, yes I will,' Katie said, counting out the money to pay him. Thank God, there was just enough in her purse. Maybe Jason wouldn't mind picking up her last paycheck from work.

'Hubby know you're comin' home today?' the driver said, staring up at the darkened windows in the house.

'Yes,' she said quickly. 'He should be home from work in another fifteen minutes or so.' Katie wasn't afraid of living alone, but neither was she fool enough to advertise the fact. The man looked harmless enough, but you couldn't stake your life on appearances, as her aunt used to say.

'You want some help carrying these things up to the house?'

Katie was about to accept the offer gratefully, then realized it wasn't gratitude he was interested in. He expected a tip, and right that he should. But unfortunately she had no more money.

'I can manage. Thanks, anyway.'

He shrugged, clearly miffed, climbed back into his cab, gunned the motor and sped off, spraying gravel in his wake.

Alone now, Katie gazed up at the old farm-house that stood like a sentinel on a slight rise in the land. Despite its being badly in need of repairs and a paint job, the house was a welcome sight. Even the surrounding trees rustled their leaves as if in greeting.

Katie gathered her belongings from the ground where the cab driver had set them, and, with the wind cutting through her thin coat and her hair blowing wildly, trudged up the path and on up the stairs where she deposited her burden on the tiny landing. Fumbling in her purse for the key, she grimaced as one of Jason's dried flowers was carried off by a gust of wind.

At last her fingers closed around the key, and she opened the door and slipped into the familiar hallway with its hardwood floor and dark panelled walls. Her gaze fell for a moment to the leaves littering the hall floor, as if someone had stood here with the door open.

Jason. Of course. When he came to get her clothes. Odd, though. Jason usually came in through the back way. Shrugging, Katie closed the door behind her, hurried on through the rarely used high-ceilinged parlor and dining room, her feet soundless on the carpets, and in through the French doors to her studio. As she'd expected, the house was damp and cold and smelled musty. She lit the kerosene lamp, and set about making a fire in the fireplace. An old hand at fire-building, Katie had the flames crackling and leaping to life in no time, sending shadows to dance on the pale, papered walls.

Hugging her coat to her, she crossed to the sliding glass doors that led out onto the small balcony overlooking the lake. Her favorite spot in nice weather, it now offered little but the cold, and the darkly churning waters below. She drew the heavy drapes closed to keep in the heat.

Placing another log on the fire, Katie then left the room to return shortly with a steaming mug of tea. The room had warmed, and Katie slipped out of her coat and settled down in the large stuffed chair in front of the fire.

In the dim, amber light, she looked around at her surroundings, smelled the familiar, soothing smell of paints and turpentine, mingling with the scent of the wood-fire. Though everything was as she remembered, she had the feeling of having returned after many years' absence.

The old Remington typewriter, on which

110

her Aunt Katherine's own dreams and fantasies had found voice in children's stories, was on the floor beside the wall bookcase, covered now to keep off the dust. How often Katie had sat in this room putting paint to canvas, listening to the tap-tapping of the typewriter in the background.

She could almost picture her aunt at her desk now, her strong, lovely face softened by lamp-light, the wisps of grey hair escaping the bun she always wore at the nape of her neck.

Aunt Katherine had completed only four slim volumes and a few short stories over her lifetime, but the books had gone into reprint many times, and allowed her to live modestly on the royalties. She'd found an equal joy in her gardening, bird-watching and reading (especially Agatha Christie) as she did in writing. She'd lived as she wanted, never marrying, and died quietly in her sleep three years ago at the age of eighty-four. And Katie had never stopped missing her.

Once Katie had asked her why she wrote for children since she'd never had any of her own, and her aunt had answered simply that her readers were her children. And when Katie asked if she ever got lonely, her eyes had shone with mystery and secrets. 'Now and then,' she said. And then she shared one of those secrets with Katie. There had been a man — a Matthew Kingsley, an English teacher. He died of tuberculosis in the forties. 'I suspect, Katie, dear,' she said, 'that I'm one of those impossible romantic women who can truly love only once. I had my love, and no one could ever quite come up to Matthew in my eyes.' Her twinkling eyes hinted mischief as she added, 'And that would hardly be fair to another, now would it?'

Smiling at the memory, and suspecting she was of the same romantic bent as her aunt, and not particularly pleased about it, Katie checked her watch. It was six-fifteen. Darkness came early now. The domed antique clock on the mantel read eleven twenty-five. Katie rose to rewind and set it properly, not only for the correct time, but because she took pleasure in the sound of the chimes. As she did, she heard a car door slam down below. It had to be Jason. He was the only one she knew who drove around the back. A brief unease passed through her, remembering the leaves littering the front hall floor.

She parted the drapes eagerly just in time to see her friend scurrying from his red Volkswagen, the wind whipping his fair, longish hair about his face. Then, he was flying up her back stairs. She opened the doors to greet him. 'Oh, Jason,' she cried, 'I've never been so glad to see anyone in my life. Please, come in before you blow away.'

Inside, they hugged, and Katie revelled in the good, comfortable feel of his cuddly, teddy bear frame. 'I've made a pot of tea, and there's a warm fire.'

'Sounds marvelous,' he said breathlessly, unbuttoning his coat. He shrugged out of it and tossed it with Katie's on the cot. He was smiling at her, his square teeth showing the slight overbite of which he was self-conscious, but that Katie found appealing. His figure, beneath the coat, was, in Jason's own words, 'pleasantly plump.' He wore a roomy, fishnet, turtle-necked sweater and blue jeans.

'I called the hospital,' he said, rubbing his hands together and holding them over the fire. 'They said you'd gone. How are you, darling?' He rushed on before she could answer. 'You look a little peaked, but not too much the worse for wear. Is there anything serious under that bandage?'

Her hand went automatically to the bandage above her eye. 'No. A slight laceration. The doctor says it probably won't even leave a scar.'

113

He nodded, beginning to fish into his coat pockets for, Katie knew, his cigarettes. He found them and lit one while Katie went to fetch his partially filled ashtray from the square oak table set against the wall facing the fireplace. She grimaced at its scarred surface strewn with art magazines, pages of sketches and a large peanut butter jar containing her brushes. Her aunt would have been dismayed at her niece's housekeeping, or lack thereof. Katie dumped the contents of the ashtray into the fireplace and handed it to Jason, who had settled himself in her chair in front of the fire. She pulled up another to join him.

'Sorry I didn't visit you in the hospital,' he said, 'but you know what a ghastly effect they have on me.'

She smiled. 'Yeah. On me, too. I didn't have a whole lot of choice.'

'No, you didn't, did you, dear.' He patted her hand resting on the arm of the chair, then combed his tangled hair with his fingers. 'My God, it's wild out there. Did I bring the right clothes to the hospital?'

'Everything was fine,' she said, stifling a giggle. She'd nearly forgotten how Jason's mind flitted from one thing to another with barely a pause. She found it endearing, but sometimes it was hard to keep up.

Katie suddenly remembered she'd left Jason's flowers on the front landing, along with everything else. 'There probably won't be a flower left in the vase,' she called after him as he hurried to bring them inside

Miraculously, most had survived. Jason dropped the overnight case at her feet, set the basket of fruit and the flowers on the table, having to clear a place, then flopped down on the chair. 'Well, what's new, darling?' he blurted. 'Silly question. We do have the damndest conversations, don't we? My God, Katie, I'm exhausted.'

She laughed. 'No wonder. And why don't you pull your chair up a little closer to the fire, Jason? You still look half frozen to me. Actually, now that you mention it,' she said, going through the small packet of get-well cards in her purse, finding the one she was looking for, and handing it to Jason. 'From Allen. What do you think?' It was a particularly pretty card, long and narrow with a single rose on the front, and inside a note that said simply that he was sorry about her accident, and hoped she would feel better soon. Innocent enough on the surface. And thoughtful. Yet she didn't have a good feeling about it.

Jason was studying the card, frowning. 'Hmph. He's not starting up again, is he?'

'I hope not,' Katie said, an understatement. 'It's been some time since you heard from him.'

'Almost two years.' Katie slipped the card back into her purse, wondering why she didn't just tear it up. Allen Parker was a policeman, a Burt Reynolds lookalike, and the last man with whom she'd had a brief involvement, one that ended with her wishing to God she'd never laid eyes on him. She'd liked him well enough in the beginning, attracted by his good looks and his sense of fun. But it wasn't long before another side of Allen, one not so pleasant, began to assert itself. He was possessive to the extreme, bullying, questioning her every move, criticizing her friends, accusing her of sneaking around behind his back. (Ironically, it was Allen, she found out later, who was doing the sneaking around.) When she broke it off, he became enraged. Though not at first. At first came the pleas and promises, the blaming of his behavior on job stress, on booze. When none of it worked, he grew obsessed with getting her back. That was when the harassment began. And Katie's fears for her safety.

Jason had been there for her through it all. She didn't know what she would have done without him.

The last she'd heard Allen had been transferred to Los Angeles — at his own request. But the card had a Belleville postmark.

'Forget about it,' Jason advised. 'There's probably nothing ominous about it. The guy just had a monstrous ego; he couldn't handle your rejecting him. Maybe the card is just his way of apologizing for being such an ass.'

'Maybe.'

'The paper said you ran into a telephone pole,' Jason said, changing the subject. 'Seemed odd to me, rain or not. You're usually such a careful driver, Katie.'

She slid her hand along the velvet chair arm. 'It's a strange story, Jason. And of course I'll tell you everything. But not just now, okay?'

He looked at her for a long moment, arching one blond eyebrow in his long, sensitive face — an artist's face. 'Sure, love. Tactless of me to bring it up. You must be absolutely destroyed.'

'Not absolutely,' she said smiling. 'Anyway, I feel much better now that you're here. How's Peter?' Peter Machum was Jason's live-in lover, had been for ten years now. He was younger than Jason, maybe thirty, dark-haired and slim. Unlike Jason, there was no hint of effeminacy about him, and

117

also unlike Jason, he was shy and withdrawn. Jason said Peter became animated in the courtroom — that he was a fine lawyer.

'He's in New York this week,' Jason said. 'A lawyer's convention.'

'Lonely?'

He shrugged and tapped the ash from his cigarette into the ashtray. 'Not really. I think short separations are good for both of us.'

Jason had been open about his gayness from the beginning, letting Katie know that he wanted only her friendship. Well, he certainly had that. She respected and admired him. Not only because he was, in her opinion, the most talented student in the art class they both attended weekly, but because he was one of the most sensitive and gentle human beings she had ever known. He was the brother she never had; a kindred spirit.

Remembering that even spirits occasionally need sustenance, she rose from her chair. 'I'll get your tea. I nearly forgot. Did I miss anything important at class?'

'You come back here and sit down,' he commanded. 'I have something here much more interesting than tea.' He surprised her then by producing a bottle of Mateus from beneath his bulky sweater. 'You're certainly not to wait on anybody today.' His eyes

118

danced. 'You are going to join me, of course.'

Katie sat back down. 'Well, maybe just a drop.'

Jason brought two wine glasses from the cabinet in the parlor, and was intently polishing them with a paper napkin. 'There was one interesting chap who came and gave a talk. He brought along some of his own work, abstracts, mostly. Quite good, too. It seems the fellow is a direct descendant of Renoir.' Handing Katie her glass brimming with the white wine, he said, 'Careful love, don't spill it. Anyway, Raymond, in his usual good form, proceeded to insult him.'

'Oh, no.' Raymond Losier seemed to Katie to be pursuing a career in meanness rather than painting. 'What did he say?'

'Told him that talent obviously didn't run in the family.'

Katie grinned in spite of herself. 'Well, I'm sorry I missed his talk.' She sipped her wine. 'Will he be coming back?'

'Would you?'

Katie laughed.

'Actually, he did promise a return visit. A good sort.' Frowning, he waved his cigarette impatiently at the air. 'But I'm darned if I can remember when. You know how I am with dates, Katie. I don't even know what today is.'

She grinned. 'Monday. October 31st.'

'There, you see. I even saw a few ghosts and goblins on my way out here, and it completely left my mind.' He gave his cigarette a hateful look and tossed it into the fireplace. 'I really ought to quit these disgusting things,' he said, as he so often did. 'Anyway, the date will be on the bulletin board. But that's not the most important matter at hand as far as you're concerned.'

'Oh?'

'The main reason I came out here tonight, aside from wanting to see with my own eyes how you were, is that I didn't want you to miss placing an entry in the state competition, especially since your show is garnering some lovely comments, and many from the right corners, I might add. The time is right, dear. Carpe diem.'

'Seize the day. You're right, of course. Oh, Jason, I'd completely forgotten about the competition with all that's happened . . . '

'I'm not surprised. But the prize is five thousand dollars, to say little of the nice tidy feather in your cap if you were to win. Good God, an honorable mention alone would be well worth the effort. But you've only got until the end of the week.'

'Thank you, Jason. You really are sweet to come all the way out here to remind me.' She gestured to the finished painting propped on her easel. 'Actually, I had considered entering my painting of the full moon on the lake. What do you think?'

'You're fishing, dear,' he said, wagging a finger at her. 'You know very well I'm mad about it.' Setting his glass on the floor, he rose and wandered over to the painting. Hands clasped behind his back, he cocked his head. 'Oh, yes. Yes. You've managed to capture all the beauty of the scene, certainly. But there's more. The painting evokes a powerful feeling of longing — a deep, collective human longing that's somehow primal and ancient. Yet at the same time the thing scares the hell out of me. I expect to see at least one self-respecting werewolf rising out of the mist.'

Katie laughed, and realized how often she had laughed since Jason's arrival. 'You're good for me,' she said softly.

He smiled at her.

'Speaking of lawyer's conventions . . . '

His eyebrows shot up. 'Were we?'

'No, but I wanted to tell you — Jason, I met someone.'

'Well, this is news.' His interest peaked, he

refilled both their glasses. 'And about time, I should think.'

'Don't jump to conclusions. I want your advice.'

'This has something to do with lawyer's conventions?' He was unconsciously pulling another cigarette from his pack.

'No, but the person I'm talking about is a lawyer. He just recently passed his bar exam, in fact.' She went on to tell him about Drake, and about her own confusing feelings toward him. 'Let me show you what he brought to the hospital.' Leaving her chair, Katie knelt and opened the case and, one by one, displayed each of Drake's extravagant gifts to her while Jason looked on in silent astonishment. 'I — I tried to give them back,' she said feebly. 'But on the night he was to take me to his graduation dinner — the same night I had the accident — his father suffered a stroke. At the suggestion of the doctors here, Drake took him to the clinic in Boston. When he went back to visit him, he uh . . . ' she gestured to the open case, 'did a little shopping.'

Jason blew a smoke ring at the ceiling. 'I'll say.'

'His father is home now, recuperating, and I just didn't have the heart to insist that Drake drive all the way back to Boston just to return these gifts. It's a three-hundred mile trip.'

There was a mischievous grin on Jason's face. 'He's got great taste, I'll have to say that for him. It's obvious the man has a real thing for you, Katie, m'dear. He spent a bundle.'

Sighing, Katie shut the case. 'I know.'

'But you don't feel good about keeping these things.'

She shook her head, returning to sit down. She felt weary.

Jason flicked the half-smoked cigarette into the fireplace, and made a careful pyramid of his long fingers, studied them. 'Then give them back, regardless of the inconvenience to the gentleman. It was presumptuous of him to buy them, of course. They've become a weight, haven't they, love.'

'You ever hear of a cement nightgown?'

He grinned. 'Give them back, Katie. The sooner, the better.'

She breathed a sigh of relief. 'Thanks. You always seem to know intuitively what's best for me, Jason.'

'You already knew what was best. You just wanted confirmation.'

He was right, of course. She was such a child, sometimes.

'Do you feel up to talking about the

accident, now? It might help.' He refilled her glass which she hadn't realized was empty. The combination of wine and the warm fire were making her drowsy. 'You don't have to, of course, if . . . '

Again, he was right. She did need to talk about the accident. She knew the moment Jason left and she was alone, the eyes would come back to haunt her. As well as the vision of the boy. She couldn't really call it a dream, could she. Could she?

'Jason,' she began tentatively, 'would you answer me truthfully about something? I mean well, don't worry about sparing my feelings.'

'Sounds serious.'

'Yes. It is.'

His expression at once grew thoughtful, concerned. He settled back in the chair. 'All right. Shoot.'

'Jason, do you think — I'm the sort of person who is easily given to hysterical imaginings — hallucinations?'

'Dear girl,' he said, looking relieved at the easy question, 'I don't know a single soul with their feet more firmly planted on the earth than you.' He allowed himself a small grin. 'Actually, some of my other, less well-grounded friends, shall we say, could take lessons.' He leaned forward in the chair. 'Maybe you better tell me what this is all about.'

She did, choosing not to meet his eyes until she'd finished her story. When she did look up, he was staring at her.

'Well, am I crazy?'

'Of course you're not crazy, love,' he replied, just a fraction too quickly. 'My God, you've been through a ghastly experience. Perhaps you just — I don't know. It was raining torrents, and dark. Could it have . . . ?'

'I've heard all the theories, Jason,' she cut in wearily. 'I tried to find one that made sense. But, no, I know what I saw in that rearview mirror. Eyes — dead eyes. And they were staring straight at me.'

Jason dragged nervously on a new cigarette. 'But the police found nothing.'

'No. I was quite alone in the car.'

'Eerie,' he muttered. 'Damned eerie.'

Not exactly an answer to the mystery, but what did she expect? It *was* a crazy story. Even Dr. Miller had thought she needed a psychiatrist, and worse, Jonathan Shea had implied she was making the whole thing up. Jason finished off the wine in his glass, and she saw him shiver just before he went to get his coat. 'Horrible business,' he said, shrugging into the coat.

125

It was suede, olive-green. Katie brushed an imaginary piece of lint from the collar. 'New?'

'I needed a treat. Do you like it?'

'Smashing.'

He looked pleased. Each button he buttoned took him farther away.

'Do you really have to go right now? I haven't had any supper. I could make us both some.' She heard the near-pleading in her voice and realized how very much she didn't want to be alone right now.

'Your road's a hazard at the best of times, love,' he said, touching her arm affectionately. 'I'll call you tomorrow, okay? Now just try and put — the whole, nasty business out of your mind.' He moved toward the patio doors, flipping the collar up on his coat. 'I'm sure there's a perfectly logical explanation.'

'Yes,' Katie said. 'You're probably right.' She was glad she hadn't told him about her vision of the boy. It would really have freaked him out.

'Get some rest, Katie,' he said, and she smiled at the familiar, easy advice.

'Thanks, I will.'

Jason lingered, looking anxious, as if sensing he was letting her down. 'Will you be all right? Have you enough wood for the fires? God, when are you going to install central heating in this place, love?'

'Probably about the same time I'm discovered as the next Rembrandt. But I'm fine, Jason, really. And thanks for coming out on such a terrible night — and thanks for the wine.' She kissed his cheek. 'I really do appreciate it — and you.'

He looked at her, shifted his feet. 'You know, I think you're quite mad to stay here all by yourself. No pun intended.' He peered behind him through the part in the drapes. 'God, I hate it when the lake looks like that,' he blurted. 'So black and angry.'

Katie was surprised at the vehemence in his voice. 'I didn't know you had a fear of the water, Jason. You never told me.'

'More like a terror. I can't swim a stroke. I nearly drowned when I was a kid. A couple of bullies threw me into — well, it doesn't matter now. It was a long time ago. But I guess that has something to do with it.'

Katie stood on the little balcony, chilled to the bone in only her linen dress, until he reached his car. 'Drive carefully,' she called out, but her voice was lost in the rising storm.

Poor Jason, Katie thought. I've spooked him. Once inside, she quickly closed and locked the patio doors behind her. And then,

127

too late, she remembered that she'd meant to ask him if he'd used her front door the last time he was here. She would call him tomorrow.

A gnawing uneasiness, which she knew had been further fueled by Jason's reaction to her story, had crawled inside her skin. Maybe Jason was right about the wisdom of her living alone out here. Maybe everyone was. Yet she'd never minded before. Black Lake was her home; she loved it here. Katie stood before the fire, rubbing the goosebumps from her arms, thinking. She'd always been independent. Even before she came to live with her aunt she'd had her own apartment, working as a hostess in the town's one good restaurant. By then her mother had already remarried and was living with her new husband in Florida, their own relationship having become more and more strained. And then when Todd didn't come back from the war there was no longer any reason to remain in Lennoxville — no longer anyone to wait for. And so she'd accepted her aunt's invitation to come and live with her here at Black Lake.

More than a decade ago. In some ways, only yesterday.

Holding the lighted lamp in one hand, and the glasses she and Jason had drunk from in the other, Katie headed out to the kitchen.

In the living room, she paused, frowning at the muddy footprints on the rug. She'd missed them on her way in. Jason? It didn't sound like her friend to track mud into someone's house. But footprints didn't lie. Someone else's? The thought sent a blade of ice straight to her heart. She played the lamplight over the tracks — definitely a man's. He'd actually walked around in here.

Allen? After all this time? He was capable of breaking and entering, she knew that.

Well, it was stupid to jump to conclusions until she talked to Jason. Katie continued on to the kitchen. Here, the air smelled of wood-smoke and of the apples Katie had picked a few weeks earlier. It was a large country kitchen, painted ivory, with the trim a robin's egg blue. (Katie's only attempt at redecorating, aside from having the glass patio doors installed in her studio, which were meant more to be functional than decorative, allowing more and longer light to work by.)

The kitchen's windows looked out on the grounds that sloped down to the road. Beyond the road were dense woods. Already, there was a smattering of stars in the sky. The nights came early now. Some of the trees

129

nearer the house had lost their leaves (*there were fallen leaves on the floor on her front hallway*), and the stark branches whipped in the wind. About to turn from the window, Katie's heart skipped as she thought she saw something move down by the big white pine near the path. She stood at the window for several minutes, her eyes fixed on the spot where she'd seen it, or imagined she had, but there was nothing. Just nerves, Katie thought, turning away. Or maybe a hungry raccoon, or a squirrel foraging for fallen pine cones.

At the porcelain sink, she rinsed and dried the glasses, set them upturned on the counter. On either side of her was an ivory painted door. The one on her right led into a walk-in pantry, while the one on her left opened onto a narrow flight of steps descending into the cellar where the wood was kept. Thankfully, there was enough wood in the woodbox to last at least until tomorrow, Katie thought, reaching for another chunk and feeding it into the monstrous cast-iron wood stove that took up most of the back wall. It occurred to her she was hungry, but the thought of preparing something, or even eating it, would take far more energy than she had at the moment. Sleep was what she needed most right now. Hours and hours of sleep.

She would face the world tomorrow.

The wide stairs leading to the bedrooms rose up through the center of the house. Gripping the handrail for support, Katie climbed them on legs that felt weighted with lead chains, the candle's flame guiding her steps. Once, she stumbled slightly and realized that having had nothing to eat, together with all the wine she'd consumed, were taking their toll. Katie was halfway up the stairs before she noticed the same muddy tracks as in the parlor. Bending to examine them closer, she picked up what appeared to be a few pieces of straw. She shoved them into her dress pocket, refusing to give any of it another thought until she had a chance to talk to Jason.

She thought instead about her car in the garage for repairs. The insurance would cover most of the cost, but in the meantime she was without a car. She would have to walk the mile and a half to the highway; from there she could catch a bus into town. Not a happy thought, what with the weather having turned so damned cold, but she didn't have a whole lot of choice. She had to work. Well, no sense moaning about it. She supposed she should be grateful that the car wasn't beyond repair, or she herself, when it came right down to it.

As she stepped onto the landing, a cool draft brushed the fine hairs on her arms, and in the next second the candle went out, leaving Katie in inky blackness. Fear made her heart race, dried her lips.

Get hold of yourself. There's no reason to panic. You're not a child; there is nothing to fear in the darkness. Reminding herself there was a lamp in her room, and matches with which to light it, she felt calmer. Katie continued down the hallway, feeling along the papered wall like a blind woman trying to negotiate her way in a stranger's house. At last she was outside her room, her fingers closing around the cool porcelain knob. Pushing the door open, she stepped carefully over the threshold.

Inside, she crossed to her dresser, feeling relieved when her hand touched the glass base of the lamp. After fumbling briefly among familiar objects, she found the box of wooden matches. Striking one against the coarse strip on the side of the box, she then gave a delicate turn of the wick, and lit the lamp. At once, the room was bathed in soft light.

Fitting the chimney back into place Katie picked up the lamp, thinking she would read awhile. Reading always helped her to fall asleep. As tired as she was, she knew she would lie awake, otherwise.

Half-turned from the dresser, Katie froze. Her breath clogged in her throat, escaping in a tiny whimper of shock and horror at the grotesque sight before her, now spotlighted in the flickering circle of lamplight.

Outside, the wind howled and raged, rattling the window in its casing, but Katie heard only the blood rushing in her ears, and the scream of terror she did not recognize as her own — a scream cut off as she sagged in a faint to the floor.

12

The ringing of the telephone downstairs pulled Katie up from the darkness, dazed and disoriented. She felt as if she'd been passed out for hours instead of the few minutes it had been. Although a deep chill seemed to pour from the very walls of the room, Katie's skin was clammy with perspiration.

What happened? Why was she on the floor? The edge of the braided rug dug into her cheek. The smell of kerosene oil was strong. Struggling to her feet, Katie reached out to the chair for support, and as she did, clutched a handful of thick, coarsely textured fabric. Memory jolted, and her hand jerked back.

'Todd?' she whispered.

Only the wind answered.

She licked dry lips. Was she losing her mind? Had she merely hallucinated? She must have. If not, then Todd was here in the room with her, and of course that was impossible because Todd was killed in the war.

Then what? Even in the dim light, Katie could make him out, could see the dark outline of his still form in the chair.

Retrieving the lamp from the floor, which, miraculously, was still lit and hadn't set fire to anything, Katie stepped nearer. The telephone downstairs stopped ringing.

Katie raised the lamp, stifling a gasp as the light threw a great looming shadow on the wall behind 'it'. The shadow quivered as Katie's hand, holding the lamp, shook. 'Oh, my God, why?' she whispered. Her words hung ominously in the room. She tore her eyes from the hideous sight, taking a backward step, wanting with every instinct in her to run from the room. But she couldn't let herself do that. She had to know what she was seeing — had to make sure it wasn't her imagination this time.

Steeling herself, Katie looked again. She forced the lamp steady.

The eyes were a pale, icy blue, the whites threaded with tiny veins. They were as real looking as those in the life-sized figures in Madame Toussaud's museum, which she'd toured with her art class two years ago.

There was no doubt in Katie's mind that the eyes that looked at her now were the same eyes she saw in her rearview mirror — the eyes that caused her to lose control of her car.

She lowered the lamp. The throat of

'the thing' oozed a dark, sticky substance that looked like blood, as if it had been slashed. Unable to look any longer, her heart thumping in her chest, Katie slowly backed out of the room.

The eyes followed her.

In her studio, fighting nausea, tasting the sour, acidy wine in her stomach, Katie thumbed frantically through the telephone book for the number of the Belleville Police Department. She couldn't find it, and only later remembered that it was clearly displayed on the front cover. Frustrated, and trying to quell her panic, she dialed 'O' for the operator. Her breathing, as she waited for someone to come on the line, seemed amplified in the silence.

'Operator,' a nasal female voice said at last, and Katie forced her own voice calm and even as she asked the woman to please connect her with the police — that her house had been broken into.

After giving the police her name and directions to her house, Katie hung up and went to place more wood on the live embers, then she wrapped herself in an afghan, and sat on the cot to wait for the police. Seized by a sudden, violent trembling, Katie hugged herself, and tried to stop her teeth from chattering. What if he's still here? she thought. What if he's still in the house?

When the hammering sounded on the front door, she jumped up and, ignoring the afghan that fell from her shoulders, grabbed up the lamp, and hurried to answer. She threw the door wide to a gust of wind and rain.

But it wasn't the police.

Katie stared in astonishment at the man towering above her in the doorway.

★ ★ ★

'Dr. Shea. I — I was expecting the police.'

'I know.' He pushed his way past her, shutting the door behind him, fading out the sounds of the storm. 'I heard the call come in over the police band.' His eyes darted about like an animal's sensing danger.

'There's no one in the house but me, Doctor,' she said in a small voice. 'At — least I don't think so.' Why is he here, Katie wondered. And why is he looking at me with such anger.

'I telephoned earlier,' he said, his voice sharp and cold, and bewildering to Katie. 'There was no answer.'

'Oh, was it you? I remember hearing it ring. I . . . '

'My God, woman, this place is like a barn. Are you trying to catch pneumonia?'

'There's a fire in the studio fireplace,' she defended, 'and the kitchen is comfortable. It's just these rooms . . . ' Her voice drifted off, and her body convulsed in harsh, wracking sobs. It was as if a dam within her had burst, a flood once began, she couldn't stop. She heard herself raving incoherently about something upstairs in her room, and before she could realize what was happening, Jonathan Shea had lifted her in his arms as though she were as weightless as a baby.

'So, where's your studio?' His tone had softened a little.

Katie pointed, at the same time trying to disengage herself from his strong arms. 'Put me down, please,' she choked out, ashamed of her loss of control.

'Hold onto the lamp. I can't carry both you and it.' His voice had lost its steely edge, and Katie let herself sag against him.

In the studio, he deposited her gently on the cot and covered her with the afghan. His eyes were questioning.

'Upstairs,' she said numbly. 'You'll know I'm not making it up this time. First door on the right at the top of the stairs.'

He nodded. 'I'll be right back. You stay here. I'll bring an extra blanket. Is there a flashlight in this mausoleum? The lamp is a damned nuisance. Anyway, you'll need it yourself.'

'In the desk drawer.'

As he started from the room, Katie suddenly flung the afghan from her. 'Wait, Jonathan. I'm going with you. I'm all right, now.' She needed to see the thing again herself, to know she hadn't imagined it. Also, she did not want to be alone just now.

'Katherine, no,' he said, turning. 'I won't be long. You're in no state to . . . '

'I'm going with you,' she said flatly, and stared him down despite his intimidating manner.

He gave her a long-suffering sigh. 'Please yourself. But stay behind me.'

She needed little coaxing to do just that. As they climbed the stairs, Katie followed close at his heels.

'Don't pull me backwards,' he said, his voice hushed, and Katie dropped her hands, realizing with embarrassment she'd had a death-grip on the hem of his jacket. 'It wouldn't do if we both fell downstairs.'

As the flashlight's beam paved their way through the darkness, she heard him say, 'It's bad enough you're living in isolation out here, but to endure this place without electricity or central heating . . . ' He glanced over his shoulder. 'I'm surprised you have a telephone.'

'I thought it a necessity. How did you find my house, Dr. Shea?' They were on the landing, and her voice had dropped to a whisper.

'I told you, the directions came over the police band. Anyway, most folks in Belleville know where Katherine Summers, the writer, lived. My kid sister has all her books.'

'Oh.'

'You are either a very courageous woman, or you're quite mad. I haven't decided which. I'll reserve diagnosis until we at least have a few sessions together.'

'Spare me,' she hissed. 'Anyway, I like it here. It's that simple. I'm with people all day in my job. I'm an artist. I need the quiet. Besides, it's rent free.'

They were standing at the bedroom door now, and talking ceased. Katie heard their combined breathing. She heard the wind. Her nerves were as taut as guide wires.

'You all right?'

'I'm fine.'

'Stay behind me.'

She had no intention of doing otherwise.

'Maybe you should wait out here.'

'No, I'm going in with you.'

'You're sure.'

'Yes.' Then she was following the wide-shouldered man, with his straight black hair coming just to his collar, into the room. He shone the light around, spotting the flowered wallpaper, her bed. As 'it' came into focus, Katie's hand instinctively darted out to touch Jonathan.

His back muscles beneath her palm tensed, and she heard him mutter a curse. Moving to stand beside him, she spoke in a whisper, as if they were in a funeral parlor. 'Someone must have put it here while I was in the hospital.' With Jonathan in the room with her, the effigy did not seem quite so terrifying. 'And I'd been thinking about Todd lately. I suppose it was the army uniform . . . '

'Todd?'

'Todd Raynes. We were going to be married. It was a long time ago. He was killed in Vietnam.'

Jonathan touched a finger to the bloodied throat of 'the thing' (as Katie was coming to think of it), drew back his hand and sniffed the red substance clinging to his finger. 'Paint,' he said. He lowered the flashlight. Her tube of red paint was under the chair. He picked it up. He was about to say something else, when Katie gasped. He followed her gaze to the picture on the

141

dresser. As with the effigy, Todd's throat in the photograph was smeared with the red paint.

'Todd?' he asked.

She nodded.

Jonathan studied the photograph a moment, then returned his attention to 'the thing' in the chair. There really was no resemblance to Todd. Even to the blue eyes, Katie thought. Todd had had beautiful brown eyes.

As if reading her mind, he said, 'I can see why you thought it was Todd. Our sick friend did a crude job, but effective nonetheless. Your imagination supplied the finishing touches.'

They both turned at the sound of distant police sirens. 'They might be able to lift some identifiable prints,' Jonathan said. 'I imagine they'll want to take that photo along, but I'm sure they'll return it in a few days.'

A shiver passed through Katie. 'It doesn't matter. I doubt that I'll ever want to look at it again.'

As the sirens rose in volume, he took her arm. 'Come on,' he said, 'let's go down and let them in.'

They were halfway down the stairs when the telephone rang. It was still ringing when they reached the studio. Darting ahead of her, Jonathan picked up the receiver.

'No, I'm sorry,' he said in his authoritative doctor's voice. 'Miss Summers is not available to come to the phone just now. Yes, I'll tell her.'

'Who is it?' Katie demanded, reaching for the phone. 'I can . . . '

But he'd already hung up. 'That was your lawyer friend, Drake Devlin,' he said off-handedly. 'The guy with the rose garden.'

13

'Straw stuffed into an army uniform,' the policeman with the hard eyes and jowly cheeks said unnecessarily. He was down on one knee examining the effigy, which was laid out on the floor at the foot of the stairs.

Katie sat on the bottom step, hands folded together to keep them from shaking. She deliberately avoided looking at Jonathan, still annoyed at him for not giving her the phone, or at least identifying himself to Drake. 'Does that mean the person responsible for this could be in the service?' she asked.

The policeman grunted to his feet, hitched up his pants which stopped just short of his protruding belly. 'Maybe. Maybe not.' There was an air of self-importance about the man that irked Katie. 'The uniform could have been picked up in any army surplus store,' he said, motioning to the younger policeman, who at once began working the strawman into a plastic bag and zipping it up. 'Do you have friends partial to playing practical jokes?'

'No. And even if I did, this is hardly a joke, is it?'

He glanced down at the clear plastic bag, through which the blue eyes were still visible. 'Well, then, I'd say we're dealing with a first rate sicko, ma'am.' He turned to Jonathan, who was standing off a little to one side, hands thrust in his pockets. 'Dr. Shea, you're a shrin . . . psychiatrist. All that book learnin' tell you anything about this guy?'

'Well, first of all we really don't know that it is a guy, do we?' Jonathan said. 'And I really don't think much expertise is required to deduce that whoever did it is a few bricks short of a full load.' With that he folded his arms and fixed the surprised policeman with a steely gaze.

Despite the seriousness of the situation, Katie grinned, and caught a matching grin from the blond young policeman who stood quietly by, appearing to wait his next command. The humor of the moment fled. Katie rose to her feet. 'Who would want to frighten me like this?' At a wave of dizziness, she sagged back down the step. 'I can't believe I've made such a terrible enemy.'

'Maybe you haven't,' the older policeman replied, his eyes sweeping over her. 'Could be someone you don't know — a secret admirer.' There was a trace of a smirk on his face. 'Anyway, we're as much in the dark as you are at the moment, but we'll do our job. If we come up with any answers, Miss Summers, we'll be in touch.'

When they were gone, taking the effigy with them, Katie said, 'That was rather rude of you. And not terribly professional.'

'Really? Well, I'm not my charming self these days. And I'm also no longer practicing the profession of psychiatry. Besides, I didn't like the son-of-a-bitch.'

'What do you mean, you're no longer practicing psychiatry?' Katie asked, ignoring his remark about the policeman, no doubt because it reflected her own opinion of the man.

'It's a long and boring story.' He moved toward her. 'Are you thinking there was a strawman in your car that night?'

'I know there was. Whoever put it there must have been following me in their car and removed it before the police and ambulance arrived on the scene.'

He laid a comforting hand on her shoulder. 'Why don't you leave here with me tonight? I've only got a small apartment, but there's a spare bed. You're welcome to stay. Or if you prefer, I'll check you into a hotel.'

Touched at the kind offer, for the moment Drake's call to her was forgotten. Frankly, she didn't know what she would have done without Jonathan Shea here tonight.

'Thanks, but I'll be fine here. I'll sleep in the studio,' she said, knowing no amount of persuasion in the world could convince her to go back upstairs tonight. Her thoughts curved back to his comment about not practicing psychiatry anymore, and she wondered if it had something to do with the young girl who committed suicide. Though tragic, Katie couldn't help thinking that tragedies could hardly be an uncommon occurrence in Jonathan's line of work.

'Have you had any supper?' he asked, breaking into her thoughts.

'No, I wasn't hungry.'

'You're a maddening woman, Katherine Summers,' he said, giving a sigh of exasperation. 'You don't eat. And I know you conned Dr. Miller into letting you come home far sooner than he thought wise. He was under the impression, as I was myself, that there would be someone staying with you.'

'Then I don't know where you got that impression. I never lied to Dr. Miller. Or you.'

'No. You just conveniently hid the truth.'

Katie's annoyance flared to anger. 'I have a job to go to, Dr. Shea.' Obviously, he hadn't lost his arrogance at all. He'd just misplaced it.

'Do you remember what I told you about there being a fine line between courage and martyrdom?' he said, as if speaking to a dull-witted child.

Seeing the anger leap to his eyes, Katie was more than a little pleased with herself.

'Where's your kitchen? Never mind, I'll find it myself.' With that, he picked her up bodily off the step and carried her into the studio, with Katie fighting him every step of the way. He stood her on her feet. 'There. Now lie down.'

'You're crazy,' she snapped, straightening her clothes.

'So you've said. Now I'm asking you nicely — lie down.'

'Look, I said I'm not hungry. Now I really do appreciate all . . . '

'Lie down,' he repeated, his voice low and dangerous. He levelled his eyes at her. 'Or would you like a little assistance?'

She lay down on the cot, glaring up at him.

He smiled. 'Good girl.' He covered her with the afghan with its knitted squares of brown and orange and beige, and as he leaned close, Katie caught the spicy scent of his aftershave mingling with a faint, darker scent that was Jonathan.

She lay still and stiff as a mannequin

while his hands moved deftly over her body, pressing here, smoothing there.

'I'm not cold, for God's sake.'

'Be quiet.'

Her muscles tensed. Did his hand linger just a little longer than necessary on the curve of her waist? Before she could decide, it had slipped lower, pausing dangerously near her thigh. She darted a look at him, but his face was impassive, revealing no hint of lecherous intent.

How little she really knew about men. In particular, a man like Jonathan Shea. Where did the doctor end — and the man begin?

He tugged the edge of the afghan up over her breasts and, as he did, his fingers brushed her nipples, sending a jolt of electricity through her clothes. To Katie's horror, her body quivered involuntarily. Their eyes met, and Katie writhed inwardly. She tried to look past the thatch of black hair that had fallen over his brow, at his firm, sensuous mouth. She fought an almost overpowering impulse to reach out her arms and draw him down to her. My God, what was wrong with her? And she knew it wasn't Jonathan Shea she didn't trust as much as she didn't trust herself.

His eyes held hers in bold challenge. 'Comfortable?' he asked innocently.

To her deep shame, she saw the tiniest

play of a smile at the corners of his mouth, and knew that that policeman had not been the only son-of-a-bitch in the room. Jonathan had known exactly what he was doing, just as he now knew what she was feeling. And he was laughing at her.

Had he done it simply to pay her back for her remark about his 'adoring nurses'? To show her she wasn't immune to his charms? Don't you dare cry, Katie Summers! Don't you dare!

'You really do have wonderful green eyes,' he said, before turning from her and leaving the room.

Katie lay there seething and hating Jonathan Shea almost as much as she hated her own treacherous body.

It was a good half hour before he returned carrying a tray, from which wafted a familiar tomatoey aroma. Katie'd had sufficient time to regain her composure. She thanked him, realizing with some surprise that her hunger was greater than her wounded pride.

'Compliments of Campbell's,' he said.

'I don't think I can eat all this,' she lied, biting into a piece of buttered bread.

Again, he left the room, and Katie couldn't help noticing the way his broad shoulders strained against the soft blue fabric of his sweater, or how his back tapered to narrow, taut hips. Her hatred of him, as she continued to eat, subsided just a little. She wondered idly where he was off to this time.

Her question was answered when, moments later, he returned with a blanket, and what looked to be her flannel nightgown and robe draped over his arm. He nodded approvingly at her tray, emptied of all but a few bread crumbs.

'I knew you could eat it all if you put your mind to it.' He removed the tray from her lap, fitting it among the disarray on the table. 'I think you'll sleep more comfortably if you get out of that dress and into your bedclothes.'

She hugged the afghan to her. 'I'm fine.'

'No, Katherine, you're not fine. You've had a stretch in the hospital, part of that time in a coma, and you've just had one hell of a shock. You're not fine at all. You need a little looking after.'

Maybe she would feel better out of the dress. She hadn't had a chance to change with all that had happened. She thought wistfully of a hot bath.

'All right. I'll put them on. If you'll just step into the other room . . . ' She certainly had no intention of changing in front of him.

'Don't be silly,' he said, and pulled the

afghan from her before she could stop him. 'Get up. I'll help you. You might pass out if you're alone.'

'I don't need your help,' she said more sharply than she meant to. 'I mean — well, you've already done more than enough.' Her face flamed at her poor choice of words. 'Look, I honestly do appreciate your concern, but you needn't stay any longer. I'm sure you have things to do. And I'm not going to pass out. I'll change as soon as you leave, I promise. You can just leave the bedclothes.'

He looked at her, surprise registering on his face. 'I have no intention of leaving you alone here tonight. And I don't really think you're up to tossing me out bodily.'

She burned at his bullying tactics. 'And before you go,' she said pointedly, 'I think I should tell you that I didn't appreciate your intercepting that call from Drake. He's a very sensitive man, and he's been worried about me. You might at least have told him who you were.'

'Or he'll think what?' he said, with a trace of amusement that grated on Katie. 'Doesn't he trust you? And if he's so damned concerned about you, why isn't he here?'

'That's not your affair, Doctor, but if you must know, Drake would be here if he'd

152

known I was coming home today.' In a burst of anger, Katie leapt to her feet. As she did, the room tilted crazily, and she would have fallen flat on her face had Jonathan not been there to catch her.

'Steady now,' he said, and held her so close she could feel the strong beat of his heart against her breasts. 'Are you all right?' he asked softly after a moment.

'Yes. I — I just stood up too quickly, that's all.' She was disturbingly aware of his warm, moist breath on her cheek, and of the way his chin brushed the top of her head.

'I don't think you're up to doing battle just yet,' he said, his tone lightly teasing.

Outside, the wind raged on, and the rain beat against the patio doors. The storm seemed to echo her own soaring emotions — emotions that both confused and frightened her. The room, with its crackling fire and the pale lamplight, seemed to encompass them, cutting them off from the rest of the world.

My God, you hardly know this man, Katie reminded herself, and tried to slip from his embrace, but he held her fast. 'Be still,' he murmured against her hair, and then she felt cool air brush her skin as the zipper at the back of her dress parted beneath his fingers, the fabric falling away, leaving her back naked to his touch. Over her feeble protests, his firm yet gentle hands moved down over her shoulders, and the dress fell to a puddle at her ankles.

Now he was undoing the hooks of her bra, and Katie knew sheer panic. 'Don't,' she pleaded. 'Don't please.'

'You're such a child, Katherine,' he chided. 'I am a doctor, after all. Do you think you'll be the first woman I've seen without her clothes on?'

Removing her bra, he tossed it somewhere behind her, in the same moment releasing her to reach for her nightgown. But in the instant before he did, Katie caught the unmistakable flicker of interest in his eyes.

Agonizingly aware that she was standing before him clad only in thin bikini panties, she instinctively crossed her arms over her breasts and lowered herself onto the cot, swiftly drawing the afghan up to her chin.

He handed her the nightgown.

She flashed her hatred at him.

'Guess I'm not as immune as I thought,' he said matter-of-factly, a devilish grin sweeping his features. 'But then it's been quite a few years since I've been in general practice.'

In a temper, Katie pulled the nightgown over her head, and when he tried to cover her with the blanket, she snatched it from him, slapping his hand away.

'It's rude to grab.'

'I'll cover myself.' Doctor, be damned, she thought, and wanted more than anything to puncture that inflated ego, that conceit. 'Do you always chase ambulances and police cars?'

He flinched as if she'd struck him, and she at once regretted the remark, though it seemed to her to have had a greater effect on him than it should have warranted. 'I'm sorry,' she said, not understanding the pain she saw in his eyes, nor, surprisingly, taking any pleasure from having put it there. 'Look, you've been very kind, and believe me, I am grateful.' Feeling the last of her strength ebb, she lay her head back on the pillow. 'But you confuse me,' she said quietly.

He looked at her for a moment, then, without replying, turned from her and extinguished the flame in the lamp. Now only the light from the fire kept them from being in total darkness.

The earlier drumming of rain on the glass doors had softened to a light patter, and it was with an unsettling blend of relief and longing that Katie watched Jonathan's silhouetted form move from her to go and sit before the fire. She watched him reach for the poker standing against the wall to stoke the fire, exploding sparks into the air like fireflies.

Now, his head lay against the chair's headrest, bringing into profile the strong chin, high cheekbones, the faintly hawk-like nose. Light and shadow played about the terrain of his craggy features.

What is he thinking about? Katie wondered, sensing that he had withdrawn into himself.

She was suddenly struck with the unlikeliness of Dr. Jonathan Shea being here in this room with her at all. Why was he? What had brought him here? He'd told her he'd overheard her call on his policeband radio. Also, that he'd known where her house was located because of her aunt's local celebrity status.

Had it been vanity on Katie's part that made her so readily accept explanations which now seemed to her contrived? She saw in her mind's eye the muddy tracks throughout the house which she'd at first assumed were Jason's. With a slight quickening of her breath, she lowered her gaze to Jonathan's shoes.

Fire danced in the black leather.

His voice came soft and deep out of the darkness, startling Katie. 'You're perfectly safe, Katherine. Go to sleep.'

She hadn't thought he could see her in the dim light. Perhaps he hadn't. Perhaps he'd only sensed her watching him.

'I wasn't worried,' she said.

14

Jonathan was gone when she woke up.

The day had dawned bright and sunny, and Katie ate a stale bran muffin and was finishing her second cup of coffee in the kitchen, trying to get up the nerve to call Mrs. Cameron at The Coffee Shop, when she heard a car slow down outside. Through the window, she saw the police cruiser, red dome twirling silently, drive by her house. Seeing it brought a measure of comfort, and at the same time frightened her, bringing home the reality that she might be in real physical danger.

Surely — whatever — whoever it was had meant her no harm, she reasoned, otherwise 'he' could have been in the back seat of her car instead of just the — strawman. Or he could have been waiting for her in her room last night. At the thought, the coffee turned suddenly bitter in her mouth.

She got up and made the rounds, checking all the locks on the doors. Old doors. Old locks. Some of the windows didn't even have locks. Someone could get in easily if they had a mind to. Someone already had. In her aunt's day, there seemed no need for locks.

Satisfied she could do no more, Katie started up the stairs to take a much longed for bath. Halfway up, a foreboding gripped her, and she had to force herself to keep going, not to turn and run.

She hesitated at the door to her room, her hand raised but not quite touching the doorknob. Was he in there now? Waiting? She opened the door.

And then she was standing in the middle of the room looking warily about her. Her brass bed with its multi-colored quilt, the night table, the dresser — all as she remembered. Nothing out of place except for the empty spot on the dresser where Todd's photograph had sat for all these years.

She noticed the dark, sooty smear on the rug where she'd dropped the lamp when she'd fainted and again said a silent prayer of thanks that a fire hadn't been started.

It came unbidden — the image of a shadowy figure moving stealthily about her room, opening drawers, sifting through her personal belongings. She tried to block it out, but it was impossible, filling her with a sensation of uncanniness. For although the room might look the same, she knew that in some intangible way, it was changed forever. It was almost as though, she, Katie, had been

159

personally violated.

Why Todd? she wondered. Why had the strawman been made to appear as Todd? She moved to the window, pushing aside the long, sheer drapes in a need to escape one possible answer that tugged at her consciousness.

No. It couldn't be. That would be too — incredible.

Outside the window, the sky was an unbroken blue. Although the wind had lessened considerably, there was still enough to ruffle the surface of the lake below and cause the nearby trees to brush against the house making a sound like fingernails on wood. Impatient with herself, she shut out the image the eerie thought had evoked. Never had she found the wind a thing to fear; she had in fact often done her best work to the accompaniment of a violent storm outside her studio doors.

Still, the leaves of the red maple trembled precariously as if echoing her own uneasiness. Always, Katie had drawn comfort from the trees surrounding her house, like the embrace of old friends. But now they held an ominous quality, like those same friends had, while her back was turned, gone over to the side of some unseen enemy.

'You're being ridiculous,' she said aloud,

and was mildly reassured by the sound of her own voice in the quiet room. Taking a change of underclothes from the bureau drawer, she went into the bathroom where she turned on both taps full.

A half hour later, Katie was back in her studio dialing the number of The Coffee Shop.

'Katie,' Mrs. Cameron's cheerful voice cried over the line. 'How are you, dear? It's so good to hear your voice.' Not waiting for a reply, she went on. 'Such a terrible thing, your accident. I would have come to visit you in the hospital, but I've been pretty well tied up here.'

Katie could hear Francine calling out to Frank for a ham and cheese omelet and a side of fries. She sounded harried. In the background, above the familiar buzz and chatter of the early lunch crowd, Kenny Rogers was singing *Lady*.

'I know, Mrs. Cameron, and I really am sorry. I hope I haven't caused you too much inconvenience,' she said, knowing full well that of course she had. There was never enough staff even at the best of times. 'I was planning on coming in this afternoon if — if you still want me to. I mean, I realize you can't hold my job open indefinitely.'

She heard a surprised chuckle. 'Still want

you to? My dear girl, I'm going quite mad here without you. You possess a certain knack of calming the staff and customers that I no longer seem to have. I suppose I don't have the patience I had as a young woman. But I don't want you coming in here, Katie, unless you're sure — absolutely sure — you're feeling up to it. We can manage to struggle along until you get back on your feet. Andrea, dear,' she called out, 'there's a customer at the cash; will you take care of it, please?'

Katie let out the breath she'd been holding. She'd been even more worried about losing her job than she realized. 'I'm feeling fine now, Mrs. Cameron. Being back to work will be good for me.' It will bring back some semblance of normalcy into my life, she thought. She was about to thank her employer, and ask her to convey her appreciation to the staff for the basket of fruit, and the lovely card everyone had taken the trouble to sign (even Joey had signed his 'X'), but then decided it would mean more if she did it in person.

Thoughts of gifts given to her in the hospital made her glance guiltily down at the overnight case on the floor. She'd almost forgotten about it. Probably because subconsciously she wanted to. Poor Drake.

162

What must he be thinking? She would telephone him if she knew his number, but she didn't, and there was little point in trying to look it up since she had absolutely no idea where he lived except that it was 'up country', wherever that was.

Katie opened the case. Gazing in at the lovely fabric, and smelling the exotic fragrance of French perfume, she tried to imagine Jonathan Shea buying expensive gifts to impress a woman, and couldn't. He would probably think he was quite enough in himself. But she'd promised herself she wouldn't think about Dr. Jonathan Shea. There were just too many confusing emotions when she did — too many unanswered questions. She was clearly physically attracted to the man, yet in a deep part of herself, she sensed a hidden side to him. An angry, darker side. She'd felt unsure in his presence, vulnerable. Even a little frightened.

Think about Drake, she told herself. Drake had tried to convince her he just wanted to be her friend, but she knew better; he was hoping for much more. Maybe she was herself. It would be nice in a way not to be alone anymore.

No. She'd made her choices. Safe choices. Holding up a lace trimmed coral negligee, intending to refold it properly, she noticed a small, glossy card fall from one of the folds in the skirt. Idly, she picked it up and read the gothic script.

Thank you for shopping at Natasha's, Belleville's first store in fine lingeree. We are pleased to have served you. Come again.

The Management

For several seconds, Katie simply stared in bewilderment at the card in her hand. As realization dawned, she began a slow burn. Drake had lied to her. He hadn't bought these things in Boston at all. So determined to have her accept his gifts, he'd actually gone so far as to trick her into believing he would have to drive three-hundred miles to return them.

Katie dropped the negligee back into the case and snapped the lock. Well, this would certainly make giving them back a whole lot easier. Relief gradually replacing her anger, Katie went upstairs to change into her work clothes.

As she entered the room for the second time that morning, there was a split second when she saw the strawman sitting propped up in the chair just as it had been last night. She turned away and reached into the closet, snatching up a white tailored blouse and straight black skirt from their hangers, leaving the empty hangers to swing and clatter together. Taking care not to peer too closely into the cavernous darkness beyond the rack of clothes, Katie shut the door and hurried from the room.

★ ★ ★

Rose Nickerson had seemed pleased, if not terribly surprised, when she answered her door and found her neighbor, Betty Martin, standing there. Which was mildly odd, since neither was the visiting kind.

'Come in, Betty,' she smiled, opening the door wider. 'How nice to see you. I've put the coffee pot on. Of course you'll sit awhile.' Mrs. Nickerson was a big woman, and solidly built. She was a cheery, capable sort.

Probably saw me coming up the path, Betty Martin thought as she followed Rose into the big yellow and white kitchen, where the aroma of freshly baked bread filled the air. Yet it did seem to her that Rose already knew why she was here — that she'd been expecting her.

'It certainly has turned cold all of a

sudden, hasn't it?' Rose Nickerson said, taking down two earthen mugs from the cabinet and filling them with steaming coffee. She set out a plate of cookies. 'I surely do hope we don't have a winter like we did last year. How's Earl, Betty? I hear the school bus drivers are talking about going on strike. Well, I for one think they should be making a decent wage. It's a darned responsible job they have.'

Earl Martin had been driving a school bus for nearly twelve years, and loved it. He had a way with the kids, and rarely did a problem arise he couldn't solve with a little diplomacy. Earl didn't want to strike. But when you belonged to a union you went along, and Earl was a union man down to his toes.

Even as they talked, Betty was listening intently, but except for her and Rose and the hum of the refrigerator in the background, there was no other sound in the house. She'd looked discreetly around as she was coming up the path, but saw no sign of the man. She wasn't sure if she was glad or not. She didn't like confrontation. Just the same, she would have liked to get a closer look at him, hear his side of things while looking him straight in the eye.

166

Now, seated across from her neighbor at the kitchen table, stirring sugar into her coffee, the small talk (which had been just the slightest bit strained) soon behind them, Betty Martin began to wonder if coming here had been a mistake. She didn't want to offend Rose. Maybe she was making too much of the incident with the children. And then she saw that they weren't quite alone as the big orange tabby came silently into the room, blinked at them, then came up to Betty and rubbed its side against her ankles, purring loudly.

'Tiger likes you,' Rose Nickerson said smiling, as Betty reached down to stroke its soft fur.

* * *

Before draping a soft cloth over the painting, Katie stepped back to appraise the work one last time. Never terribly confident about her talent, she wondered if it was good enough to enter in such a prestigious competition. Reminding herself of the success of her show, she felt mildly reassured. She'd done the water color in subdued blends of blues and greys, setting it off perfectly in the silver frame she'd picked up for next to nothing in a flea market. It both excited her and made her nervous knowing her work would be judged with the best.

She, too, was pleased with the eerie quality at which Jason had remarked. It had just happened in the process of painting, quite unplanned. Proof, Katie thought happily, of the superiority of the subconscious mind.

Or maybe it was a sign, came a small inner voice. A harbinger of evil to come. She shook the chilling notion and returned her thoughts to the competition. City Hall was only a five minute walk from The Coffee Shop; she would dash over there this afternoon. Things generally quieted down around three.

She was getting into her coat when the telephone rang. 'Hello,' she said, half-hoping it was Drake, and at the same time afraid it was. She wasn't up to running the scene she knew was inevitable. Anyway, she had to get to work.

There was no answer.

'Hello,' she said again.

At first the breathing seemed to come from far off, striking a little note of fear against Katie's heart. 'Yes, who is it, please?'

Hang up, she told herself. Hang up now.

But she didn't.

Allen used to phone her. In the middle of the night after she broke up with him, the phone would ring, dragging her out of a sound sleep. He never said anything. But she always knew it was him. But that was two years ago. She didn't know anymore. She didn't think so.

'Hello . . . hello . . . ' Standing with the receiver pressed to her ear, Katie's heart began to beat queerly as if it already knew what she was only beginning to suspect.

As the breathing reached through the line, Katie could almost feel the hot, vile breath against her ear. 'Who are you?' she cried, knowing now that it was 'him'. 'What do you want?'

'Y O U U . . . ' came the deadly whisper, and Katie jerked the phone from her ear as if she'd been burned. It was the bogeyman of her childhood, a thing shrouded in darkness that hid in her closet, and sometimes waited under her bed. It was now at the other end of the line.

She dropped the receiver.

It swayed on its cord as the whisperer called to her . . . 'K A T I E . . . K A T I E . . . '

Click.

Silence.

She stood absolutely still, her eyes riveted on the dangling receiver. In its muteness it seemed a thing alive, mocking her. The dial tone returned. But it was a full minute before Katie could bring herself to touch the receiver to hang it up.

Clutching the large painting awkwardly under her arm, Katie grabbed up her purse from the desk and left the house.

15

An hour later, having arrived near the end of the lunch hour, Katie was busily clearing away dishes and setting up fresh tables, glad of the familiar routine that left little room for thinking. Also, she appreciated the warm building. By the time she'd reached the main road from her house, she'd been numb with the cold, and then there was a ten minute wait at the bus stop. She'd had to keep changing the painting from one arm to the other, so that she could alternate putting her hands in her pockets to warm them. She'd been in such a state from the phone call, she'd forgotten to take her gloves.

The moment there was a lull, Katie phoned the repair shop about her car, and was told by a man with a bored voice that they were waiting on parts; her car wouldn't be ready for a couple of more days at least.

Katie resigned herself to a week of walking. It couldn't be helped. She would just have to remember to dress properly, that was all.

Some of the regulars questioned her about her accident and she'd answered as best she could, blaming it on the weather, remaining politely vague on the details. Though a few were genuinely concerned, she knew that someone's misfortune often brought out a morbid curiosity in others. It would pass.

'I was thinking . . . '

Katie jumped at the voice behind her.

'Oh, I'm sorry,' Andrea said, alarm leaping into her own dark eyes. 'I didn't mean to scare you.'

'It's okay,' Katie assured the petite, red-haired girl. 'I'm just a little unnerved, Andrea. What is it?'

'I sneak up on people,' Andrea said in self-disgust, her French accent delighting Katie as always. 'Francine says it's a fault. I don't mean to do it, though.'

Katie smiled. Francine and Andrea were twins, which sometimes played havoc with the cook and the customers, but Francine was the more aggressive of the two, managing to assume the role of the bossy, older sister, and Katie could always tell them apart. 'You didn't sneak. I'm on edge, that's all. What was it you wanted to say to me, Andrea?'

'Oh, just that you're welcome to stay with Francine and me until your car is okay. I saw you getting off the bus. Was that one of your paintings you were carrying?'

'Yes, it was. And you must be psychic. I was just thinking about my car. I phoned,

172

and they tell me it won't be ready for another day or two. But I don't really mind the walk,' she lied. 'The exercise will do me good. Thanks for the offer, though. I really appreciate it. And I'll keep it in mind.' She laid a hand on the girl's shoulder, and felt her slightness under the white nylon uniform. 'Really, Andrea — thanks.'

'Okay. You know where we live, Katie,' she said before hurrying off to serve a waiting customer. Katie felt touched and somewhat comforted at the thoughtful gesture. Andrea had asked no questions — merely offered her help.

But Katie had no wish to impose herself on anyone. Besides, she would be miserable living with two women, even for a few days. She liked — no — she needed her own things around her. She needed her privacy.

Threading her way to the table by the window where two overweight women in fur coats had just sat down, and were now lighting cigarettes and talking animatedly, she wondered if she was becoming too set in her ways. As she handed each of the women a menu, she saw that her hands were shaking.

In the kitchen, she called out: 'Two cheeseburgers, well-done with fries and cole slaw, Frank.'

'Food for pigs,' he grumbled, his back to her, steam rising from the grill in front of him. Frank was a short, compact man with closely cropped, curly salt and pepper hair. 'People don't know how to eat, anymore. Junk food, that's all . . . ' He turned, his face opening in a smile that revealed crooked, though white teeth beneath the neat fringe of a mustache. He had deep-set, piercing eyes in a narrow, lined face. 'Katie, for a minute there I didn't recognize your voice. It's good to have you back again, my little one. How are you feeling?'

With the exception of Mrs. Cameron, Frank called all women 'my little one'. 'I'm not sure, yet, Frank,' Katie answered truthfully.

'Soon you'll be your old self again,' he said, turning from her to plop two hamburger patties on the grill where they sputtered and hissed. The smell of frying grease made her feel queasy. 'You'll see.'

She welcomed Frank's lack of curiosity. She wanted only to put the past weeks out of her mind, if only for a few hours.

This more admirable side to Frank's nature, however, did not blind her to other, not so becoming, qualities. He had a violent temper that something so simple as a steak being sent back for further cooking could set off. Then he would fly into a rage, ranting and raving about his talents being thrown away on bores who had no appreciation of his skills. These outbursts always unnerved Katie, but she thought she understood the real source of his frustration, and knew that his anger was aimed mainly at himself. Occasionally, she managed to calm him, but mostly she'd learned it was best just to let the tantrum run its course.

Frank Cramer had been chef at some of the most famous restaurants in the world until his addiction to alcohol forced him down the ladder to where he was now — a short order cook. He'd even taught gourmet cooking for a time, but Frank could rarely manage to stay sober for more than a couple of months before all the signs began to appear: restlessness, irritability, a frequency of the tantrums. The drunken bender that followed would sometimes last up to a week and occasionally longer.

Restaurant proprietors of more elite establishments weren't as tolerant as Mrs. Cameron, but then Mrs. Cameron knew that liquor hadn't in the least dulled Frank's culinary talents, which together with the homey atmosphere and reasonable prices, were the reasons The Coffee Chop enjoyed the success that it did, and Mrs. Cameron was first and foremost a business woman.

Picking up her orders and placing them on a tray, Katie made her way through the narrow hallway that separated kitchen and restaurant and spotted Joey out in the alley through the open back door. He was frowning hard, intently stuffing garbage into a can to make more room for the listing green bag at his feet.

'How are things with you, Joe?' she called out smiling at him, feeling the familiar surge of compassion he always brought out in her.

He looked up. His long, child-like face framed in greasy, dark-blond hair, reddened with pleasured. 'G — good, Katie,' he stammered. 'I'm glad you back now.'

Joey Smith had come to work at The Coffee Shop when he was sixteen, straight from the orphanage where he'd been raised. No one knew his last name, and so he'd been tagged with 'Smith'. He would be twenty-two now, Katie thought. Katie suspected that Joey's retardation was social rather than mental.

His shy grin showed bad teeth. 'You still m — my gurfriend. Katie?' came the inevitable question. His feet shifted in their big, clumsy boots. Katie just smiled, but she didn't say yes as she usually did. Joey didn't seem to notice, and went back to stuffing garbage. Katie watched him a moment longer, taking in the hair that curled just above the collar of a faded green workshirt covering a large, no longer boyish, frame. She found herself suddenly wondering what Joe's whisper would sound like over the telephone line.

It was ten past four when Katie left the Coffee Shop with her painting tucked under her arm. In the late afternoon sun, the air had warmed considerably, and Katie's spirits rose as she strode along the sidewalk absorbing the sights and sounds and smells of the city. The blaring of traffic, people passing dressed in brightly colored scarves and hats, but with coats now thrown open. Store windows displaying fall and winter fashions. Plaid was big this year. Two teenage boys lounging against the red brick building with the sign CHAN'S CHINESE hanging over the door, hunched over a suspicious-looking cigarette, an intensity about them as they passed it back and forth.

In the square, the bench-sitters had been chased away by the cold snap. Only the pigeons remained, cooing and waddling about the legs of the benches, optimistically awaiting their benefactors. She would pick up a couple of rolls from the bake shop on her way back.

By the time Katie arrived at her destination, she was feeling better. Relaxed, and more rational. It was ridiculous to think Joey was the one doing these horrible things; Joey wouldn't hurt a fly.

★ ★ ★

Four blocks away, at 16 Highland Place, Dr. Jonathan Shea, dressed casually in cords and a denim windbreaker, entered the grey stone building that housed Belleville Police Department. Inside the building, the walls were a greasy green throughout, some hanging with wanted posters yellowed with age. The tall ancient windows hadn't been washed since *Dragnet* played on television. The smell was one of accumulated human desperation, degradation, and fifty years of stale coffee and cigarettes. The department had been pushing City Hall for years now for a new location and getting nowhere. Conversation was lively . . . a break out of raucous laughter from the back corner . . . phones jangling off their hooks.

He stepped to one side as an aging prostitute, black wigged and handcuffed, was being led toward him by an amused officer. Tottering on spiked heels, she winked as she passed him, wiggled her bottom at him in its silver miniskirt. Further on, a boy maybe fifteen, sat on a bench, sprawled there, legs akimbo, white knees protruding from holes in his jeans, trying to look like this was 'no big deal.' Jonathan smiled at him. The boy mouthed 'f . . . off,' and looked away.

'I'd like to see Captain Peterson, please,' Jonathan said to the officer at the desk. 'He's expecting me.' The captain had, over the years, sent some of his men to Jonathan, to talk. Men who 'had a problem'. Some were just average guys trying to do an insane-making job, idealists in the beginning, intent on cleaning up the streets, soon becoming jaded by the realities of a cop's life. Others couldn't handle it at all, and either quit, or found sustenance in a bottle. And then there were those who were already cold and mean even before they joined the force. It was why they'd joined.

He'd always tried to be there when the captain needed him, no matter how busy he was. This time he was the one who needed a favor.

★ ★ ★

'Mommy, that man lied,' Billy cried, fairly bouncing on his Nikes, his eyes flashing his indignation. 'We didn't go anywhere

179

near that truck. We didn't do nothin'. Just walked up the path like I told you and said 'trick or treat'. We didn't touch nothin'.' His little sister, Rachael, fervently backed him up. 'We didn't do nothin', Mommy, honest. We didn't do nothin'.'

'Didn't do anything,' Betty Martin corrected absently. Rose Nickerson had told her the reason the man had been a little rough on them was because he came out of the house to find them playing around the truck, with Billy actually sitting up in the cab fiddling around with the gears. He was sorry if he'd been a little too harsh with the children, but he'd been afraid they might harm themselves, and wanted to throw a scare into them.

Well, he'd certainly done that, all right.

Billy and Rachael were normal kids like any other kids, and certainly capable of getting into mischief from time to time. But even while Rose was explaining to her what happened, the story had a false ring. It didn't sound like Billy's and Rachael's sort of mischief. Betty thought she knew her kids pretty well; they were sensible kids, not foolhardy. She also knew when they were lying and when they were telling the truth. And right now they were telling the truth.

'I believe you,' she said, tousling Billy's hair. 'Now change into your playclothes, both of you, and get started on your homework.' As an afterthought, she added, 'And stay away from the Nickerson place from now on.'

'Don't worry,' Billy yelled behind him on his way to his room. 'I wouldn't go back there if you paid me a billion trillion dollars.'

★ ★ ★

Katie was swept through revolving doors, and a minute later was being carried up in the elevator to the third floor of City Hall. A young woman shared the elevator with her. She held a child in her arms, a little girl, maybe five or six months old, with alert blue eyes and silky brown hair wisping out from beneath a pink frilly bonnet. The mother took the tiny fingers gently in her teeth, and the baby grinned and made a sweet gurgling sound.

'She's lovely,' Katie said, and the woman thanked her, beaming with pride at her child. Katie felt a deep, sharp longing within herself.

She was at the desk registering her painting with the receptionist when she heard a voice speak her name. A familiar, particularly irritating voice, thick with a phony French

181

accent. But it wasn't the accent (a silly ploy she might have found merely amusing in someone else) that irked Katie. It was Raymond Losier himself. 'Katie, dear,' he said, coming to stand beside her, eyeing her painting which now stood against the wall with some others, 'surely you're not entering that 'Moon over the Moors' thing, are you?'

The receptionist was staring at him in unabashed admiration. Katie understood why. Raymond was a strikingly handsome man, dark-haired, deeply tanned, and just now beautifully turned out in a soft brown leather coat with a fox fur collar, an unlit pipe caught between his flawless teeth. The perfect ad for some expensive men's cologne.

Katie's eye moved to her painting. As had been his intention, Raymond's words gnawed at her confidence. She tried not to let it. 'Yes, of course I'm entering my 'Moon over the Moors' thing, as you've so unkindly titled it, Raymond. Why else would I have brought it here?'

He stroked his chin, looked at her in mock puzzlement. 'Surely not for criticism, darling — unless, of course, under that cool exterior lurks a closet masochist.'

Anger leapt in Katie despite her resolve

never to let Raymond get to her. 'I could easily have come to you for that, couldn't I, Raymond? You're such an expert.'

He smiled, satisfaction gleaming in his eyes. 'By the way, I heard about your accident. Have a few too many, did we, dear?'

Now Katie's anger was directed at herself. She was such an idiot. Why had she allowed herself to be reduced to Raymond's level? Even if she hadn't been above this sort of childish verbal ping-pong, she was no match for Raymond when it came to trading insults. But she rarely took him seriously. Why now? Why today?

'I think her painting is beautiful,' came the meek voice from behind the desk. Katie thanked her, but felt even more the fool for having put herself on display. All meanness fled from Raymond's face as he turned to the receptionist who had spoken. He was all charm now, all sweetness. 'Aren't you darling,' he said, the French accent thickening like syrup. 'But I meant no harm. I was teasing, is all. She is much too sensitive. And she has no sense of humor.' Resting the palms of his hands on the edge of her desk, he leaned down to gaze into her eyes. 'But you, darling, on the other hand — ah, yes, I see can that you do. I detect a certain devilish quality in those big blue eyes.'

The woman blushed and giggled, her hand going coquettishly to her hair.

Oh, God, Katie groaned inwardly, but was more than a little relieved at the chance to make her escape without further humiliating herself. Especially since it was clear she was about to lose an ally. Katie headed for the elevator.

Only in class in front of Mr. Jackson did Raymond bother to hide his dislike of her. Jason insisted it wasn't personal, that he was jealous. And it was true that whenever Mr. Jackson said something encouraging about Katie's work, Raymond could be counted on for a snide remark that implied something other than her artistic ability provoked flattery from their instructor. Before Katie joined the class, it was Jason who had been the butt of Raymond's meanness, but Jason had grown adept at ignoring deliberately hurtful people over the years, and Raymond didn't like to be ignored.

His own work, uninspired at best, never seemed to improve from week to week. Not so much due to a lack of inborn talent, Katie suspected, but because of Raymond's unwillingness to accept constructive criticism. It was a mystery to her why he continued to

184

spend the money on lessons.

As she emerged from the building, Katie remembered what Jason had told her about Raymond insulting a guest speaker, and she smiled a little consoled with the knowledge that at least she hadn't been singled out for Raymond's barbs. Good luck with your entry, Raymond, she thought, realizing that, of course, Raymond had been at City Hall for the same reason she had.

As she hurried along the sidewalk, Katie tried to regain her good mood. She dropped into a boutique and treated herself to an off-white angora hat and gloves to match. A few doors further on, she went into the bake shop and bought two kaiser rolls to feed to the pigeons in the park, and felt cheered. She didn't notice the old blue truck parked across the street, or the man slumped down in the driver's seat, peaked cap pulled forward to hide his face, watching her.

★ ★ ★

The rest of the day passed without incident, but the restaurant was busy, and it was well after six o'clock before Katie was finally able to get away. It was coming on to dark when she stepped off the bus and started up Black Lake Road for home. She hadn't gone very

185

far when she began to feel the effects of her first day back to work. Every inch of her body ached, and now, with the sun gone, the cold penetrated her camel-haired coat and bit at her legs in their nylon stockings. She would remember to wear slacks tomorrow. She was glad of the hat and gloves.

Seeing her breath in the frosty air, Katie drew up her coat collar and quickened her step. Other than the sound of the wind soughing in the trees that hemmed her in on both sides, and her own hurried footsteps on the lonely country road, all was silent and still. The sky had grown a dusky purple, lightly flecked with stars now. Above the tallest trees, a crescent of white moon floated.

With the smell of wet, rotting wood and vegetation drifting to her from the deep woods, at times overriding the scent of spruce and pine, Katie thought over the day. Faces rose in her mind's eye . . . sinister faces now . . . Frank, Raymond, Joey . . .

She thought about them.

Both Frank and Raymond had a streak of self-destructiveness in their natures, which, in varying degrees, often and without warning, turned outward. Was it possible that one of them . . . ? No, she was letting her imagination run away with her again. Frank simply had a drinking problem. And

Raymond was a nasty little boy taking his frustrations out on the rest of the world. What about Joey? Poor Joey — a man-child locked in the narrow confines of a world imposed upon him by an indifferent society.

Katie knew these people. Didn't she? Knew their quirks and idiosyncrasies. And yet today she knew she had viewed each of them with different eyes — eyes that held suspicion and mistrust. Even fear.

And then there was Allen. Allen, who used to follow her in the police car, be parked at the curb when she got off work, who used to phone her in the middle of the night, and once had broken into her house, waiting there when she got home. Allen who couldn't accept that she didn't want to see him anymore. Though eventually he had.

And Allen was living in Los Angeles now, probably even married, certainly with a girl friend. Allen wouldn't remain long without a woman in his life. And yet the get-well card had been mailed from Belleville.

As Katie walked along the dirt road thinking her thoughts, the plaintive cry of a loon echoed on the night. And a moment later an owl close by hooted. Happy to set her mind on a different track, Katie wondered if the owl was calling out to its mate. Or perhaps it had babies and was warning her off. Did owls hatch their young in the fall of the year? Spring seemed more likely, but she wasn't sure. Aunt Katherine could have told her. Or had it spotted some small game with its round, predatory eyes — a rabbit perhaps. No, it would have remained silent before swooping down on the unsuspecting prey for the kill.

Katie glanced behind her at the road snaking back to the highway, suddenly nervous. Why did the walk seem so much longer than it had this morning? One thing was sure; she wouldn't be braving it at night again. She was lucky there was a moon to guide her, otherwise she would be walking blind. If there was any place darker than a country road at night, Katie hadn't found it.

As she trudged on, she heard the loon cry out again, and its mournful sound filled her with a deep sense of vulnerability, of aloneness. She walked faster, ignoring the stitch that leapt like a flame in her side. Not much farther now, she tried to console herself, not much farther.

An uneasiness had bloomed in her. The kind of uneasiness that came when she was a little girl and had gotten up in the night to go to the bathroom, and her small fingers couldn't find the light switch. The kind of uneasiness that started out small, but could swiftly become a terror that paralyzed, that brought the tears. Think of something pleasant, she told herself urgently. Yes, think about that sweet little lady who comes in to The Coffee Shop every day at exactly two o'clock carrying her own sandwich and a teabag in a Snoopy lunchpail, and always says, just as if she were the queen visiting, 'Just a pot of hot water, if you please, my dear.' She wore a ratty fur coat and a child's red and white touque.

Sometimes Katie would manage to sneak her a couple of fresh-baked cookies or a bran muffin, treats the woman accepted as her due, but Katie didn't miss the child-like delight dancing in those lively blue eyes.

Mrs. Cameron, of course, wasn't at all thrilled at having a table taken up for 'just a pot of hot water,' but she never said anything directly, and Katie would give her a good argument if she ever did.

Katie stopped suddenly, thinking she'd heard something in the woods. She peered in at the place from where the sound seemed to come, but other than shifting shadows caused by moonlight, and the deeper blackness beyond, she saw nothing. She listened a moment longer, then, with the murmur of wind in her ears mingling with the slight escalation of her heartbeat, she walked on, careful now to stay well in the middle of the road.

Every few seconds she cast a wary eye into the woods where suddenly threatening shapes lurked everywhere, crouching menacingly behind every tree, every bush, inching closer the instant she turned her head away.

'Stop it!' she commanded herself. It's probably just some mangy old raccoon. Yet the sound had suggested something heavier. A bear? That thought brought with it its own special jolt of panic, even though Katie couldn't recall ever hearing of any bear sightings at Black Lake.

If her car wasn't ready tomorrow, she would rent one and damn the expense, she vowed as she continued, pain stabbing her side rhythmically as she half-walked, half-ran toward home and the safety of locked doors.

And then she heard it again. A rustling in the woods, just to her right. She stopped, straining in the semi-darkness to see what it was. And did. Not clearly and only for an instant, but long enough to see that this shape was no shadow cast in moonlight. It had substance. It had stopped when she had stopped.

Slowly, Katie began to walk.

The rustling began.

Oh God! There was something in the woods.

And it was keeping pace with her.

16

Katie's first instinct was to run, but a deeper, saner voice warned her that if she did, she just might not make it home. Don't act frightened, she told herself, though terror clawed at her. Just walk calmly. Don't run. Don't run.

It was all but impossible to heed her own advice with the rustling so close beside her, remaining steady, speeding up as she did, slowing as she slowed. Fear tasting like rust in her mouth, Katie tried not to hear the whisperer's voice as it had sounded on the phone this morning, calling her name. She tried not to envision 'the strawman' moving through the woods, not three feet from her, fixing her with its pale, unblinking stare like some ghastly monster from a childhood horror movie.

Abruptly, the rustling stopped.

Only her footsteps now, soft and hurried on the dirt road. She dared to hope that whatever or whoever was in the woods had grown tired of following her. But her heart knew it was a vain, foolish hope.

And then, behind her, came other footsteps.

The sound catapulted Katie into a full run. With adrenaline flooding her veins, erasing all pain and exhaustion from her mind, Katie's feet fairly flew over the road, not slowing even when her house burst gloriously into view, with its dark, familiar shape through the trees filling her with a blessed relief.

Now that safety was close, her chest tore with every step, the pain in her side a searing fire as she ran toward the house. She faltered for an instant at the sight of Jason's car parked beside her own. Thank God, she thought, as she half-ran, half-stumbled toward the red Volkswagen, crying out her friend's name as she went.

But when she reached Jason's car, there was no one inside. Hesitating only an instant in her bewilderment, gasping for breath, Katie went on, not daring to look behind her. She raced up the slight incline over the dead grass, oblivious to the brittle leaves that rose in disturbance to scurry about her ankles. Then she was climbing the stairs, at the same time fumbling in her purse for her house key and praying aloud. Her hand closed around the key, but when she took it from her purse, it slipped through her gloved fingers and fell — where? She hadn't heard it drop. Had it gone through the floor boards?

Oh, please, God, no! She began to cry. The sound came out in small puppy whimpers.

Down below, the bottom step creaked.

Terror closed a hand around Katie's throat, started up a loud buzzing in her ears.

She spotted the key on the landing. It hadn't fallen through, after all. Yanking off a glove she bent to retrieve it, tears making the key a silvery blur. Dear God, don't let me drop it. Please don't let me drop it this time.

Holding the key firmly now between thumb and forefinger, every inch of her alerted for the next footfall on the steps, Katie quickly let herself into the house and locked the door behind her.

Gasping for breath, she stared at the locked door, and waited. Only after several minutes, in which there came no scratching of nails, no whispering of her name from the other side of the door, did she finally let herself sag down on the chair in the hallway, dissolving there, cradling her head in her arms, feeling her body clammy inside her coat. She remained there, unmoving, for a long time — until gradually her heart slowed to normal, the fire in her side cooled, and terror loosened its grip on her.

Why is Jason's car parked out front? came the unbidden question. He always parks around back. And where is he, anyway? Katie lifted her head slowly to stare again at the locked door as suspicion coiled around her heart. Could Jason be the one . . . ? No, that's crazy thinking. She shook her head as if to clear it of the traitorous thought. And the guilt that followed it. Jason wouldn't hurt her. Jason was her friend.

At last, Katie rose from the chair, and on legs that felt without substance, headed for the studio. Her step was silent through the carpeted rooms. 'You're becoming scared of your own shadow, Katie Summers,' she said aloud, and heard her voice echo hollowly in the empty house.

Jason probably just got bored waiting around and decided to go for a walk, that's all. (Not like Jason to walk alone out here at night.) And what you heard in the woods was exactly what you thought it was in the first place — a raccoon, or maybe even Charlie Black's old lab, Sarah.

You didn't think 'animal', she argued with herself as she lit the lamp in the studio. Only at first did you think it. You thought — never mind what you thought. You were wrong. Forget it. Enough hysterics for one night. God, it was as cold as a tomb in here. Not much new about that. Turning, she groaned at the sight of the empty woodbox.

She'd forgotten she'd used up the last of the wood this morning. Damn! She hated the thought of having to go down to the cellar for more. She wasn't even sure if she had the strength. She supposed she could wait until Jason returned and ask him to go get it for her, but then she decided that was hardly a fair way to treat a welcome guest. And neither was a cold, damp house. Giving a small sigh of resignation, Katie collected the empty woodbox, the flashlight from the table, and started back through to the kitchen, from where the narrow flight of steps led down to the cellar.

She'd taken no more than half a dozen steps when the phone rang, nearly startling her out of her skin. Setting the woodbox on the floor, she turned back. Just as she was about to answer, the whisperer came to mind. Katie's hand remained in midair for two more rings, then she picked up the receiver. 'Hello.'

'Would this be Katherine Summers?' the woman asked. Her voice was husky with a trace of British accent. Katie answered that it was, wondering if the enormous relief she felt carried over the line.

'You don't know me, my dear,' the woman said pleasantly, 'but I've recently become acquainted with you through your work.

Though most of your paintings had 'sold' signs on them, I did manage to purchase one, which I must say I'm enjoying immensely.'

Sold? Most of her paintings had sold? Katie's heart lifted. 'Well, I'm very pleased and flattered, Mrs . . . ?'

'Oh, do forgive me. I'm Hattie Holloway. Please call me Hattie. And may I call you Katherine?'

'Katie, please. Katie is fine. It's so kind of you to call, Mrs. Holl — Hattie. Which painting did you choose?'

'*Summer's Silence*. It's wonderful. The barns and that old farmhouse — the green fields. It did so remind me of the place where I grew up in the south of England. But I'm sure you don't want to hear my life history, so I'll get right to the point. Oh, by the way, if you're wondering, and I'm sure you are, they had your number at the gallery, and I took the liberty of copying it down. Since I'm a familiar old face, they didn't seem to object. I hope you don't, Katie.'

'No, of course,' she said quickly. She didn't add that her number was listed in the phone book. Intuition told her that would have been insensitive and a mistake. The woman obviously hadn't called just to compliment Katie on her work.

'Good,' she said brightly. 'Well, I was

196

wondering, Katie — do you do portraits?'

Excitement coursed through Katie at the thought of a commission. 'Yes, I've done several,' she said, not adding that she'd done them without pay, and mainly for her own enjoyment.

'Could you do one from a photograph, do you think? I know this is an unusual request, but I do so admire your style. I'd be quite willing to sit for you, of course, but I'm going out of town with my husband — a business trip. Anyway,' she said, laughing in her rich, throaty voice, 'I'm slightly younger in the photograph. So you see, Katie, I'm not without a certain vanity.'

'None of us is, Mrs. Holl . . . Hattie. When would you, I mean, I see no reason I couldn't do your portrait from a photograph.'

'Wonderful. It's to be an anniversary gift for my husband.' Her voice lowered conspiratorially. 'I'd like it completed in three weeks, if that's possible.' She went on hurriedly, as if anticipating a protest from Katie. 'I'll expect to pay you extra for rushing you, naturally. I only just thought of having a portrait done. Seeing your work inspired the idea.' And then she mentioned a sum that made Katie's breath catch — enough to pay for art lessons for a year, and supplies to boot.

Admittedly, three weeks wasn't much time in which to do a portrait, at least in Katie's case since she worked slowly, but it was enough time. She would make it enough.

Most of her paintings sold. A commission. And her car had even been returned from the shop. Letting out a squeal of delight, Katie hugged herself and did a little dance around the floor, feeling much as she used to on Christmas morning before her father went away — a long time ago, but she remembered.

Most of her paintings sold. A commission. God, she could hardly believe it. With renewed energy, her recent scare flown from her, Katie grabbed up the woodbox from the floor as if it were weightless and hurried from the room, figuring that by the time she got back Jason would be here and she could tell him her wonderful news. He would be so happy for her. They would celebrate. There were probably no more than a few drops left in the bottle of Mateus they'd shared, but Katie knew where there was a bottle of Chablis, still half full — a last year's Christmas gift from one of the regulars at The Coffee Shop.

Descending the cellar steps, Katie went straight to the woodpile stacked against the far wall. Setting the flashlight on the floor at her feet where the beam made a pale, sweeping light on the grey cement, Katie hunkered down to gather the wood. As she did, something creaked behind her.

Holding a chunk of wood in midair, she frowned. Mice? God, she hoped not. But it was an old house, after all. She would have a cat if she were home during the day. She went back to gathering the wood, smiling to herself, thinking of the cat she'd owned as a little girl. Saucy, she'd called it, and it was. Even now, she could almost feel its soft, silky fur against her cheek, the warmth of its body vibrating in her arms whenever Saucy condescended to bestow her affection.

Well, she would just have to forego that little indulgence for the time being. Again, she thrilled at the thought of her sold paintings, of her first commission. Maybe someday she really would be able to stay home and earn her living from her painting. Somehow that possibility did not seem quite so remote as it usually did.

Katie was nearly finished gathering up the wood and stacking it in the woodbox. Half-filled would have to do. Otherwise, she would never be able to carry it upstairs. Cradling a few more chunks in the crook of her arm, she again heard the creaking sound behind her. It came from high up, just off her right shoulder. And then again.

Not a mouse. No, not a mouse.

Her shoulders tensed, her new-found joy gradually fading to be replaced with a creeping, eerie sensation that prickled the hairs at the nape of her neck. Katie's hand closed around the flashlight. For a long moment she was absolutely still. Then, slowly, she turned in the direction of the sound.

On a direct level with her eyes, brown and white shoes dangled in midair. Katie gasped, dropping the wood that fell in a noisy clatter to the cement floor. Her horrified eyes were riveted on the shoes as back and forth they swayed — back and forth — like the shoes of a mindless puppet.

Screams sounded inside Katie's head, piercing, wailing screams. Yet, but for the slow, rhythmic creaking, all was silent.

Katie raised the flashlight higher, blacking out the legs and bringing into focus the tan tweed jacket she knew so well — Jason's jacket. The light rested for a terrible moment on the sloping shoulders, then, as though with a will of its own, the flashlight jerked upward.

Katie stood transfixed, staring in mute horror as the circle of light spotted the strawman dangling from the end of a hangman's noose.

At last a scream broke from her, and she stumbled backwards. As she did, the flashlight slipped from her grasp, shattered on the cement floor, abandoning Katie to complete darkness. And when the warm, moist breath brushed her cheek, her scream became a soft, strangling sound deep in her throat.

She barely heard the cellar door close.

17

Huddled on the cold floor with her knees drawn up and her back hard against the rough concrete wall, Katie stared into the almost palpable darkness. Jason wasn't dead. Only his clothes. The insane thought brought laughter — hysterical laughter that mingled with tears. The creaking of the rope had stopped finally, but the vision of Jason's dangling, twisting effigy remained imprinted on her retinas. And the warm, moist breath only now cooled on her cheek.

The laughter soon died away, and Katie wept soundlessly as she waited. For something.

In a little while, she grew oblivious to the damp chill of the cellar, to its dark, musty smell and, like a child trying to comfort itself, she began to rock. Back and forth, she rocked. Back and forth, hugging herself. Time held little meaning for her. Gradually the rocking motion soothed Katie, sending a merciful numbness to settle over her. Only when she heard a 'thump', did a little of the numbness peel away.

Katie's eyes darted about in the darkness like those of a small, trapped animal. The sound had been muffled and seemed to come from far off. Had she really heard something? She couldn't be sure. Not of anything. Not anymore. She wondered idly if she had gone mad during the long, black hours.

Slow, measured footsteps descending the cellar steps let her know she hadn't. Cowering against the hard, cold wall, she pressed her hands to her mouth to keep from crying out. It would all be over soon.

He was coming for her.

All numbness fled from Katie in a rush as the cellar door slowly opened. Struggling to her feet, she thought, I'm not ready to die. Not like this. Not without a fight, damn it!

Light blinded her. Her clenched fists flew to her eyes.

And then a familiar voice called her name, and she was suddenly being lifted in strong arms, Jonathan's arms. She clung to him, her body heaving in uncontrollable sobs. He held her without words, until at last she quieted, and then he spoke softly to her.

'I telephoned earlier. When I didn't get an answer, I guessed, being you, you'd gone into work, so I went there and they told me you'd already taken the bus home. I forgot about your car being in for repairs. Anyway, I drove out here to see if you were all right and saw two cars in the drive. It was enough to know you weren't alone, so I turned around and headed back to town. Something, I'm not sure exactly what, stopped me. Made me turn back.'

'Thank God,' she whispered into the rough texture of his coat. 'He locked me in. I was so frightened, Jonathan.'

'Who? The door wasn't locked, Katherine. You must have . . . didn't you just come down here and take a weak spell?'

Not locked? But she'd thought . . . Katie moved out of his embrace reluctantly. Her legs felt weak, and her eyes burned from crying. 'What time is it?' she asked.

He shone the flashlight on the face of his watch. 'Eight-thirty.'

Only a little over an hour, she thought, disbelieving. It had seemed so much longer. 'Behind you, Jonathan. Shine the flashlight behind you.'

He did and she felt his shock. 'It's dressed — in Jason's clothes. Jason Belding. We're good friends. He's in my art class. That's his car you saw — the Volkswagen. The Comet's mine. They delivered it today while I was at work. I wasn't expecting . . . ' Her momentary calm broke. 'Why would anyone do such a horrible thing, Jonathan? What madman . . . ?'

'That's your answer, Katherine,' he answered

quietly. 'We are dealing with a madman. What were you doing down here anyway?'

She told him.

'I'll get the wood. Then, let's get the hell out of here. You're freezing. I'll light the fires and make some coffee — or better still, a drink.' He finished filling up the box with wood. Hefting it easily, he added, 'Yes, a drink is definitely what you need right now. Do you have anything in the house?'

'There's the better part of a bottle of wine in the cupboard,' she said vaguely.

Upstairs, after telephoning the police, Jonathan lit more lamps and set about building fires in both the studio fireplace and the kitchen stove. Even before the house had had a chance to warm, uniformed men were flooding Katie's house and grounds. Through parted drapes, she watched as circles of powerful lights flitted here and there among the black trees, and made sweeping paths on the lake's surface and over the land. Men shouted to one another, and every shout was a tiny blow to Katie's heart. What happened here? she asked silently. Where are you, Jason? Where are you, my good friend?

Long after the policemen were gone, Katie sat clutching her glass of wine and staring into the fire. Within the flames pictures formed. Nightmarish pictures that seemed to exist in hell. My life is like that, she thought. As though some malevolent force had wrenched her destiny from her control, and was now torturing it into shapes and patterns that no longer made any sense — shapes and patterns that terrified her.

'They'll search again tomorrow,' Jonathan said beside her. 'When it's light. They'll find him, Katherine.'

Katie saw that there were a few drops of wine left in the bottom of her glass and drained them. 'Don't humor me, Jonathan,' she said, though not unkindly. 'If they do find him, he'll be dead.'

'You don't know that.'

But she did. Deep in her heart, she knew. She'd seen it in the faces of the policemen. And somehow she felt Jonathan knew it, too. She held out her glass to him. 'More, please.'

Without hesitation, he rose and refilled her glass. 'Sip this one,' he advised in a fatherly tone. 'You don't want to get sick.'

'I'm sick already.' She sighed heavily. 'Thank you for not letting the police hound me with questions, Jonathan.'

He nodded. 'We can't stall them forever, though. You'll have to be prepared to answer those questions tomorrow. And we do want to find whoever is responsible for what's been happening, don't we? The police are just doing their job, Katherine.'

She knew that. She just didn't want to think about it anymore. At least not right now. Taking a sip of her wine, she said, 'Tell me about you, Jonathan. What made you decide to become a psychiatrist. Or is it a secret?'

He didn't answer right away. Then, 'As a matter of fact, yes, it is.'

Katie looked at him. The bluntness of his reply both surprised and stung her. She wasn't even sure why she had asked the question, but she was angry at herself that she had. 'I'm sorry. I didn't mean to pry.'

'You weren't. It's a reasonable question. And I'm the one who's sorry.' When Katie gave no response other than to drink more of her wine, he added, 'Perhaps one day, if you're still interested, I'll tell you the story of my life.'

Not missing the bitter amusement in his voice, Katie shrugged as though it was all the same to her if he did or not, and concentrated on her wine. Then she felt the slight, warm pressure of Jonathan's fingers as he slipped behind her and began to massage the back of her neck. 'You're terribly tense,' he said. 'Not so surprising.

You've been through a lot these past weeks. You're a very strong woman, Katherine. But, of course, I knew that about you the first time I saw you.'

Continuing to stare into the fire, thinking she should remove his hand, but without the will to do so, Katie replied, 'No, I'm not strong at all.' She closed her eyes. His touch felt so soothing, so good. 'The truth is I'm confused and scared as hell.'

'Anyone would be.'

His hand moved around to her cheek and lingered there a moment, while Katie gazed into her glass and realized sadly that it was empty again. She passed it behind her. 'More please.'

Jonathan took his hand from her face to accept the glass. Reaching for the bottle on the floor, he laughed softly as he shook the few remaining drops into her glass. 'You're trying your damnedest to get drunk, aren't you? Not that I blame you, but I'm afraid we've depleted our source.'

The wine was flowing warmly and sensually through her veins, giving her a pleasant sense of floating. 'There's some cooking sherry in the pantry,' she said, congratulating herself for remembering. 'Left over from last Christmas. Just like the Chabee — I got it for a present.'

He laughed again, more heartily this time, and Katie thought it a beautiful sound. 'I don't think that's a particularly good idea right now. Why don't you lie down? Try to rest awhile. I'll be right here.'

Lie down. Rest. Yes, she thought. A good idea. Her lips felt numb. 'Hand me the afghan and a pillow from the cot, Jonathan. Just put it here on the floor.'

'The floor? Why don't you lie down on the cot? You'll be more comfortable there.'

'No, no, I want to see the fire. I like the fire. 'S pretty.'

He grinned and took the empty glass from her hand. 'I think you're already a little tipsy.'

Was she? And what did it matter if she was? It would be so nice just to float away on this warm, liquidy feeling, not to have to think anymore, not to be afraid . . .

When Jonathan had spread the afghan in front of the fire, Katie curled up on it. He sat above her watching the firelight play over the gentle curve of her cheek, the soft fullness of her mouth. There was such a toughness about her, and yet, lying there she seemed so vulnerable, so like a little girl. But there was nothing fatherly in the way he was feeling at the moment. He wanted to make love to Katherine Summers more than he had ever wanted to make love to any woman in his lifetime.

Katie was not oblivious to the way he was looking at her. His arms, folded across his chest, were bronzed and muscled below rolled-up shirt sleeves.

'You look like an Indian chief.'

He smiled. 'Do I?'

'Or an intelligent Rambo.' She giggled.

Jonathan laughed.

'No, no, more like an Indian chief. Mmm. A very nice Indian chief.' Her words sounded strange and distant in her ears. Maybe she really was drunk. She suddenly ached to feel Jonathan's arms around her again. She'd felt so safe when he was holding her, like nothing bad could ever happen to her again.

'You can't see the pretty fire with your back to it,' he said in a gentle, teasing way.

'Jonathan?'

'Yes.'

'Will you lie down with me?'

He didn't answer right away and when he did, the 'no' came out in a hoarse whisper, and Katie was encouraged by the struggle she'd heard in his voice. 'Just for a little while?' she coaxed. Her words sounded like they belonged to someone else — someone she didn't know. 'Hold me, Jonathan. It felt so good when you were holding me. I wasn't afraid then.'

She heard the small sigh of defeat as he rose from the chair. 'All right. Just for a little while. You try to sleep, okay?'

'Okay.' She hid a small, triumphant smile.

He stretched tentatively out on the afghan beside her and drew her into his arms, leaving a careful space between their bodies.

Katie murmured in protest and cuddled closer, burying her face in the warm hollow of his neck. Her mouth brushed his skin and came away with the faint taste of salt. She kissed him there lightly.

'Go to sleep,' he said, and she could feel the tension in his body although he had moved farther from her.

'You always seem to be rescuing me, Jonathan.'

'That's me. Regular dragon killer.'

Behind Katie, the fire crackled softly, while outside her door she heard the wind stirring in the trees and the water lapping against the shore.

She thought of Jason. Where was he? Lying hurt and bleeding somewhere out there in the darkness? Would the police find him? If they do, he'll be dead, an inner voice taunted. You know he'll be dead.

Hot tears slipped down her cheeks. 'What's

happening, Jonathan? Who is doing these terrible things? Why?'

His arms tightened about her, caution forgotten for the moment. 'I don't know. I wish to God I did. Please, don't cry, Katherine. Try not to think about it.' He stroked her hair. 'I know it's difficult, but at least *try* to get some sleep. There's still hope, you know.' His lips brushed her forehead. 'You have to hope.'

Katie closed her eyes. And at once saw the hanging 'strawman' dressed in Jason's tan tweed jacket, his brown and white shoes, both part of Jason's spring wardrobe. Her fashion-conscious friend wouldn't have been caught dead wearing those things in the fall. She cringed at the unintended pun. The monster must have broken into Jason's apartment and stolen the clothes and stuffed . . . No, don't think about it anymore — don't think about it, she repeated like a chant. Katie licked a salty tear from the corner of her mouth and longed to return to her earlier state of numbness.

Lying in Jonathan's arms, gradually she became aware of his firm body pressed against her own. She remembered the way his hands had felt on her body, even through the blanket, and a slow heat began to throb within her. She moved closer.

'Katherine . . . '

She ignored the note of warning she heard in his voice, the same warning that echoed, in her own mind. This was crazy, reckless behavior, and she was going to be sorry. The old adage about 'playing with fire' came to her and she thought, Yes, that's what I need right now, to be consumed in the fire of my senses. Senses don't think. And safety was only a delusion, anyway. Who was safe? Not Jason — not her . . .

Her fingers moved through Jonathan's slightly coarse, thick hair, and revelled in the feel of it. She felt the quick, momentary pressure of his hand at the small of her back. 'No,' he whispered. 'Not like this.'

Katie's hands moved over the planes of his back, broad and smooth and muscled beneath the cotton shirt. 'Like this?' she teased.

'You're not yourself, Katherine.'

I was never more myself, she thought and, treating his protests as feathers on the wind, deftly undid the buttons at the front of his shirt and slipped her hand inside. She was gratified to hear the small sucking in of Jonathan's breath as she caressed his warm skin beneath its soft mat of dark hair. His heart beat strong and steady beneath her palm.

213

'Katherine, stop it! I'm your doctor.'

The statement struck her as funny, and she laughed.

'That was dumb, wasn't it?' he said, and she heard the smile in his voice.

'Mmm. A little. Who hired you, anyway?'

'I'm self-appointed, I guess.'

'Then unappoint yourself. I don't need a doctor. Right now I . . . '

'Katherine . . . ' With a little moan, he removed her hand from beneath his shirt and sat up. She saw his own passion reflected in his eyes.

'Undress me, Jonathan.'

'No, I . . . '

'You did before,' she joked lightly.

'That was different.'

'Why? Because it was your idea?' She reached up and took his face in her hands. It felt warm and a little stubbly. 'I want you.'

And then his lips were on hers, a kiss as tender and sweet as that kiss born of first love, and Katie floated out of herself on it, but she wanted more, and parted her lips beneath his. His arms tightened about her. His kiss grew more demanding. Katie flicked the tip of her tongue over his upper lip. Jonathan drew away, trembling, barely perceptibly, but she knew, and knowing gave her a sense of power.

214

'You're a little devil,' he said.

She smiled. 'Yes.'

'Katherine, you don't know what you're . . .'

'Make love to me, Jonathan. Please.'

He looked at her for a long moment, and she knew he was fighting with himself, and she also knew when he muttered 'damn' under his breath, that he'd lost. And then his hands were undoing the buttons on her blouse, and she closed her eyes. The warning flashed back to her through the fog of wine and passion, but Katie ignored it.

When she was naked, she felt him watching her, not touching her, and a stirring of self-consciousness made her open her eyes.

'You're beautiful,' he said.

'Am I, Jonathan?'

'You know very well you are.'

'No, I don't. Really.'

He smiled at her, his teeth a startling white against his dark skin. 'I don't believe you. You know, Katherine, you're going to hate me tomorrow.'

'Maybe. But I'll love you tonight.'

He laughed softly and stood up. Slowly, methodically, he began to take off his clothes, his eyes never once leaving hers.

When at last he stood naked before her, Katie said, 'You're magnificent. Like a fine jungle animal.'

He knelt on the floor beside her, amusement mingling with desire in his eyes. 'I don't know that I'll ever find my way out of this particular jungle,' he said, then he was kissing her brow, her eyelids, kisses like moth wings brushing her skin, moving to the hollow of her throat. 'Sweet, sweet Katherine,' he murmured.

Katie heard herself moan softly as his lips trailed downward to her breasts. This was a dream, wasn't it? She would never think of giving herself with such boldness, such abandon, to a man she barely knew. She had one small instant of cold sober thought, and then, willing the dream to last forever, Katie lifted her arms to him.

18

November 2nd

The soft pink glow of dawn filtered through the drapes and through Katie's closed eyelids. She opened her eyes just long enough to see Jonathan's navy topcoat hanging on the halltree beside her paint-spattered smock, and closed them again.

She was on the cot, lying naked beneath the blanket and afghan. Vaguely, she remembered Jonathan carrying her here sometime during the night. She had no trouble at all, however, remembering their lovemaking, and despite a mild, wine-induced headache, she stretched lazily, languidly. The rich aroma of coffee wafted invitingly to her. Katie smiled dreamily.

Darker thoughts prodded her consciousness, threatened to rip open her magical cocoon of love, to expose her to harsher realities. She squeezed her eyes shut tighter. Not yet. Not yet.

Voices down by the lake. Men shouting to one another. Urgent, excited sounds.

Katie felt cold in the hollow of her stomach.

At the sound of Jonathan coming into the room, she opened her eyes. He hesitated in the doorway, steam rising up past his face from the two mugs of coffee he held. One look at him and Katie knew. All the good feeling drained from her. Wrapping herself in the blanket, she sat up and accepted the coffee he handed her. Though she steeled herself for the bad news, she clung to a thread of hope. Maybe she was reading him wrong. She couldn't bring herself, however, to ask the question aloud. It wasn't necessary.

'They've been dragging the lake for the last hour,' Jonathan said. His eyes shifted from her to his coffee mug. 'They — just found him.'

A small sound escaped Katie. Her magical cocoon exploded into darkness.

He sat down heavily beside her and closed his hand over hers. They sat like that for several minutes, not speaking. Then Katie heard herself say, 'He couldn't swim, you know. Jason was afraid of the water.' Why wasn't she crying? Maybe there were no tears left.

Jonathan nodded, still staring into his coffee. 'He was — uh — fully dressed. Whoever dressed that — thing, and hung it in the cellar, must have broken into his apartment first.'

'Murder,' Katie said simply.

'We don't know that. They're combing the ground for clues, tracks . . . ' His voice faltered. 'The bank is slippery from all the rain. He could just — have fallen in.'

Katie looked at him. 'You don't believe that.'

'No, I guess I don't.' He frowned into his coffee mug as though it had suddenly been transformed into some foul-tasting brew, and set it on the floor. He released her hand. 'You'd best get dressed. There'll be questions. There's hot water if you'd like to bathe.'

She needed him to hold her, needed that badly, but he'd thrown up a wall between them. She sensed his withdrawal. He'd been caring, but in the way of a doctor toward his patient. She felt hurt and confused, but she would not reach out to him. She had her pride. Where was your pride last night? she asked herself.

Her clothes were neatly folded on the chair by the fireplace. She asked him to please pass them to her. He did.

'I'd like to be alone now.'

'Of course,' he said kindly, and a moment later she was alone.

And found that all her tears had not been shed, after all.

An aproned Rose Nickerson stood at the kitchen counter peeling apples for pies and turnovers for the church bake sale. And though her practiced hands worked deftly, her mind was on Betty Martin's visit. Rose knew, though Betty didn't say so, that she hadn't been at all satisfied with her explanation of why Billy and Rachael had fled for home scared half out of their minds, and it bothered Rose. The incident with the truck, she supposed, was a reasonable enough explanation, yet why wasn't it holding well in her own head?

Though she wasn't much for visiting, never had been, she felt she knew these people, knew their children. Hadn't she lived in this house for over forty years, ever since Harvey had built it for her when she was a young bride? Not once in all that time had there ever been any trouble with the neighborhood children. Not even a soaping of her windows, that she could recall. Maybe because she always handed out generous treats, she thought smiling to herself. She enjoyed the children coming to her house on Halloween night, and was sorry she'd missed Rachael and Billy. And sorrier still about what had taken place in her absence.

'You missed them by no more than fifteen minutes,' he'd told her as he explained rather sheepishly what had happened. It had surprised Rose to hear that Rachael and Billy were playing around in the truck, with Billy sitting boldly up in the cab. It didn't sound like them. She'd always found them to be lovely, polite children, even a little on the shy side. But he'd been so sincere in the telling.

It had, in fact, been his sincere manner which had persuaded her to hire him in the first place — that and his charm, she supposed. Rose began slicing the apples into the uncooked pie shells. She thought about that day nearly three months ago now that he'd stood in her doorway, cap and suitcase in hand, and told her he was a writer and needed a quiet, private place to work for which he would do odd jobs in exchange. She had to admit, she'd quite enjoyed the thought of having a real writer living in her house. When she showed him the attic room, he said it suited him just fine, and when she quoted him the meager wage she could afford to pay him, he didn't bat an eye, just smiled and said that that was just fine, too.

Odd, Rose thought as she bundled up the peelings in newspaper, that I never hear any typing coming from up there. But perhaps he wrote in longhand.

Rose carried the small bundle to the garbage can by the back door, passing the kitchen window as she did. She stopped there and adjusted her bifocals.

He was busily raking leaves down by the path, wearing that old faded army jacket, head bent to the task. He was a good worker; she had no quarrel with that. Nor that he made his own hours and came and went as he pleased. For all she knew, he might even have another job he went to. Now that she thought about it, she realized she really knew very little about this stranger who shared her house.

Had she made a mistake?

A woman alone couldn't be too careful.

Yet he did seem a sincere fellow.

Rose moved from the window and dropped the bundle of apple peelings into the garbage can. 'What do you think, Harvey?' she said aloud. 'Should I have another talk with him, spell it out that he'll just have to watch himself with the neighbors? Or do you think I should let him go?' Harvey was dead seven years now, of a sudden heart attack, and Rose had never stopped missing him. Talking to him comforted her, as did believing he heard every word she uttered, and even that he offered Rose advice in his quiet way.

222

At the sound of her voice, Tiger came trotting into the room, his big, yellow eyes looking questioningly up at Rose. 'No, I wasn't calling you, Tiger-poo,' she said laughing, bending to gather the now loudly purring cat up in her arms. As she scratched beneath his chin, Tiger arched his neck and closed his eyes in ecstasy. 'What a baby you are, Tiger-poo,' she laughed again. 'What a big, old baby you are.'

It was at that moment that Harvey spoke to her — not in a human voice — but in a voice similar in a way to her own inner one. But there was no mistaking it was Harvey she heard. No mistaking at all. 'Get him out, Rose!' Harvey said. 'Get him out of your home, now!' Gooseflesh rose on her bare arms as Tiger let out a soul-chilling howl and sprang from her embrace.

* * *

'Dr. Shea tells us you were a close friend of the deceased.'

'That's correct,' Katie said with outward calm. She was sitting in a worn, overstuffed chair in the parlor, dressed in grey slacks and a white blouse, her face bare of makeup. Her hands, folded in her lap, clenched at the reference to Jason as 'the deceased.' The policeman was the same one who'd been here before. His voice was no longer skeptical, but hard as the steely eyes that were nearly lost in the puffy folds of skin surrounding them. In the midst of pacing the floor in front of her, he fired off a question like a bullet from a gun. 'How good, Miss Summers?'

If she were not so sick at heart she might have laughed at his posturing. Instead, she said, 'Very good, as Dr. Shea has already told you.'

He was standing before her, hands clasped behind his back, looking down at her as if she were in a courtroom, and he was the supreme judge. 'We found fresh tire tracks — large tracks, probably a truck — on the property. And erratic footprints, both leading down to the lake. It's clear to me that whoever was behind the wheel chased your friend down until there wasn't any place for him to go but into the water. Mission accomplished, the vehicle in question sped off.'

His words drew a picture in Katie's mind that made her want to cry out. It was as if the nightmarish experience of Jason's childhood had returned to claim him. She nodded her head involuntarily, wanting to, but unable to deny the sergeant's horrible conclusions. 'How can I help you, Officer?' she asked.

'This is Sergeant Miller, Katherine,'

Jonathan said, and the sharpness with which he said it made her glance at him. He was glaring at the sergeant. It took a moment for it to dawn on Katie that Jonathan was making a point of the officer not bothering to introduce himself to her. As if it mattered.

The sergeant shot Jonathan a look of annoyance. Then he cleared his throat and returned his attention to Katie. 'Do you happen to know anyone — friend, co-worker — who drives a truck?'

'No, I . . . '

'Take your time, Miss Summers. Think hard. It could be important.'

Important? Was anything important anymore? Jason was gone. Dead. She supposed she would just have to accept that. As she'd had to accept that her father was gone. And Todd. And Aunt Katherine. Even in an ironic way, her mother.

'Joey Smith sometimes drives The Coffee Shop van,' she said. 'To deliver take-out orders, or run errands for Mrs. Cameron, the owner.'

Interest glinted in the small, ice-grey eyes, and at once Katie felt guilty. 'But he wouldn't be the . . . '

'We'll decide, Miss Summers.' He smiled to take the sting from his words. 'If madmen always looked like madmen, they'd all be locked up. Our job would be a whole lot easier. Now, let's get back to this Joey. You say he works at The Coffee Shop. That's on Cavendish, isn't it? You're employed there, yourself?'

She nodded.

He scribbled in a small black notebook. 'Anything else?'

'What?'

He looked up from his notepad. 'You know anyone else who drives a truck?'

'Oh. No, I — well, Charlie Black has a truck. He lives about three miles from here. He owns a woodlot which has provided my Aunt Katherine, and now me, with fuel for many years. When my aunt died, he simply carried on. I've had no reason to be anything but grateful. Anyway, the man is in his seventies.'

'He live alone?'

'His wife passed away years ago.'

'Does he have access to this house?'

'He has a key to the cellar. He's had one for as long as I can remember. But anyone intent on getting in here wouldn't need a key. The windows fit poorly, and the locks on the doors aren't that secure. It's an old house.'

'Maybe you oughta consider moving. Doesn't sound too safe for a woman alone.'

226

'This is my home. I'll decide if I'm to move. And when.'

'You know a Peter Machum?'

The question caught her by surprise, which, she understood at once, it was meant to. She had a sinking sensation she knew where it was leading. Jonathan was right about one thing: Sergeant Miller was a son-of-a-bitch.

'Yes, I know Peter Machum. He's a — he was a friend of Jason's.'

His grin edged very close to an out-and-out sneer. 'Jeez, you never know, do you? You couldn't tell by that one. A lawyer, too. I guess it can't hurt the investigation to tell you we found a letter in Belding's wallet, in the plastic part where decent people usually keep pictures of their wife and kids. It was from this Peter Machum — a pretty cozy letter considering it was from one man to another.'

Katie said nothing.

'You know this Jason Belding was a faggot?'

Katie's cheeks burned with anger. 'Yes, I knew Jason was homosexual.'

'And you two were good friends.'

'I've already told you that.'

'But you didn't tell me how good.'

Katie could only stare at him as her thin veneer of calm began to peel away and a trembling began deep within her.

The sergeant's voice grated on. 'Maybe Belding swung both ways. Maybe the boyfriend didn't like you two being so cozy, and maybe he got a little jealous and . . . '

Jonathan suddenly sprung between them, towering over the policeman. His mouth was a grim line. 'I hate like hell to interrupt this class act of yours, Sergeant, but you seem to have forgotten Jason Belding is the victim here — as is Miss Summers.'

Sergeant Miller stood his ground. 'And you seem to forget, Doctor, that you're treading dangerously close to obstructing an officer in his line of duty.'

'I doubt that your 'duty' includes obnoxious and inexcusable behavior. Any further questions will have to wait until tomorrow, I'm afraid. And you can bet your badge, Sergeant, I'm going to do my absolute damnedest to make sure you're not the one asking them.'

'It's all right, Jonathan,' Katie said. The interruption, and maybe the passionate defense, had allowed her to regain a little of her composure. 'Let him ask his questions. I want them to find whoever did this as much as anyone.' Maybe more. Except for Peter, she thought suddenly. Oh, God, she would have to get to Peter before someone else did — before he heard it on the news.

'Are you sure?' Jonathan said anxiously. 'You don't have to subject yourself to this, you know.'

'I know. But it's okay.'

He nodded. To the sergeant he said, 'Speed up your questions, then. And use a little care in asking them.'

The man appeared totally undaunted by the attack, although when he began to speak again, both his manner and his tone of voice had softened considerably. He was almost pleasant.

'This Charlie Black,' he was saying, 'he any relation to the Blacks who used to own most of the land around here? Goes back a bit before your time, though,' he said, scratching absently at his head beneath the police hat.

'Yes, he is,' Katie replied, recalling her aunt telling her about Black Lake being named for the Black family, and that Charlie was the last living member. They'd been farmers. She related what she knew.

'Yep,' the sergeant said, adjusting his cap, then reaching inside his jacket to take a crumbled pack of Pall Malls from his shirt pocket. 'Biggest farm around way back then.' He popped a cigarette from the pack, had it halfway to his mouth. 'Mind?'

Katie nodded that she didn't. After lighting up he dragged deeply on his cigarette, did his little walk across the floor, eyes narrowing to slits as the smoke spiralled upward. He turned. Waving his cigarette at Katie, he said, 'Tell me a little more about this Joey Smith.'

At some point during the questioning, a part of Katie seemed to detach itself, hearing the dialogue and watching the scene unfold as if viewing some macabre play.

'We can start with Smith. It's possible the person responsible — that's if the drowning wasn't accidental, mind you — which I doubt — is someone you know. Or at least someone who knows you. There could be some small incident, something that seemed insignificant at the time, but which could prove important now.' He tossed Jonathan a challenging look. 'Maybe the good doctor here might help in that area. Maybe he could even put together — what do they call it — oh, yes, a psychological profile of the man we're looking for.'

'I'll do whatever I can to help, of course,' Jonathan said. 'But there's not always the domineering mother in the background, Sergeant. Or the brutal father. Sometimes there's just — evil.'

After a long silence, Sergeant Miller turned impatiently from Jonathan, grumbled something that sounded suspiciously like 'freakin' witch doctor.'

At last, all the questions asked and answered, the policemen left, and she and Jonathan were alone. Katie dragged herself out of the chair and went into the studio where she watched through the glass doors as two men in white coats fitted what she knew to be Jason's body into a green bag which looked horribly like a garbage bag. As one of the men began to zip it up, Katie jerked her head away.

'You mustn't stay here alone tonight, Katherine,' Jonathan said. 'Is there someone who could stay with you? What about Drake Devlin?'

The suggestion struck her like a blow to the heart, and she felt her remaining calm threaten to slip away. No, dammit! No, she would not let him see her cry. 'I'll be fine,' she said. 'Please don't worry about me.' As Katie followed him out the door into the bright sunshine, fresh pain washed over her. The perfect autumn day seemed somehow a final betrayal to Jason.

Part way down the steps, Jonathan turned. 'Oh, by the way, Devlin called while you were upstairs. He was quite concerned.'

She hadn't heard the phone ringing. She must have been in the shower.

'I identified myself this time,' he added, giving a sheepish grin. 'But he hung up before I could get his number. But I except you know it anyway.'

'Yes,' she lied. 'Did you tell him . . . ?'

'He already knew. Heard it on the radio.'

Suddenly she did not want Jonathan to leave. She did not want to be alone. 'Will you be going back to the hospital?' she asked. She had dismissed his remark about no longer practicing psychiatry. 'I imagine your patients must be feeling neglected by now.'

'Oh, I guess I didn't tell you. I'm not seeing any patients, except on an emergency basis. I've taken a year's sabbatical. You will call Drake Devlin — ask him to stay with you?'

Not trusting herself to speak, she could only nod. Jonathan came back up the stairs to where she stood holding the door open. He cupped her chin in his hand, tilting it upward so that she was forced to meet his eyes. 'About last night,' he said softly. 'Don't make more of it than what it was, Katherine. You were distraught. You needed someone. I was there, that's all. No one but you and I need ever know. Somehow I don't think — Drake would understand.'

232

The gesture, the words, the half-grin seemed to mock her.

Fighting tears of pain and humiliation, she said, 'I'll call him the moment you leave.'

Alone now, Katie tracked down Peter Machum in New York. She dialed the number of the hotel. When she hung up, she hoped she would never have to do anything so difficult in her life again. But at least Peter hadn't had to hear the news through the media.

As Katie turned from the phone, it rang.

It was Drake. 'Katie, my God, what the hell's going on out there? Are you all right? I heard the news on the radio. Please, can I come out there? I want to be with . . . '

'I'm going in to work, Drake,' she said with a calmness she did not feel. 'Will you come to The Coffee Shop this morning?' Surprisingly, she was glad to hear Drake's voice. Glad he had called. 'I — really do want to talk to you.'

'Going into work? Katie, are you . . . ? All right, I'll see you there.'

She would tell him what she had to in person. She at least owed him that much. She hoped she would still have his friendship. She could use a good friend right now. Oh, Jason. She sagged into a chair and let the tears come.

When she arrived at the restaurant, a flushed and clearly disturbed Mrs. Cameron met her at the door. 'I certainly didn't expect to see you in here this morning, Katie. You should be home.'

'I thought it would be better if I was working. Anyway, I've missed too much time already.' Mrs. Cameron said nothing, but her expression spoke loudly. She didn't want Katie here, and it was not out of any concern for Katie's welfare. 'I'll just put this overnight case behind the cash,' Katie said quietly, not understanding. 'If that's all right.'

Her employer glanced curiously at the overnight case Katie held, shrugged her indifference and left.

As the morning wore on, Katie found herself confusing orders, dropping dishes, and trying not to see the curious, suspicious glances of both staff and customers. Yet no one came right out and questioned her about what had happened, or offered a word of sympathy. One customer, a woman who always seemed so pleasant, refused to be served by Katie. From behind the cash register, Katie could feel Mrs. Cameron's sharp eyes, like burning coals, watching her. What was going on? It was as if she were being blamed for something. Why? What had she done?

It occurred to her as she refilled someone's coffee mug that she must seem terribly callous coming in to work with her friend lying on a cold slab in the morgue. The thought conjured up a picture in her mind, and she began to shake, spattering the back of her hand with the scalding liquid. Bursting into tears, Katie fled to the kitchen where she lay her head against the large refrigerator. Its hard coolness felt soothing on her forehead, contrasting with her burning hand. Mrs. Cameron had been right. It had been foolish to come in to work this morning. She was a mess. Katie whirled at the slight pressure on her shoulder.

Frank Cramer drew back his hand, his smile quickly fading at Katie's expression of fear. 'Katie, I only wanted to . . . ' His thin, deeply creased face turned beet red as Katie rushed past him. In her haste to get away, she came face to face with Joey out in the hallway. He was carrying a pail of blackened, soapy water, and some of it was spilling onto the floor. A sour smell mixed with creosote wafted to her. Joey was staring at her. Then he smiled. Why did he always wear that stupid smile — that stupid, mindless smile? Joey? Was it Joey? Did Joey murder Jason? Oh, God.

He set the pail down, spilling more water

onto his big boots. 'Hi, K — Katie, you still my gurfriend,' came the inevitable question.

'No, I'm not your girlfriend, Joey,' she cried, tears blinding her. 'I never was. Please, just leave me alone.'

Like a child unjustly punished, Joey's face crumbled, hurt filling his eyes. He lowered them and reached for the pail.

Katie's hand went out instinctively to touch him. 'I'm sorry, Joey,' she whispered.

His pathetic attempt at a smile of forgiveness wrenched her heart. Despising herself, she watched him turn his face from her, hefting the pail of water with the strength of a man and the awkwardness of a child.

Heaviness descended on Katie like a wet, black shroud.

'You go home now, Katie.'

Mrs. Cameron stood before her. Her eyes and voice were firm in their decision. Unyielding. Obviously, she'd witnessed the scene with Joey.

'I'll be all right. I just . . . '

'Get some rest,' Mrs. Cameron interrupted. 'Francine is managing quite well.'

'I need this job,' Katie said, and hated the plea she heard in her voice.

'We'll see, Katie. Right now, there's — too much talk. Take some time until it dies down.'

'Talk? I don't understand. What kind of . . . ?'

'I've made up a month's severance pay for you.'

Clearly, it had been decided even before she arrived that her services would no longer be required. But why? She knew it had to be something other than her losing time? But what? What had she done? What were they saying about her?

Forcing herself to stand taller, she said, 'Thank you. You're more than generous. Could I ask — just one last favor of you, Mrs. Cameron?'

'Of course.'

'Do you remember Drake Devlin — the man I was planning to go out with on the night of my — accident?'

'I remember,' she said without hesitation. 'A nice young man he was.' Flushing a little, she added pointedly, 'A real man.'

Looking into the woman's eyes, seeing the unveiled contempt there, even embarrassment, Katie suddenly understood everything. The media (probably thanks to Sergeant Miller) had not ignored the homosexual angle in the case, and she was somehow being made part of something sordid, something unhealthy.

'He'll be in later this morning,' she said, refusing to even acknowledge the unspoken accusation. People believed what they wanted to believe. 'The overnight case is his.' Here was something else they could discuss among themselves, she thought bitterly. Something else they'll enjoy speculating on.

'I'll see that he gets it,' Mrs. Cameron said stiffly.

Katie scribbled a hasty note to Drake and slipped it inside the case. After rezipping it, she went back out to the kitchen, knowing she couldn't leave without first apologizing to Frank. Surely he would know the strain she was under and forgive her. Yet, she managed only to say his name before he turned on her, his face livid with rage and indignation.

'You're just like all the rest,' he lashed out, waving the egg turner dangerously in the air. 'You think you're so good Frank Cramer shouldn't put his dirty hands on you. But I listen to the news, Katie — you're not what you pretend. You think Frank Cramer is nothing, only a useless drunk. Well, I'll show you. I'll show everyone.' With that, he picked up a stainless steel pot and flung it against the side wall where it made a loud 'thunk' against the bricks, then bounced along the tiled floor. 'Frank Cramer is an artist!' he proclaimed to Katie and the world at large.

'Frank, you're wrong,' Katie stammered into the tirade. 'I mean . . . '

'I don't care what you mean,' he yelled, the vein pulsing visibly in his forehead. With that he turned from her to furiously scrape two scorched, smelly eggs from the grill into the garbage disposal. The back of his neck was purple.

Katie walked out of the kitchen feeling totally numb, as if something in her had shut down. As she reached for her coat on the rack, Mrs. Cameron came up to her. Wisps of white hair had escaped her usually neat braids. 'You know Frank,' she said in a kindly voice. 'He gets a little crazy sometimes. He'll be okay. You know as well as I do what the real problem is. Frank likes you, Katie.'

It was the only warmth the woman had shown her since she got here, but Katie was far removed from its having any effect. As she left the restaurant, she heard Mrs. Cameron's voice, sharp and angry, behind her. 'Joey, when you take the truck out to do an errand, don't stay half the day. And don't leave here again at night without mopping up this floor.'

Poor Joey, Katie thought as she let the heavy door close behind her for what she knew would be the last time. And yet she couldn't really blame Mrs. Cameron for chastising Joey — he could be irresponsible.

239

Anymore, she supposed, than she could blame Mrs Cameron for firing her.

She did, after all, have a business to run.

Katie drove home in a daze. In her studio, still wearing her coat, she curled up on the cot in a fetal position and fell into a sleep so deep and sound she might have been drugged.

Soon, she dreamed.

She was sitting in a corner of a cold, dimly lit room surrounded by dark forms — human forms? Straining in the near-darkness, she saw that they were not human forms at all — but strawmen. The throat of each lay open, a gaping wound oozing blood that dripped onto the cement floor, where each drop became a small puddle, quickly spreading its red-blackness over a larger and larger area, until all the floor was covered in blood. Katie felt its warm stickiness under her.

Where the strawmen had stood unmoving, they now, like grotesque wind-up toys, began to move toward her. Stiff-legged they came, zombies whose greedy, dead eyes burned into her, dead eyes that she knew could somehow see. Katie's flesh crawled, her knees drawing up ever tighter to her body pressed hard against the rough, cold wall, but there was no where to go. No escape. She watched

240

in helpless terror as skeletal hands reached out to her. As the strawmen came closer, their limbs made a dry, raspy sound that to Katie was more horrifying than the thunder of boots. Insane with terror, she fought to move, to get away, but it was as if she was bound with invisible ropes. Then she felt a hand on her cheek — light as spider legs — and saw that the straw fingers had become pale bones, and the nails touching her face were long and curled and yellow from an eternity spent in the grave . . .

She screamed.

And sat bolt upright on the cot, hearing the echo of her scream all around her. Her breathing ragged, her body drenched in perspiration, Katie scanned the room, peering warily into dark corners, not yet certain if she was really awake or still locked into her awful dream. At last she got up and lit the lamp.

Only when the lamplight had chased all the shadows from the corners, did Katie breathe a sigh of relief. She was safe — at least for the moment. She tried not to hear the whispery sounds of movement that lingered at the edge of her nightmare.

She'd lit the fire and was taking off her coat when the phone rang, jarring every nerve in her body. She snapped it up on the second ring. Drake, she thought, and half-hoped it was. She would be grateful for his company. He'd probably read her note by now. She hoped he would understand and take no for an answer, but she also knew it wasn't like Drake to give up without a fight, and she had no strength for a confrontation. She said hello, her voice sounding small and weak in her ears.

At the sound of breathing, her heart gave a little skip. Not Drake. It was *him*. 'Hello,' she said again foolishly. 'Who's calling, please?'

No answer.

Suddenly more angry than frightened, Katie slammed the receiver down. Before the phone could ring again, she took the receiver off the hook.

For a solid hour she sat staring into the fire. At last she rose and walked to the desk, picking up the Manila envelope that had come in the mail along with a postcard from her mother. Ignoring the postcard for the moment, she slid the photograph from the envelope, and moved closer to the lamplight.

As Katie studied the photograph, she gradually began, both consciously and unconsciously, to slip into a different world. A world detached from all the terrible things that were happening.

Hattie Holloway was neither young nor beautiful, not in the traditional sense, yet her face was far from uninteresting. The word 'aristocratic' came to mind to describe it. Her eyes were her best feature — deep-set, wide, intelligent, almost black in color. Her mouth bordered on thin. Her dark hair was softly styled in a rather out of date pageboy, framing an oval face accented by high cheekbones. Wonderful bone structure, Katie thought, not without a mild stirring of excitement. It was a face that begged to be captured on canvas.

As she gathered her brushes and paints together, arranged the canvas on the easel and uncapped a tube of flesh-tone paint, Katie realized this was exactly the sort of therapy she needed right now. Painting required nothing short of her full concentration.

After donning the yellow, paint-spattered smock that hung on the halltree, she turned up the wick and placed the lamp just to her left on the table so that its flame spotlighted the canvas. Holding her brush delicately between thumb and forefinger, Katie began the deft, fine strokes that would form her outline.

Deeply immersed in her work, Katie did not hear the car when, two hours later, it pulled into her drive. She whirled at the pounding of feet up her back stairs, knocking the jar of brushes to the floor.

'Katherine, are you in there? Katherine?'

Letting out a breath of relief at the familiar voice, Katie unlocked and slid open the doors. 'Jonathan, I wasn't expecting you,' she said, more pleased at the sight of him than she wanted to be.

'I know. I'm sorry to barge in on you so late. I tried to call you, but all I could get was a busy signal.'

He looks tired, Katie thought, and realized she was herself. Her shoulders ached, and her eyes felt as if someone had rubbed them with sandpaper. Yet, on a deeper level, working had calmed her. 'I took the phone off the hook,' she said, taking his coat and hanging it on the rack. 'I didn't want to be disturbed. What time is it, anyway? My watch seems to have stopped, and I keep forgetting to wind the clock.'

He held his wrist up to the lamp to look at his watch. 'Twenty to ten. I called you this morning, too, but — uh, I guess you went in to work.'

She chose the moment to gather her brushes from the floor. Jonathan bent to help her. 'I thought I should,' she said. 'It seemed important at the time.' It occurred to her that losing her job wasn't the tragedy

244

she'd expected it to be. In a way, it was even a blessing. She had a month's pay in her purse, and there would be the money from the portrait, and from the sale of her other paintings. For a little while, at least, she would be free to do her real work. Odd, that something in her life should still matter to her.

'I dropped in to The Coffee Shop,' Jonathan said, handing her the brushes he'd picked up off the floor. 'I spoke with Mrs. Cameron.'

'And she told you she fired me.'

'She chose a nicer way of expressing it. I'm really sorry. People can be so . . . '

'It doesn't matter,' Katie cut in. 'Look, I was just about to have some coffee. Would you like a cup?' She might as well be civilized. He had, after all, been kind to her. She couldn't very well hate him. There wasn't enough emotion left in her for that, though it might have been easier. Besides, she could hardly consider herself his victim when she knew full well she'd boldly and willfully thrown herself at him.

He accepted her offer of coffee. 'I — uh, need to talk to you, Katherine.' As he ran a hand through his thick, black hair, Katie's senses flashed to the way it had felt to her touch. She remembered its clean, soapy fragrance. The memory shattered when Jonathan added, 'What happened to your lawyer friend? I half-expected to see another car in the drive.'

She briefly considered telling him the truth, that Drake wasn't coming, but knew he would then feel obligated to stay with her, and further obligating Jonathan Shea was the last thing she wanted to do. 'He was tied up. He'll be along later.'

That was good, he said, and told her there was a police cruiser in the area, so she could feel relatively safe anyway, which Katie found comforting. She saw him looking at her canvas.

'The commission I told you about,' she said. 'A portrait. There's not much to see yet, but maybe when it's finished, you'll give it a review.' She managed a smile at him, then showed him the photograph of Hattie Holloway.

As Jonathan studied the woman in the photo, Katie saw recognition come into his eyes. 'I know this lady,' he said. 'Or rather, I know her husband, George Holloway. He's a land developer. They've just donated a new wing to Belleville General Hospital. They're wealthy people. And good people.'

Katie had figured with what Mrs. Holloway was paying her, they weren't exactly paupers.

'I suppose she must be a patron of the arts,' she said. 'Otherwise she would have chosen a name to do her portrait.'

'Don't underestimate yourself, Katherine. I'm no expert, but your work looks damned good to me.'

Katie warmed at his compliment. 'Thanks. Actually, I never imagined it could be anything but a hobby.'

'Well, I won't press you on that,' he said smiling. 'Is this your first portrait?'

'The first one I'll get paid for. Please, sit down, Jonathan. Make yourself comfortable,' she said, suddenly uncomfortable talking about herself. 'I'll get the coffee.'

When she returned he was sitting on the cot, legs angled out in front of him. She handed him his coffee. 'You said you wanted to talk. Do the police have any leads?'

'Nothing solid.' He patted the place beside him. Katie tensed for a second, then, not wanting to create an issue, sat down.

'I've been at the police station most of the day,' he began, 'going through reports, computer files . . . ' He shook his head despairingly. 'I thought we might stumble on something helpful if we went back to the beginning. To the night you saw the strawman — assuming that's what it was — in the back seat of your car.'

'It's what I saw all right. I'm sure of that now.' Her nightmare came back in a rush. She forced it away. 'But I don't know what I can add that I haven't already told you.'

'Neither do I. But humor me for the moment. Unfortunately, we don't know anything about that particular one,' Jonathan went on, talking more to himself than to her, his forehead creased in concentration. 'But we do know about the effigy of Todd. We have the physical evidence of that one. Of course, they could easily have been one and the same. I had hoped it was just some sick Halloween prank, but too much has happened for that to stand up.'

Meaning Jason was dead and that Jonathan believed as she did that he'd been cold-bloodedly murdered. How terrified her friend must have been seeing that monster truck bearing down on him, the cruel deliberateness of the madman behind the wheel. She could almost feel his panic when at last he went into the lake, as the icy water closed over him, blocking out sun and sky, feel his desperate struggle for air as the lake roared its deadly message inside his head as it sucked him down, down, pounding it triumphantly through his very marrow. What must it feel like to know you were dying? How long? How long did it take to drown? When had

248

he lost consciousness? Two minutes . . . three
. . . four . . . Katie gasped in air as though her
own lungs were about to burst. She closed
her eyes against the bombardment of images
and sensations. Somehow, I'm responsible for
Jason's death, she admitted to herself for the
first time. Knowing it was true, she could
only stare at her hands.

'Are you all right, Katherine?' Jonathan
asked beside her.

She opened her eyes and looked at him,
almost surprised to see him sitting there.
'Yes,' she said. 'Yes, I'm fine.'

'I know this is difficult, Katherine, but we
really do have to talk about it.'

'I know. I'm just not sure what it is
you want me to say.' Recalling Sergeant
Miller's suggestion, she said, 'I guess you're
trying to help me remember something of
significance, huh?' Might as well get on with
it, she thought. Maybe she would remember
something that would help. Why not? It
worked all the time in the movies.

'If there is anything,' he said hesitantly.
'Anything at all. Katherine, I was wondering
— do you have any suspicions, yourself?'

'No, not really.' No one and everyone, she
thought. Allen Parker not excluded. But she
did not want him drawn back into her life,
not unless it was absolutely necessary. Allen

was certainly capable of slapping a woman around and of harassment. She could attest to that. But murder? It didn't seem likely. Still, she couldn't be sure. Whether or not he was still in Belleville was something she planned to check out herself.

'There has to be some connecting link,' Jonathan was saying. 'Some pattern. It's all so damned bizarre. Oh, I guess I should tell you, the police are interviewing everyone you worked with, the people in your art class . . . '

'That should make me popular,' Katie quipped. She dropped her gaze to a burn spot, shaped like a black teardrop, on the floor near the fireplace. Well, her popularity was at an all time low, anyway. And maybe they would uncover some important clue. 'I suppose it's not entirely true that I have no suspicions,' she said slowly, her eyes shifting from the floor to Jonathan. He was studying her intently. 'Lately, it seems I've come to suspect just about everyone I come into contact with. So I really don't know how much stock you could put . . . '

'Katherine, what is it? What happened?'

'Well, there was an incident with Frank today, but it probably didn't mean . . . '

'Frank Cramer? The cook at The Coffee Shop?'

'Yes,' she replied, knowing how Frank would have bristled at the term 'cook.' He was a chef, dammit, he would bellow when any unwitting soul made the mistake. An artist! Katie related briefly the incident to Jonathan who listened without interruption. ' . . . and when he shouted that he'd show me, that he'd show everyone — I guess I couldn't help wondering if his words implied some sort of threat.' Frank? she mused. Not the most stable individual she knew — but a murderer?

'Right you should wonder. Anything else?'

She thought a moment, remembered her encounter with Raymond Losier at City Hall, then dismissed it as too ludicrous to have any importance. All the while, Jonathan was scribbling in a notebook. When he stopped writing, she said, 'There is something. Last night when I was walking home from the bus stop, I heard something in the woods, just off the road. It seemed to be — keeping pace with me. I didn't see what it was.'

Jonathan frowned. 'An animal?'

'It's what I thought at first. And what I tried to convince myself of when I got home. But I sensed a person. I wasn't about to hang around to find out.' She envisioned herself running, recalled the blind terror that had pushed her on. 'Anyway, we can't keep blaming everything that happens on animals, can we? That's just about as bizarre as anything else we can think of.'

'You're a perceptive woman,' he said. 'If you sensed a person in those woods, I'd be willing to bet on it.'

'Thanks,' she said, not certain if that made her feel any better. If she hadn't been such a coward, if she'd just stopped to turn around, even for an instant, she might have seen the face of her tormentor — of Jason's killer. She could have told the police, and it would be all over by now. (*It would be all over because you would be dead. You know very well you didn't really outrun him. He was standing at the bottom of the stairs while you were scrambling around for your key. He was watching you. Smiling. Look hard, Katie. See him. See his face.*) 'Did the police talk to Charlie Black?' she asked, snapping herself out of the almost hypnotic state.

Jonathan gave a wry grin. 'Poor old fellow was scared half to death. I don't think we need include him in our list of possible suspects.' He looked at his watch. 'Your friend's a little late, isn't he? It's five to eleven.'

Katie rose to refill their coffee cups. (*Please, don't go, Jonathan. I don't want to be alone.*) 'His father's been ill,' she said.

'I expect he'll be a little detained. He'll be here though. Drake is reliable.' She thought about the police car cruising the area and told herself she had nothing to fear.

'Live far from here, does he?'

'Who?'

'Devlin. He live far from here?'

'On a farm with his father.'

'Oh? Where?'

Katie let out a nervous laugh. 'Why? Does it matter?'

He shrugged and sipped his coffee. 'No, I suppose not. I just thought you told me he was a lawyer.'

'Yes. Well he's had to put aside his plans to open a practice to help his father on the farm.'

'I see.' Jonathan checked his watch again. 'Commendable.' He stood up. 'Well, I suppose I should be leaving . . . '

'Oh, I'd almost forgotten,' Katie said, standing to face him. 'Jason's car was parked around front when I got home last night.'

'Yes, I remember. Is that important?'

'Jason never parked at the front. Always around back.'

Jonathan shrugged into his coat, his face thoughtful. 'He must have come upon the intruder as he was leaving your house. Stopped the car and got out.'

'Yes,' she answered sadly. 'That's what I concluded. And that's why he's dead.'

'The police found truck tire tracks on the property — right down to the lake. But you say you didn't hear or see a truck — only someone in the woods.'

'There are lots of little side roads leading into the woods. Old logging roads. It wouldn't be too hard to hide a truck.'

He was standing at the door now, hands jammed into his pockets, and from the way he was looking at her, she got the distinct impression he didn't want to leave any more than she wanted him to. But maybe that was just wishful thinking on her part.

'That strawman — that was planned,' Jonathan said suddenly. 'He had to have broken into Jason's apartment to get those clothes.'

Katie nodded. 'Are the police really convinced the man they're looking for is someone I'm acquainted with?' she asked, knowing even as she did, the question was merely a stall to keep Jonathan with her a little longer. God, would she never learn?

'They're not convinced of anything at this point, but you have to go with some premise, otherwise we really are faced with looking for the proverbial 'needle in the haystack'.'

Again, he checked the time. 'Are you sure Drake is coming?'

She was on the slippery edge of ending the charade, of telling him she never had been expecting Drake, when the phone rang. She walked calmly over to answer it. Maybe it was Drake now. She wasn't sure if she wanted it to be. Or maybe it was 'him' calling to further torment her. Then, she would simply hand the phone over to Jonathan.

But it was neither. A woman's voice, soft and cultured, asked to speak with Jon Shea. 'Tell him it's Lona, will you, dear?'

Katie handed him the phone. 'For you. Lona. This case must be playing hell with your social life.' As he spoke into the receiver, Katie headed for the kitchen, fighting hot pangs of jealousy. She could imagine the owner of that voice — gorgeous, sexy, smiling up at Jonathan, lips moist and parted, eyes inviting. She saw Jonathan's hand reach for the zipper at the back of the expensive dress (a Dior), saw the dress fall from alabaster shoulders to puddle at her feet, revealing a perfect body — Jonathan's eyes glazed with passion . . .

'Sorry about that,' he said, coming into the kitchen where Katie at once busied herself polishing the kettle on the stove with a dish cloth. She saw her face in the chrome. It looked pale and distorted. 'I don't know how she got your number. Probably from the police department. Lona can be very persuasive.'

'I'm sure,' Katie said coolly. God, she was being so obvious. She didn't want to be obvious. She couldn't seem to help herself.

He was looking at her oddly, then, to her shame, she saw the hint of a grin touch his mouth. Her own face flamed as she fought the urge to slap it off. He was as arrogant as ever. There was nothing, she supposed with a twist of malice, like a pursuing 'Lona' to inflate a man's sagging ego.

'Well, I'd best be leaving before your company arrives,' he said. But he made no move to go, instead stood looking at her, indecision coming into his cobalt-blue eyes. 'Don't hesitate to call, Katherine,' he said solemnly, all trace of the grin gone now. 'Not for any reason.'

'I won't.' She turned abruptly from him, moving to the sink where she began rinsing the few dishes there. He came up behind her and reached past her to turn off the faucet. Then he placed both hands on her shoulders and turned her to face him. 'I mean it, Katherine. Not for any reason.'

'Yes. I heard you.'

Seeming satisfied with that, he released

her. 'Lock the doors when I leave. I'll be in touch.'

She thought about telling him of the ominous phone call she received today, then changed her mind. He would probably just see it as a ploy to keep him here.

As Jonathan was getting into his car, Katie saw the police cruiser drive slowly by, dome light flashing silently as a beacon, bringing her a small measure of security.

In the studio, Katie recapped her tubes of paint and set her brushes to soak, wondering as she did if 'Lona' was the society woman Linda Ring had told her about — the woman Jonathan had almost married. And why was he taking a year's sabbatical? Surely, it had to be more than the death of a single patient, as tragic as that was. Weren't doctors conditioned to expect that not all of their cases would end successfully? Especially psychiatrists. Jonathan did not seem so fragile as to be bowed by one failure.

But perhaps there wasn't just one.

Well, he was no concern of hers, she told herself, beginning to make up her bed on the cot. And he certainly owed her no explanations. Let Lona help him work through whatever was haunting him. And hadn't she, Katie, already mapped out her own life? A life free of personal commitment?

No husband. No children. She would travel light. A no-risk life. What a joke that was. There was no guarantees of safety, no matter how carefully you planned your life. She was proof enough of that.

As Katie mechanically changed the pillow case on the pillow, she thought of those people who had once been an integral part of her life — her father, Todd, Aunt Katherine, even her mother . . . they moved across the screen of her mind like a parade of ghosts from a past lifetime.

Now Jason would join them. She pushed the morbid thought away.

The postcard from her mother was on the desk. She hadn't read it yet. Mainly because she knew in essence what it would say. 'George bought a bigger cruiser . . . met some people who really know how to party . . . how's the painting going? You must come for a visit soon.'

They both knew, of course, that Katie would never take her up on her invitation, which was born out of a sense of duty, and to her mother's credit, perhaps even guilt.

From the time Katie was eleven, she'd known that because she bore such a strong physical resemblance to her father — tall, green-eyed, even to the same gold highlights in otherwise brown hair (her father was probably grey by now, or maybe bald, if he was alive at all), her mother found it a strain to have her around. 'You're just like your goddamned father,' she would shriek whenever Katie did anything to displease her.

Stan Summers, a salesman for a pharmaceutical company, had betrayed her mother by running off with the office secretary (what a cliché, Daddy) never to be heard from again, and Katie's presence was a constant, bitter reminder of that fact.

Laying a piece of wood on the fire, Katie directed her thoughts to a more pleasant subject. A cat. A grey momma cat. She could get one now that she was home to take care of it. Probably, she thought, it would make more sense to get a dog. She would feel safer with a dog. She would get both, she decided with the smallest uplifting of her spirits. A cat and a dog.

She opened the drapes a little and looked out on the darkness. No wind now. No raging water. Just calm. A terrible, waiting calm. She let the drapes fall back into place and came away from the window. The house, too, was silent.

What if someone tried to break in here right now? What would she do? How would she protect herself? She vaguely remembered the handgun her Aunt Katherine always kept upstairs in her room in a dresser drawer. No doubt it would be considered an antique by now. Did the gun even work? And if it did, were there any bullets?

She was being ridiculous, of course. Even if the gun was functional and she did manage to find the bullets, she didn't know the first thing about guns. The intruder would probably take it from her and shoot her with it. Providing she didn't shoot herself first.

Bone tired, Katie switched on the radio for a time check. It was ten minutes to midnight. After resetting both her watch and the mantle clock, she picked up the postcard on her desk and saw with surprise that the picture on the face of it was of her mother lounging on a lawn chair under a palm tree, holding a tall drink with one of those striped straws angling out of it, and smiling happily at whoever held the camera. George, most likely. With her champagne-blonde hair and the new face-lift, she looked at least as young as her daughter. Katie smiled. Despite her own deep hurt, she was glad that her mother was finally happy.

Setting the postcard down on the desk, she went to turn down the covers. But before getting under them, she grimly removed the stove poker from its usual place against the wall and placed it on the floor within her reach.

Katie got into bed and closed her eyes. But despite her need for sleep, it did not come. Tomorrow, she thought, she would definitely drive out to the pound and inquire about a dog and a cat who could at least tolerate one another.

She turned on her side, tugged at the blankets, tried to fall asleep. But the harder she tried, the more awake she became. The house, too, wakened. She lay listening to the creaks and groans caused, she knew, from boards and nails complaining under the stress of too many seasons — of simply the house settling — harmless sounds that up until now had all but escaped her notice. But now they fed her fears, provoked her worst imaginings, making her uncomfortably aware of how alone she really was, and how vulnerable.

Not until the sun was coming up behind the hill did Katie finally fall asleep, but it was a sleep plagued with dreams of herself running down endless corridors, the sound of breathing all around her. Like giant waves it came, rising and falling, flooding her mind and heart — drowning her. Soon the breathing became laughter — insane laughter echoing off walls and ceilings, while Katie,

261

herself half-mad with terror, ran blindly on, knowing even as she did that there was no escape. And then the dream began to change, and she was in a different place, a cold place with high, white walls, and she saw that the laughter came from Jonathan and an elegant dark-haired woman with blood-red lips and vampire teeth, named 'Lona'. They were standing together looking down on her, while Katie crouched small before them, trying to cover herself with her arms, trying in vain to hide her nakedness.

She woke at noon to a dull, punishing headache, her body cramped and cold, the blankets kicked away.

The laughter lingered.

There was a moment of sick bewilderment before she understood that the laughter was coming from the radio, which she'd left on. Canned laughter. The station was airing some old, near-forgotten radio comedy show.

19

Rose Nickerson dabbed Mercurochrome on the inside of her wrist, painting the scratch Tiger had left when he'd leapt from her arms yesterday. About three inches long it was, deep, and right now, on fire. She blew on it, suspecting infection. 'What's got into you, Tiger?' she said to the orange cat reflected in the medicine chest mirror. Tiger sat on his haunches, looking up at his mistress in that patient way he did when he was waiting for her to put food in his dish. But she'd already done that.

'Don't worry, Tiger,' she said, lowering her voice conspiratorially, 'we'll get rid of him.' Tiger at once seemed to relax, began washing his face. Rose knew very well what had 'got into' her old friend. Tiger had heard Harvey's voice just as she had, heard his warning. She didn't know how he had, but she didn't question it. Weren't cats known for their mystic powers? It was just that nothing similar had ever happened with Tiger before. Which only served to further convince her of the rightness of her decision.

'We will banish this stranger from our

kingdom,' she said, stroking Tiger behind his ears. He purred his approval.

She tried to tell him this morning as she was setting out his plate of bacon and eggs, that he had to go, that she had no further need of him, but something, perhaps his silence, the absence of his usual charming self, which now seemed false, made her hesitate, stopped her. But she would not be stopped again. She would not be unkind about it, of course, she thought as she returned the bottle of Mercurochrome to its place on the shelf. It was not in her nature to be unkind. But she would be firm. She would make the excuse that her cousin was coming to stay, and she had to free the room. Surely the good Lord would understand and forgive her small white lie. She went into the kitchen, the cat padding behind her, where she turned the fishcakes browning in the frying pan for lunch, and put on the peas to heat. Perhaps, when she disposed of her immediate problem, she would do up a couple of bags of treats and just take them down to Betty's tomorrow. She certainly had no wish to have her house labelled among the neighborhood children as 'that mean old hag's place.' She chuckled at the thought.

As she began setting out the plates (old blue

windmill china on a white linen tablecloth which Rose used even when she was alone) and cutlery, she found herself listening with growing apprehension for the sound of the back door opening.

★ ★ ★

At Belleville Police Station, Captain Peterson sat behind his massive desk, his door closed, going over the list of names of those people who had been interviewed, the profiles of each, the questions posed in three different ways, the answers, never varying, and the added info Jon Shea had dropped off this morning. A growing stack of paper that brought him no closer to solving the mystery.

Captain Mike Peterson, a big man, completely grey now, a scant two years from retirement, but still muscled and solid from a disciplined regimen of working out with weights, tapped out a new series of blue dots on the blotter with his ballpoint like he was sending out some new form of coded message, an old habit to help him think. It wasn't working. Behind the opaque glass in his door, officers in silhouette moved about. Jangling telephones were muffled.

He went back to rereading the reports, trying to make a connection, again coming up empty. The captain had a history of solved cases behind him, but this one clearly had him stumped. Nothing added up. What did any of these people have to do with the effigy left in the Summers woman's bedroom? To the drowning victim?

He went over it all again looking for something he'd missed. There was always something. He just couldn't find it. Heaving a sigh of momentary defeat, he set the papers aside and picked up the photograph of the kid in the army uniform, its throat smeared with red paint, made to look like blood. The long-ago boyfriend, Todd Raynes.

Was it possible he was back from 'Nam after all these years, not dead at all, but screwed up from the war, a full-fledged killer, a raving psychotic? Of course he was a killer. It's what we did; sent off young innocents filled with romantic notions of war, and developed their dark sides. We all had our dark sides. We're a world of Christless Jekylls and Hydes, he thought, laying down the photograph, pinching his lower lip between thumb and forefinger.

Shea had persuaded him to put on an extra black and white to patrol the area around the Summers woman's house. He would have to call it off soon, despite favors owed. They were already short-handed.

He considered Sergeant Miller's theory that Katherine Summers herself needed closer surveillance, but for reasons other than her safety. And though Miller was a dyed-in-the-wool redneck, and not one of the captain's favorite people, it was Mike's own opinion that Shea, as brilliant as he knew him to be, wasn't exactly showing objectivity in this particular case.

Maybe Miller's theory did warrant a closer look.

20

She'd been up an hour. Having taken two Tylenol, Katie now sat at her kitchen table, bundled up in her robe, picking at a stale bran muffin and sipping hot tea. With the sun pouring through the window, laying a pool of yellow over the wooden table, exposing old scars and the lack of varnish, catching dust motes in its path, her situation somehow did not seem quite so threatening.

She thought about the phone call she'd deliberately not mentioned to Jonathan. What good would it have done? The call probably came in from Belleville anyway, so she hadn't been in any immediate danger. Then she remembered seeing a phone booth out on the highway, near the bus stop. And there was an all-night diner about a mile and a half toward town. Ralphie's, it was called.

If she'd reported the call the second she'd hung up the phone, the police just might have been able to converge on him. Well, nothing she could do about it now. It was a good bet she would get another chance to redeem herself — and a better one that she hadn't heard the last of 'the strawman'.

Katie shivered as if a cloud had just passed beneath the sun.

Upstairs, she hurriedly dressed in jeans and a warm sweater, then she raced back down and immediately telephoned the animal shelter. Yes, the man told her, they had a good choice of homeless dogs and cats, and he was sure they had just the right pets for her. Come in and shop, he said. After promising she would be there before closing time, Katie hung up the phone. She stood looking at it for a couple of seconds, then, as she had yesterday, she took the receiver off the hook.

21

At the sound of the back door opening, Rose, who had her back to it turning down the heat under the peas, nearly jumped out of her skin. Slowly, she turned to face him. He was taking off his jacket, hanging it on the hook by the door. Then he washed his hands at the kitchen sink and sat down at the place she had assigned him — not at the head of the table. No one sat in Harvey's place. Tiger had leapt up on the counter and was glaring at him. Rose didn't swat him down as she usually did.

'Smells good,' he said, smiling at her. 'You're a wonderful cook, Mrs. Nickerson.'

But his eyes didn't smile. Rose had the feeling that he knew what was coming. But of course he couldn't know. She sat down across from him. Say it! she thought. Get it over with.

She plunged in.

' . . . I hope you understand,' she finished lamely. 'It has nothing whatever to do with your work. I'll be more than happy to give you a written recommendation.'

He seemed to find her offer amusing.

'That's good of you,' he said, 'but it won't be necessary. Actually, I wasn't planning to stay on much longer, anyway.'

'Oh? Have you finished your book?'

'Book?' He looked puzzled. And then his smile widened. 'Oh, yes the book. No. But it's coming on to hunting season. I'm planning to do a little hunting.' He left the table and went to where his jacket was hanging on the hook. He was fishing something out of the pocket — something Rose couldn't see until he turned around, and then a ripple of fear, as cold and bright as the knife he held in his hand, went through her. He stroked the blade and smiled at her. 'A hunter needs a good knife,' he said softly. 'Don't you agree. Did your husband like to hunt, Mrs. Nickerson?'

'No,' she said in a voice barely audible, unable to tear her gaze from the deadly blade. 'No, Harvey didn't hold with killing things.'

22

For the remainder of the day, Katie worked on the portrait of Hattie Holloway, stopping only when nature called, and once to make herself a cheese sandwich, half of which remained uneaten on her plate. It was nearly six o'clock when she finally gave it up. She was tired, her body one big ache, but it was a good kind of tired. Pleased with the day's accomplishment, she gathered up her paints and brushes. The work was coming along well. She hoped Mrs. Holloway would be pleased with the results.

Just as she was replacing the receiver in its cradle, the phone rang, vibrating in her hand, making her pull it away as if she'd received a shock. She let it ring twice more before she answered. 'Hello.' Her voice sounded deceptively strong, if wary.

'Hi there,' Jonathan said cheerfully, and Katie wondered if the gravity of her relief travelled through the line. 'Just checking in. How are you holding up?'

'Fine. I've been working.' It was the first time she'd heard Jonathan's voice on the telephone, and aside from the relief she'd felt at hearing it, its deep, masculine resonance sent a warm thrill coursing through her.

'Everything's okay, then?'

'Yes — well, as good as can be.' Then, surprising herself, she blurted, 'I didn't get very much sleep last night. I kept hearing things.' She gave a small laugh that sounded hollow.

After a lengthy pause, Jonathan said, 'You mean you were alone last night?'

Along with the incredulity and accusation, she heard alarm in his voice and decided to abandon the foolish game about expecting Drake. 'Yes,' she said simply and was grateful when he didn't push for further explanation, saying only, 'If I'd known, I wouldn't have left you.'

What about Lona? she wanted to ask, but of course didn't. She remembered her dream and felt a momentary hatred for him. 'I'm sure I was perfectly safe,' she said, her voice gone the slightest bit frosty. 'After all, the police are watching the house.'

She heard his sigh of exasperation. 'Do you really think, Katherine, that some maniac intent on getting his hands on you wouldn't be resourceful enough to get past one police car?'

'If one is not enough then why don't they put on more?' she snapped, but his question had had the intended effect. Thinking she'd heard a noise, Katie darted a look over her shoulder. Her gaze went quickly to the stove poker on the floor.

She heard another sigh as Jonathan began explaining that it wasn't so simple as she might think. The department was understaffed, underequipped, and they really couldn't even spare the one car they'd assigned to her. 'Katherine, all I'm asking for here is a little cooperation on your part. Please trust me. If not me, then someone. Don't try to be brave.' He paused. Then, 'It could end you up in a body bag.'

This last called up the image of Jason being zipped into the body bag as she watched out the window. Tears sprang to her eyes. Why was Jonathan doing this? Why was he trying to frighten her? The dog! Dammit! She'd forgotten to go to the pound, and now the place was closed.

'I'm sorry,' she heard him say, more gently now. 'It's just that you don't seem to realize the seriousness of your situation.'

'I do. Really, I do. And I'll be more careful, I promise,' she said, feeling not entirely unlike a child properly chastised. Wanting to redeem herself, she added, 'I've been considering getting a dog.'

'That's an excellent idea.' She knew he

was smiling now. She could hear it in his voice. 'Then I'll stop lecturing,' he said.

'I'd be grateful.' Intending to hold him to his word, Katie thought it was an opportune time to tell him about the phone call. She thought he showed remarkable restraint when he calmly asked her if the voice had sounded at all familiar, or if she could even tell whether it belonged to a man or a woman.

'No, not really,' she replied, though she had thought 'man.' And there had been some small thrill of recognition — something in that hideous laugh. Like a name on the tip of your tongue. Or maybe she was just getting it confused with the laughter in her dream — like déjà vu. Yet the phone call had come prior to her having the dream. 'It never occurred to me,' she said, 'that a woman might be doing these . . . but then you're the detective.'

'Psychiatrist,' he corrected lightly.

'Same thing.'

He laughed. 'I'll be there in a little while. I'll stay with you tonight.'

'No,' she said quickly, switching the receiver to her other ear. 'That won't be necessary. I — uh, I'm planning to stay with a couple of friends — girls from The Coffee Shop.' The lie just popped out. But perhaps it needn't remain a lie. If the invitation was still open, it might not be a bad idea to accept it. It was highly possible, of course, that Andrea and Francine were among those whose good opinion of her had changed. Possible she would no longer be welcome in their home. Well, there was only one way to find out. If she detected even the slightest hesitation, she would simply book herself into a hotel. She hoped she wouldn't have to. With Jason being buried tomorrow, she would like not having to be alone tonight.

As if reading her thoughts, Jonathan said, 'I could try to arrange for a policewoman to stay with you if you prefer.'

'No, Jonathan, really. And I'm not making it up, I promise. I really do plan to stay with friends tonight. I'll even call you with the number.' She didn't add, From wherever I end up.

'Well — that's good, then.'

Did she detect the smallest note of disappointment in his voice just then? No, she must be mistaken. He wasn't apt to want to leave the gorgeous Lona just to babysit her.

Katie glanced at the clock on the mantle. The girls wouldn't be home for a couple of hours yet. In the meantime, there was something she had to do, something she'd been putting off. Flipping the phone book open on the desk, Katie ran her finger down the list of names beginning with 'P', stopping when she got to Mrs. E. Parker, 42 Queen St. S.

Edwina was a frail little woman, one of the truly good souls, long widowed and the mother of Allen Parker, whom she clearly adored. Allen had lived with his mother in the days when Katie knew him, and Katie had been to the house a few times. A small, cozy house, smelling faintly, Katie recalled, of old roses. Mrs. Parker had a great fondness for fancy, heavily starched doilies, knickknacks, and for pictures of her son.

They were everywhere, taken at every stage of his life, seemingly filling all available wall and surface space. No matter in which direction you cast your eyes, a handsome Allen would be smiling back at you. Allen as a baby, Allen as a boy, Allen as a man. There were numerous pictures of him in uniform.

You could actually watch him growing up in Mrs. Parker's parlor.

So many pictures, and yet Katie wondered if the woman really knew her son.

With each number she dialed, her stomach knotted a little more, the memory of Allen's face as it had been that night, ugly, distorted with rage, grew more vivid. He'd broken into her house and was waiting for her when she got home from work.

Katie was barely inside the door, when he'd grabbed her, his fingers digging into her arms. 'Who were you with?' he hissed, bringing his face down close to hers, his breath reeking hot and sour of booze. 'Who is he?' Katie had been sure he was going to kill her.

But he'd only slapped her across the face. The sound echoed sickeningly in the room. He'd seemed as surprised as she was that he'd actually struck her. He dropped her hands, launching at once into the familiar litany of apologies, the begging for forgiveness.

But she was cold to his pleadings. Cold to everything about him. By the time the shock and sting of the slap faded, any feeling she might still have harbored for Allen Parker faded with them. After weeks of terrorizing her, Allen seemed finally to understand that. To accept it, then. Perhaps he'd seen it in her eyes. Because he left her house that night, and it was the last she saw of him.

The phone rang once . . . twice . . . Hang up! Hang up now! What good to dredge it all up again, all the ugliness of that time in her life? But she had to know. There was no other way. Maybe Mrs. Parker wouldn't recognize her voice. After all, it had been two years since she'd heard it.

'Hello?' At the sound of the dry, aging

278

voice, Katie remembered again how fond she'd been of Mrs. Parker, and hated deceiving her this way. But she had no choice.

'May I speak with Allen, please, Mrs Parker.' If she went to call Allen to the phone, Katie would simply hang up. She would have her answer.

'I'm sorry. I'm afraid Allen doesn't live here anymore. He lives in Los Angeles now. With his wife and little boy.'

'I see. Well . . . '

'If it's important I can get you his number. I have it . . . '

'No, no. That won't be nec . . . '

'Katie? Katie, is that you, dear?'

Hearing the warmth in the woman's voice, Katie felt doubly guilty. And trapped. 'Yes, yes, it is, Mrs. Parker,' she said, beginning to absently twirl a length of hair about her finger. 'I — uh, received a get-well card from Allen when I was in the hospital, and I just wanted to thank . . . '

'I'm so pleased to hear from you, dear,' she cut in. 'How are you feeling after your terrible accident? I wouldn't have known a thing about it but for Allen. I don't listen to the news — can't abide it — all that killing, you know, and my eyes aren't what they used to be. Allen was down visiting me for a few days, and he read it aloud from the newspaper. We both felt just terrible, Katie.'

'Thank you. But I'm pretty well back to normal now.' She almost laughed aloud at her choice of words.

'You know, dear,' Mrs. Parker said, her voice lowering secretively, 'I think Allen will always have tender feelings for you, never mind that you've both gone your separate ways.'

'Well, I'm flattered, but I'm sure he's very happy,' Katie muttered, not knowing how else to respond, and having no wish to be cruel by telling her she had no interest in Allen's feelings, one way or the other. He was, after all, her son.

'I think so, Katie. Arlene's a lovely girl. Not that they haven't had their share of troubles, mind you, but I suspect you've seen Allen's unpleasant side a time or two yourself. I expect I've spoiled Allen — always felt sorry for the boy, you know, having no father and all.'

Mrs. Parker was apologizing for Allen. She was not so blind to his faults as Katie had thought. 'I understand,' she said. And strangely, for the first time, she did. Though it didn't serve to make her like Allen any better, at least she no longer hated him.

They talked a little longer, mostly about Mrs. Parker's grandson, Christian, who would be a year old on Christmas Day, and 'a precious boy', and Allen, who, apparently, was going through a transformation for the better. He'd quit the police force, was working days as a truck driver while attending school at night studying for his real estate agent's license. He'd stopped drinking, and he and Arlene were seeing a marriage counsellor. Katie ended the conversation by asking Mrs. Parker to please not mention to Allen that she'd called. 'It's better that he doesn't know,' she said. 'It would be — awkward.'

'Of course,' Mrs. Parker said, seeming to understand at once. 'Sometimes it's wiser not to open doors that have been closed.'

After they hung up, Katie stood quietly by the phone going over the conversation and all that she'd learned about the 'new' Allen. These thoughts on her mind, she headed out to the kitchen, intending to make herself a bit of supper before calling the girls. She was looking forward to a full night's sleep, even in a bed not her own. She would have to get back early in the morning, though, to get ready for the funeral. This thought settled over her like a heavy shroud. Please, God, she prayed silently, let them find the monster who took his life.

She was passing in front of the stairs leading up to the bedrooms, when someone knocked on the door. Her heart lurched. She stood staring at the door, unable to bring herself to move.

The knocking came again, more insistent this time.

'Yes?' she called out, clasping her hands in front of her. 'Who is it?'

'Peter,' came the hoarse, slurred voice. 'Peter Machum.' Katie quickly unlocked and opened the door. The sight of Peter standing unsteadily on her landing, dressed in only a dark suit and tie, which was slightly askew, his thin, ashen face revealing a young man only barely managing to hold himself together, clutched at Katie's heart. It was obvious he'd been drinking — but not nearly enough, she thought sadly as she opened the door wider.

'I'm glad you came, Peter. Please, come in. Was it difficult finding the house? Where's your overcoat?' She hugged herself against a blast of cold air. 'It's freezing out.'

'Overcoat?' He held out his arms, looked at them in bewilderment, then at himself. 'I — uh, guess I left it in the bar.' He ran a hand through his hair. It was starkly black against his pale skin. 'I've been there most of the afternoon. But there was no one to talk to — no one . . . ' She saw him straighten himself mentally, trying to appear sober before her, his dignity threatened. 'I'm sorry. I don't know why I came here. I didn't plan to, you know. I just . . . I'm sorry,' he repeated under his breath, starting to turn away.

Katie reached for his hand, icy cold, and drew him inside, saying gently, 'I need someone to talk to too, Peter. I really would like the company. I'll put on some coffee.' The pain in his eyes was terrible to see, like peering into someone's soul. His grief, she knew, was far worse than her own. Impulsively, she put her arms around him. He smelled of alcohol and of the cold night. 'I'm so sorry,' she whispered.

He drew away first, and Katie saw in his eyes that at some level, he blamed her. Looking away, he reached into his pocket for a handkerchief and blew his nose.

When she asked if he'd had any supper, he shook his head. 'I'm not hungry. He's being buried tomorrow, you know,' he said, his voice on the edge of breaking.

Katie could only nod. She wished she could find words to comfort him, but she knew there were none.

'I made all the arrangements,' he said,

stuffing the handkerchief back into his pocket. 'His parents won't be coming to the funeral; they disowned him years ago — when they found out. He has no brothers or sisters . . . '

'I should have called you, Peter. I should have called and offered my help.'

He shrugged. 'It's okay. I wanted to do it.' He suddenly swayed on his feet, and Katie feared he might pass out right there in front of her. She put out a hand to steady him. 'Are you all right? Would you like to lie down for awhile?'

'No, I'm okay.'

'Coffee, then,' she said, putting firmness into her voice. Black coffee. Gallons of it.

'What happened, Katie?' he said, as she put an arm around him and led him into the kitchen. The question might have come from a small boy, lost and confused. 'Why is Jason dead?' And then, as she guided him to a chair at the table, he covered his face with his hands, and his shoulders heaved with harsh sobs that tore from him. 'I don't understand.'

Katie's own tears spilled over as she thought, Neither do I, Peter. Dammit, neither do I.

In a little while, Peter began to get himself together. The coffee had the desired effect, sobering him somewhat. Though the tuna sandwich she'd fixed for him remained untouched on his plate, as did her own. More than food or sleep, Peter seemed to need to talk. Katie was more than happy to listen.

' . . . We never really had all that much in common you know. Not on the surface, anyway. I mean, well, I'm a lawyer — objectivity, facts and all that. Jason is . . . ' He clenched his fists on the table, swallowing hard. 'Jason *was* an artist. He liked people; they liked him.' He bit down on his lower lip. 'I've always been something of a loner. I never believed there would be any kind of real relationship for me — just out-of-town bars — just . . . ' He shook his head as though to clear it of painful images. 'And then I met Jason. I was twenty-two, still in university. Jason was active in the drama club. He was starring in a play called *Charlie's Aunt* the first time I saw him. God, he was funny. He got a standing ovation every night.' Peter gave a wistful smile, began turning his sandwich plate round and round on the table. 'Jason could always make me laugh. It was one of the things I loved about him. He thought I took life too seriously. Jason was a beautiful man, Katie. What we had wasn't — sordid. It was special.'

Katie smiled. 'I know,' she said softly.

He looked into her eyes for a long moment, then he dropped his gaze to stare into the dark swirls of his coffee. 'I don't think too many people knew about me.'

Katie said nothing. The fact that secrecy was so important to Peter, that his grief was something he need now feel ashamed of, caused her own sadness to deepen.

'They do now, of course,' he said, giving a short, bitter laugh. 'Now that the police have found the letter.' He grew thoughtful. 'Jason told me he confided in you. I was angry about that at first — I was afraid. But he trusted you, so I had to trust you, too.' Idly, he spooned sugar into his coffee, stirring it slowly. 'I think I was jealous of Jason's friendship with you — a little.'

'There was no need to be,' she said gently.

He nodded, sliding the cup away from him. 'I really don't expect you to understand . . . '

'And I won't patronize you by pretending to, Peter,' she said. 'I can't know your experience. But I do know about loneliness — and loss. Believe me, I do.'

Peter took two cigarettes from a silver case and offered her one, and though Katie hadn't smoked in over three years, she accepted it. Peter lit their cigarettes. Dragging deeply on his own, he then let out the smoke in a long, shuddering sigh. Quietly, he said, 'I can see why Jason was so fond of you.'

Despite the kind words, Katie knew that she and Peter would not share a similar friendship. The knowledge saddened her, but she thought she understood. Part of Peter would always resent her. Mainly because if Jason had not come to her house that fateful night, he would still be alive. On that, they both agreed.

It was close to eleven when Peter left. Though she'd tried her best to persuade him to stay over, he'd just shaken his head numbly and went out into the night. It was too late, of course, to call the girls. But then, Katie realized she'd never really intended to go there anyway.

She lingered over the tepid, bitter coffee for a long time, thinking of Peter. He'd come here tonight because he'd been vulnerable — and desperate for someone to talk to — someone who had been close to Jason. He'd also been looking for answers that neither she nor anyone else could give him.

A sound like pebbles hitting the window made her look up, startled. Then she saw it was hailing, and thought at once of Peter. The roads would soon be treacherous if this kept up. She prayed his depression would not cause him to drive recklessly. Damn! Why hadn't he accepted her invitation to stay over, for both their sakes?

Peter's embarrassed admission that he'd been jealous of her friendship with Jason came unbidden into her mind, calling up Sergeant Miller's ugly insinuations and speculations. She considered them briefly, guiltily, before rejecting them. The only person Peter was apt to hurt, she thought uneasily, was himself.

She went into the studio wondering if she should call Jonathan. Maybe he would talk to Peter. She picked up the receiver — put it back down. Oh, sure, you'd like an excuse to call him, wouldn't you? Okay, I admit it. The truth was, she just didn't think she could bear to stay here alone tonight.

The hail had stopped as quickly as it started. Thank God for that at least. Staring at her ghostly reflection in the night-blackened glass doors, she had an overwhelming sense of someone out there in the darkness — someone watching her. Recalling Jonathan's remark about her foolish bravado ending her up in a body bag sent her back to the phone where she dialed the number Jonathan had given her.

As the phone began to ring at the other end, Katie found herself wondering if maybe she really had heard disappointment in

Jonathan's voice when she'd turned down his offer to stay the night. Maybe she was wrong about Lona being someone special in his life. Katie's heart gave a little skip as someone picked up the receiver — then sank as a woman's voice — Lona's, she knew — called out melodiously, 'Jon, darling, would you be a love and bring me my drink?' Then she sang into Katie's ear, 'Hellooo.'

Katie gently replaced the receiver.

★ ★ ★

His hair darkly damp from the shower, Jonathan crossed the forest-green carpeting, tying a navy velour robe over his pajamas. 'Who was on the phone?'

Lona was sitting on the floor in a lotus position, her long, slender body clad in a black leotard, her hair cascading like an ebony cloud to her waist. Except for enormous brown eyes, her face was a finely chiseled, feminine version of Jonathan's.

'No one. Well, I suppose it was someone, but they hung up. Wrong number, I suppose.'

'Where's your drink?'

'In the bedroom.'

He looked at her.

She batted her eyelashes at him. 'Do you mind? I'm tied up.'

Shaking his head, but grinning, he went to get it. 'Booze and yoga,' he said, his tone lightly teasing. 'Weird combination.' After handing her her drink, Jonathan sat down on the sofa. 'Well, little sister, what's next on your varied agenda?'

She grinned up at him, her face glowing with the vitality and energy of youth, though she was thirty-three. 'New York,' she said, untangling herself and going to sit next to him on the sofa, curling her long legs up under her. 'I'm leaving tomorrow. I landed a great part in Frank Marcus's *The Killing of Sister George*. I'm playing Mercy Croft, the producer of a soap opera.'

'Saw the movie,' Jonathan said with a grin. 'Hated it.'

'The play's a comedy, dummy. Except for the story line, there's no comparison.'

'So, Broadway, huh?' He tousled her mane of hair playfully. 'I'm impressed.'

'Off-off Broadway, actually,' she quipped in her best British accent. 'But what the hell? It's work. Tell me what's been happening with you. What's this about a year's sabbatical?'

'I needed a rest, that's all.'

She gave him a mock pout, sipped her drink. 'So don't tell me. You never tell

290

me anything, anyway.' As if dismissing him, Lona rose and sauntered over to the painting that took up most of the wall facing them. 'I've been looking at this while you were in the shower. It's really good. Terrific, in fact.' She peered at the name scrawled in the lower right-hand corner. 'Katie Lynn Summers. Never heard of her.'

Clasping his hands behind his head, Jonathan said, 'You will,' so confidently that Lona turned to look at him.

'You say that like a number one fan. Someone you know?'

'Yes, I know her.'

Lona came closer, almost cat-like in her movements, her dark eyes narrowing suspiciously. 'Do I detect, after all this time, stars in my big brother's eyes?'

Jonathan laughed. 'You always were nosy.' He stood up and, crossing in front of her, went to the sideboard where he poured himself a generous shot of whiskey over ice. Standing with his drink in his hand, he returned his attention to Katherine's rendition of Madonna and Child. He'd picked it up at the local art gallery weeks before he'd actually met the artist. Aside from it being a superior work, there was an added, special reason why he'd felt compelled to buy it. At the time, there'd been a couple considering the painting, and while they were arguing about whether or not the colors fit in with their new decor, Jonathan unashamedly snapped it up, earning some icy looks for himself. He grinned, remembering. 'We're just good friends,' he said, coming to sit beside his sister. Odd, how his blood had quickened at the mere mention of Katherine. But, alas, there was the matter — however virtually invisible — of Drake Devlin. The lady, as they say in Victorian novels, was spoken for.

'Too bad,' Lona said, and for a moment Jonathan was startled, thinking she'd read his mind, then he realized she was responding to his half-truth that he and Katherine were no more than good friends. Lona shifted her position on the sofa, began rearranging the plump cushions, covered in beige and chocolate-brown corduroy, behind her back.

The sofa was tweed, matching one of the chairs. The other chair, arranged at kitty-corner by the window, was upholstered in brown leather. The walls throughout the small apartment were painted antique white. It was a typical bachelor apartment, pleasant enough, he supposed, but he knew he wasn't the apartment dweller type. He needed space. He needed to walk out of his door and see green trees, breathe clean air. And he would.

Soon. But for now the apartment served his purpose just fine.

'Ever hear from Constance?' Lona said, trying to make the question sound matter-of-fact.

Down in the street, a car horn blasted, while above their heads, someone was practicing chords on an electric guitar. Jonathan gazed into his drink, swirled the pale amber liquid lightly so that the ice tinkled against the sides of his glass like tiny crystals. 'No. Not anymore.'

'Good.'

He smiled and shook his head. 'Always the protective little sister, aren't you?'

'And why not? She was never right for you.'

'Would anyone be?' he teased.

She put on a deeply wounded face. 'Sure. You think I don't want you to be happy?'

He patted her knee. 'Tell me about your love life, Lona. It's always a hell of a lot more interesting than mine.'

'Always the psychiatrist. Get them talking about themselves; keeps the spotlight off you, right?' All the same, Jonathan watched her expression grow thoughtful as she began turning the large, fake emerald on her engagement ring finger, flashing a plum-colored nail, a secretive little smile beginning to play at the corners of her mouth. 'Actually,' she said, letting her hands drop to her lap and looking at him, 'there is someone.'

'Oh?' Jonathan tried to act surprised.

'Yeah, I met him at an audition. I don't even remember the play. Big, blond and oh, so gorgeous. Ivan Wellington. How about that for a name? Not a stage name, either. Too bad he's as dirt poor as I am, and just like me, stalking the big break.' Her face, always expressive, suddenly lit up with something close to awe. 'Oh, but Jon, what a fine actor he is. Reminds you of a young Laurence Olivier. He doesn't act; he simply becomes. He internalizes the role, makes it his own. He will make it, there's no doubt in my mind.' Then she rolled her eyes and hugged her knees, a mischievous look coming into her face. 'Not too bad in the real life department, either, if you get my drift.'

Jonathan laughed, shaking his head again. 'You're incorrigible Lona.' Then he settled back to listen, as he so often had while they were growing up, to Lona's latest love adventure. Lona's voice rose and fell like the tide, often far in the distance, as Jonathan's thoughts kept returning to Katherine. He was so afraid for her. And for himself, too, he might just as well admit it. He was terrified he would prove powerless in the face of this evil that had invaded her life, and ultimately, his own. He was terrified of failing again. He didn't think he would be able to go on if that happened. Well, at least for tonight, he consoled himself, I needn't worry. Tonight she was safe in the company of friends.

Lona was asking him a question. He had to ask her to repeat it, almost resenting the intrusion into his thoughts. Not that he didn't enjoy Lona's visits, which punctuated his life like a series of exclamation points; he did, even if she did take over his bedroom while he was relegated to sleeping on a sofa that was never meant to accommodate a six-foot-three frame.

With a twinge of guilt, Jonathan knew he would be more than a little relieved when he saw her onto the plane tomorrow.

23

It was close to one when Katie drove into the funeral home parking lot. Since the funeral was not scheduled until two, she'd thought she might have a few private moments with Jason, but now, as she searched the crowded parking lot for a space to park her car, she knew that that would not be possible.

Sometime during the night, while Katie dozed fitfully in the chair, jolting awake at every sound, it had snowed. Belleville's streets were dusted white, though the wide cement steps she climbed on leaden legs had been swept clean.

A crowd was milling about on the steps, and on the veranda. People spoke in hushed tones. Katie stared straight ahead. She heard one woman whisper, 'That's her,' and her step faltered. In that same instant, Jonathan's hand was at her elbow, and he was guiding her up the stairs. 'You look beautiful,' he said, so softly that only Katie heard.

'This was Jason's favorite outfit,' she answered foolishly, referring to the moss-green suit she wore, with its mink trim and padded shoulders, which had once belonged to her Aunt Katherine, and was now back in style. 'I didn't expect so many people.'

'Curiosity seekers, half of them,' he said, giving her hand a little squeeze for moral support.

She supposed she should have anticipated a large turnout; Belleville was a small town. Not much happened here. Her step faltered for a second time as she saw Drake Devlin just coming out of the funeral home. The collar of his tan leather coat was drawn up, and Katie thought quite objectively how attractive he was — almost handsome in an all-American way, right down to the smattering of freckles. There was even a hint of a cleft in his prominent chin. Many women would find it easy to fall in love with Drake Devlin.

He hadn't seen her right away. Now, he stood stock-still on the step above her, his grey eyes locked with hers. Katie wasn't sure what she saw there.

Seeing the exchange between them, Jonathan's hand dropped from Katie's arm. As he stepped to one side, Drake, like a freeze-frame come to life, stepped down and embraced Katie. 'I'm so sorry,' he said. 'I know he was a good friend. You've spoken of him often. I — uh, just came by to pay my respects. And to offer my condolences.

He must have been a very special person for you to care about him, Katie.'

'Yes, he was.' Katie's eyes welled with tears, guilt now blending with her grief. Drake was being so kind, so generous, much more than she deserved. She'd been less than fair with him. As she moved out of his embrace, she saw him glance at Jonathan, who stood looking strangely solitary, as if his collar was too tight. She'd never seen Jonathan look so uncomfortable. It puzzled her.

She introduced them.

'Katherine tells me you're a farmer,' Jonathan said warmly, but warmth was forced. He'd taken an instant dislike to the man. Jealously, he admonished himself. 'What — uh, do you farm?'

Drake eyed him coldly. 'A few vegetables — wheat mainly. It's my father's farm, actually. I'm a lawyer. Why? You interested in agriculture, Shea?'

'As a matter of fact . . . ' Catching the plea in Katherine's eyes, Jonathan flushed, appalled at his behavior. What the hell was possessing him to stand here on the steps of a funeral parlor making small talk with Drake Devlin? 'I'll meet you inside,' he said to Katie, then lied, 'Good to meet you, Drake.'

When he was gone, Drake said sheepishly, 'I guess I'm not a very good sport. I don't like losing.'

Katie saw the hurt in his eyes and knew she'd put it there. Leaving a scribbled note in the case for Drake had been shabby treatment. She should have faced him with what she had to say. It was fitting she should have to deal with it here — today.

Acutely aware of eyes pretending not to watch them, Katie said, 'There was nothing to lose. You and I were never more than friends, Drake.'

'Through no fault of mine.'

'I'm sorry.'

'Don't be. I — I'm just glad — well, he seems like a nice guy.' He gestured with his chin to the door where Jonathan had entered.

'Yes, he is.' Let Drake think what he would. If his assessment of Jonathan's intentions toward her were less than accurate, it at least made things simpler. She asked about Drake's father, partly to change the subject, but too, because she realized she genuinely cared.

Drake's eyes lowered. He shifted his feet. 'He suffered another stroke, Katie. He's been in a coma. Doctors — don't think he'll come out of this one.'

'Oh, Drake, I'm so sorry,' she said, her hand reaching out automatically to touch his arm. 'He's in the hospital, then.'

'He was. I brought him home. It's where he'd want to be when . . . ' His voice wavered. 'A volunteer nurse is with him today.'

He'd gone to the trouble of getting a nurse in, then, because Jason had been her friend. Impulsively, Katie kissed his cheek. 'I know how hard this must be for you, Drake. I know how much your father means to you.'

He smiled thinly. 'Can't win 'em all. Shea's a lucky man. But I do hope you and I can remain friends. I've felt like such a damn fool for lying to you about where I bought those gifts. It was unforgivable. I — I have no excuse to offer except that I wanted you to have them.'

'I know. And it's not unforgivable at all. It's very sweet. And thank you for still wanting to be my friend, Drake.'

Jonathan was standing in the lobby alongside a giant fern waiting for her, looking awkward. She crossed the silent ash-rose carpeting and took his arm. 'Seemed like an odd time for a discussion on farming.'

'Dumb conversation is not beneath me,' he said, and was rewarded with a small smile.

300

She looks so tired, he thought. So terribly tired. Makeup hadn't successfully hidden the dark circles, like bruises, beneath her eyes. 'It's over between you two, isn't it?' he whispered, knowing it was hardly the time or place, but unable to help himself.

'There was never anything to be over. I went out to dinner with him once, that's all.' Silly games, false pride had no place within these grim walls, Katie thought, trying to tune out the strains of organ music — 'Faith of Our Fathers' — that drifted to her from the sound system. Letting out a shuddery breath, she raised her eyes to the wall directory. Under today's date, November 4th, was the name of a woman she didn't know. Beneath that, she read: JASON BELDING — PARLOR 3. Seeing his name up there hit her like a shock wave, stripping away all her protection, leaving her naked to the reality of her friend's body lying only a few yards from her. This was not one of her dreams — or some little drama being staged to be ended when the curtain fell and all the players went home. Jason wasn't going home — not ever.

She moved slowly ahead of Jonathan. Parlors branched off on either side of the corridor. Parlor 3 was on her left. As she came nearer, the smell of flowers grew stronger, sickly-sweet, almost overwhelming. She was afraid she was going to be ill. The feeling passed. And then she was at the threshold. Not daring to pause, knowing that if she did she might never go in there, she stepped into the room. At once, the casket burst into view. Katie swooned.

Jonathan caught her. 'Are you all right? Maybe you should sit down for a minute?'

Whispers rose up around her. The faces that turned to look at her were the faces of strangers. Katie gathered herself to go on. 'I'm fine,' she said, stepping further into the room, moving down the aisle between the rows of occupied chairs toward the front, grateful for the slight pressure of Jonathan's hand at the small of her back.

She sensed Peter even before she saw him. He was sitting in the front row, flanked by empty chairs. He sat ramrod straight, hands folded in his lap. He did not look up when she passed. Katie did not think he was aware of her, nor, from the distant look in his eyes, of anyone else in the room. She longed to go to him, to reach out with some word of comfort, but she knew as she had when he was at her house, that there was no such convenient word, and to try would be an unforgivable intrusion into his private grief.

She looked away, and a moment later

heard herself saying in a small voice, 'It doesn't look like Jason.' Why did they always put that awful orangy makeup on people? As if with a will of its own, Katie's hand went out to touch the crisp set of his hair. 'Jason would have hated his hair like this,' she said, more to herself than to him. 'He always wore it so — uncombed.' She gave a small laugh that quickly became a sob. Jonathan pressed a handkerchief into her hand and with it she dabbed impatiently at her eyes. She would not make a public spectacle of herself. Dammit, she would not!

Regaining a surface composure, Katie felt a need to share her memory of Jason with Jonathan. 'He created so many beautiful paintings,' she whispered, gazing down at the hands that, once so talented, so graceful in their movements, were now folded and still in death. 'He was . . . ' Katie gasped suddenly, felt the blood drain from her.

Jonathan laid a concerned hand on her shoulder. 'Katherine, what . . . ?'

'Look.'

The way in which she uttered that one word sent a chill to pass over him. His eyes followed hers. He saw then what had made her gasp, what had made her already pale skin to grow ashen. His own hand unsteady, he reached into the coffin and, with some difficulty in his conscience, extracted the photograph from the stiff, lifeless fingers.

'Get me out of here, please, Jonathan.'

★ ★ ★

Rose Nickerson stood in the middle of the attic room surveying it as if for the first time. She'd known the instant she woke, from the tremendous relief she'd felt, that he was gone. He'd left the house while she slept, while it was still dark outside. Despite the jolt of fear he'd given her as he fondled that nasty looking knife and spoke so chillingly to her of 'hunting,' he had not made any move to harm her, and in fact grew quite genial soon after, returning the knife to his jacket pocket. She had not expected getting rid of him to be so easy.

His things had been cleaned out; the cot was made up neatly, the army blanket folded at the foot. Yet there was something of him still in the room, some coldness that Rose could not understand nor quite describe. But perhaps she was imagining things. Noticing the wall calendar, the fifth of November encircled in red pen, she crossed the room for a closer look. Wondering briefly at the significance of that, she then shrugged and left the room, closing the door quietly behind her, thinking she would not be so quick about bringing a stranger into her home again.

Downstairs in the kitchen, she opened a can of Puss & Boots and was mildly surprised when the buzz of the electric can opener did not bring Tiger padding into the room as it usually did. She filled his plastic dish, then donned Harvey's old plaid jacket, long since robbed of its beloved, familiar smell of pipe tobacco and of Harvey, pulled on her boots, and left by the back door.

What a lovely day it was. Crisp and cold, but sunny, the sky a perfect, unbroken blue. She would do up those bags of treats and take them down to the Martin children as she had promised herself she would. The walk would do her good. She greeted a bluejay perched in the apple tree. He squawked at her and flew away.

Feeling at peace with herself and the universe, Rose made her way down the snowy path to the mailbox. 'Tiger?' she called out. 'Where are you, you naughty boy?' It was not like Tiger not to come home all night, not since she'd had him neutered, and certainly not for a good many years. In old age, he'd long ago given up his nightly prowling for the comforts of home and hearth. She called out to him again, half expecting to hear his meowed response, to see his fat, colorful self emerging guiltily from the tall grass where the lawn ended. Maybe he was having himself a late mid-life crisis, she thought, and chuckled to herself at her own absurdity.

The mailbox was crooked on the pole, had been for as long as she could remember, its front end tilting slightly toward the ground. Rose pulled the metal door, raised her hand, about to reach inside for the mail. The half-smile froze on her face and a loud ringing began in her ears as she stumbled backward to avoid the furry, orange head that came tumbling out of the mailbox to land on the ground at her feet.

★ ★ ★

They were in the front seat of Jonathan's silver New Yorker out in the parking lot. Katie was trying to stop trembling. 'I sent that picture to Todd when he was in Vietnam,' she said, searching Jonathan's eyes as if to find some logical explanation there. 'How could . . . ?'

'I don't know,' he cut in. 'I wish I did. But I am sure of one thing: There's nothing supernatural about it. Someone very much alive put this photograph in . . . ' He let the sentence trail off. Katie could see he was nearly as shaken as she was.

'The police will want this,' he said, carefully placing the photo on a square of tissue from the box in the glove compartment. 'There could be prints. Unfortunately, ours will be among them. I expect they'll also confiscate the guest book.'

'Do you really think 'the strawman' would sign his name?'

It's a possibility. Ego can be a friend — but it can also be a formidable enemy. It's tripped up more than one criminal.' He was staring down at the photograph of her, his expression unreadable.

'What do you think it means, Jonathan?'

'It could be — symbolic,' he said, not meeting her eyes.

'Symbolic?' A chill passed through her.

'Someone with a deranged mind might think of this picture as being you. He's burying you with Jason.'

'Or plans to,' she said dully.

There was a few seconds when neither of them spoke, then Katie said tentatively, 'Do you think — Todd . . . ?' The question had been gnawing at her subconscious mind almost from the beginning. Now, finally, she had allowed it to surface, had given it voice. She hadn't needed to complete the sentence.

'No, I don't,' Jonathan replied too quickly, as if he'd been half-expecting the question all along. 'I admit,' he said slowly, 'that the possibility did occur to me when . . . '

'When you saw that strawman in my room,' she finished for him.

'Okay, it's true. But Todd Raynes is not alive, Katherine. The army is certain of that. He died in the war.'

She gave a short, bitter laugh. 'How can they be so certain? His body was never found. Maybe something happened to him in the war — something far worse than death — something with his mind. Maybe . . . ' The tears came unexpectedly, born of nerves, grief and frustration. 'I sent that picture to Todd, Jonathan,' she said, sobbing now. 'It doesn't make any sense that . . . ' Katie drew herself together abruptly, drying her eyes on a Kleenex provided by Jonathan. After a pause, she said, 'I'd like to see the photograph again, please.'

He passed it to her on the square of Kleenex as if it might be the crown jewels. He was watching her intently.

The young woman wearing shorts and halter, with shoulder-length hair blowing carelessly in the wind and her eyes shining with all the optimism of youth, smiled out at Katie. In the background was their old house, small and box-like, the picket fence in front. Who had taken the picture? Her mother, maybe? No face came to mind. But she did remember the day, the way it had smelled of sunshine and lilacs and summer rain. Another lifetime. A different person. 'I hardly recognize myself.' She handed back the photograph.

Accepting it, he said softly, 'You've grown even lovelier. Where was this taken?'

'My hometown — Lennoxville.' Taking little note of the compliment he'd paid her, she said wearily, 'When will it end, Jonathan? When I'm on display, too?'

Taking her hands in his own, he looked steadily into her eyes. 'I promise you, Katherine,' he said, 'no harm is going to come to you. You must believe that.'

'Why? Why must I believe that when the truth is neither you nor the police are one step closer to solving this case than you were in the beginning?'

His eyes dropped from hers, his hands falling away. He looks so tired, she thought. As tired as she felt. The lines in his face, especially those bracketing his mouth, seemed to have deepened even since yesterday. She wasn't being fair. He was doing his best. She supposed everyone was. 'I'm sorry, Jonathan. I'm just so . . . the truth is, I don't know what I would have done without you here, today.'

'You would have managed,' he said.

Back inside, Katie signed the guestbook, then checked the signatures above her own. Only one was familiar — the first one — Peter Machum's. Katie read down the page opposite: Clayton Jackson, Anne Jackson, Raymond Losier, Drake Devlin and printed at the bottom of the page in large, child-like letters that took up two full spaces, Joey Smith. It both touched and surprised her to see Joey's name there. It was for her, of course, that he had come. Knowing that, and recalling her recent cruel verbal attack on Joey, she felt doubly bad. 'Joey used to ask me every day if I was still his gurfriend,' she said in a hushed voice, using Joey's pronunciation, as she stepped aside to allow Jonathan to add his own name in the guestbook, beneath hers. As she had done, Jonathan was scanning the names. He stopped to give her an odd look. 'Joey — Joey Smith from The Coffee Shop?'

'Yes.'

'You never mentioned that.'

'I didn't think it was important.'

He contemplated her answer, then turned to give Joey's signature a harder look, and Katie was suddenly remembering that Joey often drove The Coffee Shop van. 'Don't keep it out half the day,' she recalled Mrs. Cameron yelling at him. Was it possible . . . the police hadn't been able to make anything solid of the tire tracks down by the lake except to say that they might have been made by a half-ton. Might they also have been made by a van?

Katie called up Joey's face in her imagination, and for the first time his smile took on a sinister cast. Perhaps his seemingly innocent daily question was not so innocent after all. Perhaps there was an underlying . . .

But what about the photograph? There was no way on earth Joey could have come upon that photograph.

The grave site was located near the top of the hill, and the paved drive was carpeted with bright fallen leaves, damp and slippery from last night's snow. They skittered among the rows of tombstones. It was a little windy here, so high up.

Katie found herself studying the many faces, some familiar, some not, for the one that would stand out among the others, one that would not be able to hide its evil in these solemn, holy proceedings. But, of course, she saw no such person. She glanced discreetly about for Peter, but didn't spot him in the crowd. The line of cars went back a quarter of a mile. Was 'the strawman' here? she wondered. Was he watching now, deriving some sick pleasure . . . ?

' . . . Yeah, though I walk through the valley of the shadow of death I will fear no evil; for thou art with me . . . ' The minister, a young, blond man in black robes that fluttered in the breeze, had begun to speak, thumbs held firmly down on the rattling pages, blue sky, soft billowy clouds behind and above him. Katie bowed her head. She let the words enter her mind, and repeat themselves in her heart.

The service was mercifully brief, and but for one terrible, gut-wrenching moment as Jason was being lowered into the ground, when she could not help thinking how her dear friend would have feared the dark and the cold, Katie managed to hold herself together. Now, feeling her legs weak under her, she gratefully accepted Jonathan's assistance back to his car. They would return to the parking lot tomorrow for hers, he said.

The New Yorker smelled faintly of Jonathan's aftershave and of showroom newness. Katie let herself sink against the plush upholstery.

Jonathan switched on the ignition, and the

big car purred to life. The same yellow sedan they had crawled behind on the way here now was leading them back the way they had come (though with urgency now — like escaping), down and through and finally out of the cemetery.

Out on the highway, Jonathan felt a rush of relief like fresh air. After driving a while, he switched on the radio, turning the dial until he found a station playing classical music — Chopin, he thought. He turned it low. Beside him, Katie appeared to be asleep. Her lashes shadowed her pale cheeks.

The familiar strains of piano together with the rolling wheels on pavement had lulled Katie into the grey zone between sleep and consciousness. Never before in her life had she felt so completely drained, both in mind and body, and almost wished she would never have to wake up. She thought of Peter. Would he be all right? Maybe Jonathan would talk to him. That was foolish; he couldn't very well go about soliciting patients. It would be different if he knew Peter. And certainly Peter would resent such presumptuousness.

Because she'd closed her eyes even before they'd left the cemetery, Katie had no way of knowing that once through the iron gates, Jonathan, rather than turning left, had taken a right turn, and that now they were heading in the direction opposite to Black Lake.

Her beige leather purse clutched in her lap like some childhood security toy, Katie sank gradually deeper into sleep, oblivious to how little by little her head had dropped down and down to where it now rested comfortably on Jonathan's shoulder.

It seemed to her she'd slept only minutes when the jostling over bumps and ruts in the road drew her partly awake. They must be getting close to home, she thought. Even so, with Jonathan's car so much bigger and newer than her own, the ride was smoother than she could remember. Suddenly conscious of the feel of soft wool fabric pressed against her cheek, Katie eased herself with a little moan to a new position, pretending to be still asleep.

At last the car slowed, and moments later came to a full stop. She was home. She heard the motor cut to silence, heard Jonathan's door open, then close again with the softest click. Reluctantly, having wanted the drive to go on and on into infinity, Katie willed herself fully awake and opened her eyes. And stared out the window. Expecting, of course, to be greeted by her own familiar surroundings — the blaze of maples, the lake, the brown house on the hill — it both startled and bewildered her to see that they were parked in front of a ranch-style house built entirely of logs, smack in the middle of the woods. Her gaze travelled to the side of the house where more logs had been cut and stacked for firewood. Beneath the huge picture window facing her, a red shiny wet wheelbarrow lay on its side.

The passenger door opened, and Jonathan was standing with a tentative smile on his face, offering her his hand. 'Welcome to Stoneybrook,' he said with a note of self-conscious pride. 'This is home. At least when I can manage to get out here. I thought you might like to see — my own haven from the world.'

Overcome by the beauty of her surroundings, and not yet recovered from the shock of finding herself here, in fact disoriented as though she were still asleep and dreaming, she stepped mutely from the car, her hand in Jonathan's.

Here and there on the forest floor, patches of snow sparkled in the sunlight slanting through the trees. Not as many maples here as at Black Lake, but instead a forest of fir and pine and cedar interspersed with bright ambers and golds among the evergreens, their branches still lightly laden with clumps of the newly fallen snow. The air was crisp and

315

fragrant with woodsy smells, blending with that of newly-sawed lumber.

'It's a little rough underfoot,' he said apologetically as Katie stepped carefully over sprawling tangled roots the size of arms, and fallen branches. 'There's still a lot of work to do. More trees to clear away, some landscaping. Maybe a bit of lawn, some flowers. There's not too much more I can do until spring.' He slid the key into the lock and opened the door.

'You built this place?' Katie said, the first words she'd spoken since they'd arrived.

'Mmm, hmm. Step into my humble abode, m'lady.' He bowed and gave a grand sweep of his hand.

Inside, the first thing that struck Katie was the warmth that greeted them. She'd been unconsciously expecting that same bone-chilling, damp cold of her own house when the fires had been out for a while.

'Electrically heated,' Jonathan said as though reading her thoughts. 'We're really not all that far from the main road — maybe half a mile. This place has all the conveniences of modern civilization.' He flashed a devilish grin. 'You see, I'm only half-Indian.'

Despite her heavy mood, Katie smiled. 'This is a beautiful room, Jonathan,' she said, taking in the warm honey-glow of natural wood walls and floor, the beamed ceiling, the rich earth tones of good but simple, comfortable furniture, all of it enhanced by splashes of colorful Indian artifacts and hanging green plants. 'I can't imagine anyone ever wanting to leave here.'

His face lit with pleasure, and, she thought, relief. It surprised her that Jonathan would need anyone's approval until she remembered that his confidence had been badly shaken recently. Her gaze moved to the mantel over the huge stone fireplace to her left, and to the photographs she saw there. Jonathan's family? Lona? She resisted taking a closer look.

'Oh, I hardly think a log cabin in the middle of the woods is every woman's dream house,' Jonathan was saying, smiling at her.

'Well, this is hardly *just* a log cabin, and you know it.' And then she thought of her mother and knew Jonathan was right. 'Considering where I live,' she said, 'it's pretty safe to assume I like trees — and the privacy.'

'And the quiet?'

She grinned. 'You know perfectly well the woods aren't quiet. Not if you really listen.' Her attention was taken with the bookcase facing them, which took up most of one wall. 'I see you like to read.'

'When I can find the time.' He followed her to the bookshelves, standing so close that Katie caught the remembered, faint scent of his aftershave and of Jonathan himself. She had an almost overwhelming urge to turn around and let herself move into his arms, knowing how good it would feel just to have him hold her. She concentrated on the books. Those on the top shelves were devoted to psychiatry, and beneath them books on Indian culture — art, medicine, religion. From eye-level on down she saw the revered names of Shakespeare, Maugham, Poe, Twain, Fitzgerald, Hemingway . . . all the classics were here. Her fingers traced their spines like the features of old friends. 'Have you read all these?'

'Most of them over the years. I'm also a big whodunit buff. Agatha Christie is one of my favorites.'

'Really? She was my Aunt Katherine's favorite, too.'

'What about you, Katherine? What do you like to read?' A casual question, but there was an intensity in his eyes. He really wanted to know. It seemed so strange that they should be standing here so calmly discussing books when only an hour before they'd been attending Jason's funeral. Katie gave a little shrug of her shoulders. 'Just about anything.

But I suppose I'm partial to the biographies of great artists — and historical romances.'

'The ones that end happily?' His eyes teased her. 'Here, let me take your coat. You sit and relax, and I'll make us a little supper.'

'Oh, I couldn't eat anything, Jonathan.'

'Some tea, then.' He led her to the Boston rocker by the window, with its velvet, burnt orange cushions. 'This was my mother's chair,' he said, and touched the lace collar of Katie's silk, ivory-colored blouse. 'Very pretty,' he said. 'Suits you.' And then he was gone.

Closing her eyes, curling her stockinged feet up under her, Katie thought how peaceful it was here, how beautiful. The house smelled of varnish and something lemony. She could hear Jonathan moving about in the kitchen, and the sound was comforting. As Katie began to rock in the chair, the house seemed slowly to wrap itself around her.

Soon, she opened her eyes and looked about her, knowing that all along she'd been halfsearching for some sign of Lona's having been here. There was none visible. Lona must be neat, she thought, and the now familiar stab of jealousy made her impatient with herself.

She was studying the wall-hanging to the

right of the door when Jonathan entered with a tray, which he placed on the round coffee table, inset with colored, polished stones.

She trailed her fingers over the smooth surface. 'Did you make this, too?'

'Yes. I got the idea when I was hauling stones for the fireplace. Do you like it?'

'Very much. I was also admiring your wallhanging. It looks hand-woven.'

He raised his eyes to the Indian version of Madonna and Child. 'It is. My mother's work.'

'It's beautiful.' She thought of her own rendition of Madonna and Child. It was one of the few paintings she'd been reluctant to sell.

'Yes,' Jonathan said, sliding the tray of assorted cheeses, cold meats and fruit toward her. 'Have something. You'll feel better.'

'You always seem to be feeding me,' she said, selecting a small square of cheese, nibbling at it. 'Lona must really love this place,' she blurted before she could stop herself.

He looked briefly surprised, then he laughed. 'Lona? Lona wouldn't be caught dead out here in 'the sticks' as she calls it. No, I'm afraid my little Lona is thoroughly citified.'

The cheese turned to chalk-dust in her

mouth. 'Oh, I just assumed when she called . . . ' But Katie was remembering her own call, and how she'd hung up after hearing Lona ask 'Jon darling' to bring her her drink.

'She was calling from my apartment in town,' he said easily, plucking a blue grape from the bunch and popping it into his mouth. 'I need a place close to the hospital — or I did. Lona stays with me whenever she's between plays — or lovers.' He grinned and shook his head. 'I expect they're both one and the same.'

Katie reached for a Ritz Cracker. She stared at it and wished she could put it back. 'She's an actress, then?' she said, thoroughly confused. Between lovers? Jonathan hardly seemed the type to be so liberal-minded. But then how well did she really know him? She ate the cracker. 'Lona must really be something.'

Jonathan looked amused. 'Oh, yes, she is that, all right.'

Yes, that's what she heard in her voice — that phony theatrical way of speaking actors often took on, she thought with enjoyed malice.

'And I guess you and Lona have what they call in our modern society — an open relationship?' Why was she pursuing this?

She couldn't seem to stop herself. It didn't help her mood when Jonathan threw back his head and laughed. She writhed inwardly, wondering what he found in her question that was so damned, hilariously funny.

'Are you comfortable?' he asked, seeing her shift around in the chair. 'We could move to the sofa.'

'No, I'm fine.' Her smile was strained.

He brought her tea from the kitchen in a stone mug. 'It's made from a special blend of herbs,' he said. 'You might have to acquire a taste.'

With a thatch of dark hair fallen across his forehead, his tie gone and his shirt sleeves rolled up, he looked disturbingly handsome, and Katie lowered her eyes to the sherry-colored tea, sipping a little, wondering if Jonathan knew she was in love with him. How often she had heard her mother say, 'You can always tell when Katie's lying; it's written all over her face.' God, she hated being so obvious.

The tea tasted bitter and coppery. 'It's good,' she lied.

He was regarding her thoughtfully, seated across from her. 'Drink it all, then. It'll relax you.'

'Have you been working on the house for a long time?' she asked, anxious to return to a safer topic, and sensing that he enjoyed talking about this special place he had carved out of the forest for himself.

'Over a year now. A couple of hours here — a few weekends there . . . '

In some ways, like now when talking about his house, he reminded her of a small boy — vulnerable, anxious to please, shyly proud of his accomplishment. She decided there were many sides to Jonathan Shea, much like a prism, each depending on a certain angle of light. She also suspected a dark side to Jonathan, of which, up to now, she'd had only glimpses.

She drank a little more of the tea. Oddly, it didn't seem so bitter now. 'You've never been married, have you?' The instant the words were out of her mouth, she wanted to pull them out of the air. 'I'm sorry, Jonathan. I didn't mean to pry. I . . . '

He waved off her apology. 'No, it's okay. Actually, I did come close once, but the lady had dreams of being the wife of a big name psychiatrist with a 'fabulous', as Constance termed it, practice in Boston. Not a bad dream, I suppose, but unfortunately, not one we shared.' He speared a triangle of ham and rolled it around his fork. 'Or perhaps fortunately,' he added, before eating it.

'Did you love her very much?' Boy, she

was really on a roll. She might just as well have a spotlight glaring down on the poor man's head. Why were her lips feeling so numb? Katie drained the few remaining drops of tea, then sat the mug, which had grown too heavy to hold, down on the table. She was having some difficulty keeping her eyes open.

'I thought I did,' Jonathan said in answer to her question, smiling at her, seeming not to mind that she had asked it. 'For a while.' He leaned forward in his chair, his face suddenly alight with enthusiasm. 'Tell me, Katherine, do you like to fish?'

'Fish?' The question caught her so by surprise, she laughed. 'I really don't know. I haven't done any fishing.'

'Oh, but you must. It keeps one out of analysis. There's a lovely little brook not ten minutes from here where the trout practically jump up on your hook.' Then softly, 'I'd really like to take you sometime.'

For a moment Katie could think of no reply, and then she wanted to ask him if Lona liked to fish, but guessed that if she wouldn't be caught dead 'in the sticks,' it wasn't likely she did.

'It sounds like it might be fun,' she said, blinking as Jonathan's face swam out of focus, became two Jonathan faces, both of them smiling at her. She shook her head as if to clear it of the gauzy fog. 'I can't seem to . . . ' A thought rose dully. 'What did you put in my tea, Jonathan?' Her tongue felt thick, her words far away and strange sounding.

'It's a secret potion,' he said, feigning mystery. 'If I tell you, it'll rain.'

'You're making that up. It only rained when your people danced.'

'And only then when there was heavy cloud cover,' he said, laughing. When had he stood up? When had he taken her hand in his? 'Come and lie down, Katherine. You need to rest. You're going on nothing but nerves.'

'Oh, I can't do that. Really, Jonathan, I must go home and work on Hattie Halloway's portrait.' Even as she spoke she saw that they were no longer in Jonathan's kitchen, but in a spacious, sparsely furnished bedroom where she was being led to a big brass bed set against the far wall. While holding one arm firmly about her waist to support her, Jonathan turned down the blankets. 'Hattie Halloway can damn well wait,' he said, beginning then to undo her clothes.

'This is getting to be a habit,' she muttered, but was far too weak and groggy to offer any real resistance. And then she was limp and naked sitting on the edge of the bed and wondering why she felt no embarrassment or self-consciousness as Jonathan began helping her into the too-big flannel striped pajamas. Instead, she felt like a little girl being taken care of, and it was a good, safe feeling.

When she was tucked in, Jonathan kissed her lightly on the forehead. His big, gentle hand smoothed her hair, and she smiled sleepily. 'I have a few phone calls to make,' she heard him say. 'You're safe here. I'll only be a few steps away if you should need me.'

Katie nodded, beginning to drift off on a soft cloud of sleep. When she heard him whisper, 'Sleep well, my sweet Katherine,' she imagined she was already dreaming.

24

Katie woke from a heavy sleep sometime in the night thinking she'd heard someone cry out. She listened. Her mouth tasted woolly, the way her mind felt. Had she really heard it or had she been dreaming? She sat up, momentarily bewildered by her unfamiliar surroundings. When she saw the figure outlined in the chair across the room, she almost screamed, sure it was 'the strawman.' But then she saw it was Jonathan and remembered where she was.

Outside the window, the moon bathed the land and trees in a silvery white. Katie glanced at the clock on the night table. The date and the time glowed green. Nov. 5, 4:31 a.m.

'No — no,' Jonathan cried out, and Katie's heart jumped. She switched on the lamp. Again, he cried out. It seemed oddly like the cry of a child, filled with pain and terror. Katie quickly slipped out of bed and went to him.

It alarmed Katie when his body began to jerk spasmodically, his head toss wildly from side to side, yet she was afraid to startle him awake. She touched his shoulder tentatively and barely had time to get out of the way when his arm shot out. His hair was damp on his forehead, his shirt clinging wetly to his body.

'Jonathan,' she said softly. 'Wake up, Jonathan. It's a dream — only a dream.'

His eyes flew open so suddenly, so hard did he stare at her, a small thrill of fear went through Katie. Then gradual recognition relaxed his features; she could almost feel the tension leaving his body. Suddenly he was on his feet, and she was in his arms, and the words broke from him like sobs. 'Katherine, you're here. Oh, thank God, you're all right.'

'I'm fine,' she said reassuringly, feeling his heart beating hard and too fast against her breasts. 'You had a bad dream, Jonathan, that's all. Just a dream.'

After a moment he drew himself away, a heavy sigh escaping him. 'I'm sorry I woke you.'

She laid a hand on his arm. 'It's okay. Do you have these dreams very often?'

'I feel lousy,' he said, ignoring her question, tugging the damp shirt from his skin, raking his fingers almost angrily through his hair. 'I'm going to take a shower. You go back to bed.'

Why hadn't he answered her question? she wondered as she lay there listening to the water running in the bathroom. He had seemed so like a terrified child in his sleep. And yet she had been the child last night. She only vaguely remembered Jonathan putting her to bed, fitting her into his too-large pajamas, though she recalled clearly her lovely sense of well-being at being taken care of. 'Sleep well, my sweet Katherine,' he had said, and kissed her forehead. But had he really? She tried to piece events together, separate fact from fancy. She recalled offering at some point a feeble argument about having to go home and work on Hattie Holloway's portrait, to which Jonathan had replied, 'To hell with Hattie Holloway,' or something to that effect. She must tell Jason about her commission, she thought suddenly. He'll be so happ . . . Memory brought her up short, pressed against her heart. Jason was no longer in the world. For an instant she'd forgotten. She knew from experience that forgetting was common in the beginning. The smallest thing: a song, a book, a mere thought could send you reaching for the phone to dial a familiar number — until you remembered.

And it hurt, dammit! It hurt.

So immersed was she in her thoughts that Katie didn't notice the water had moments ago stopped running, or that Jonathan, now clad only in a navy robe, his hair damply dark and unruly from the shower, stood watching her from the doorway. Only when he spoke did she look up.

'I thought you might have gone back to sleep. I didn't want to wake you a second time.'

Seeing him standing there, some of the soreness lifted from Katie's heart. There was no mistaking the deep tenderness she saw in his eyes, and yes — more than that. All the love that filled her own heart was reflected there for her to accept or reject.

'I wasn't tired,' she said. 'Are you all right?'

'I've recovered. How about you?'

She said she was fine, too, and then, as their eyes remained locked, as Katie's longing for him grew, fear and doubt crept over her like dark clouds blocking out the warmth of the sun. She thought of Lona. She thought of Jonathan telling her not to make more of their single night of love than what there was. Impatiently, she pushed the thoughts away. He loved her. She couldn't be wrong about this. She felt it from him — felt everything she needed to know. And her heart told her to trust — to believe . . .

She raised her arm from the bed and held out her hand to him.

Later, as they lay together, bodies damp and relaxed, smiles lazy, happy, Jonathan tracing her lower lip with his fingertip, Katie felt a blend of wonder and shyness, and thought she would be quite content to stay right here where she was for the rest of time. With perhaps the odd grape or square of cheese tossed to her from time to time for sustenance.

'I always thought magic was reserved for kids,' Jonathan said softly. 'I know different now, with you, Katherine.'

She smiled dreamily and nuzzled against him. 'Me, too.' She raised her eyes to his. 'Why do you always call me Katherine? No one has called me that since I was a little girl, and then, only my aunt and my teachers.'

He kissed her fingertips. 'Because you look like a Katherine.'

'Oh? And what does a Katherine look like?'

'You're fishing?' he teased lightly.

'Yes.' She nibbled his earlobe. 'You said I should learn.'

He laughed and drew her more firmly against him. 'Well,' he began, 'Katherine is a tall, elegant lady with eyes the color of emeralds under water, and silky brown hair that turns gold in the sunlight. She has a determined, maybe even stubborn tilt to her chin. She's a woman filled with spirit and courage that was evident to me from the moment I set eyes on her in that hospital bed — so fragile, so vulnerable, yet beneath it all, strong and fiercely independent.'

'This is a wonderful story,' Katie said, grinning, a little embarrassed, but loving it. 'Is there more?'

'I'm serious. You really are a little girl in many ways, you know.' He kissed the tip of her nose. 'That innocence and wonder of life comes through in your work, and in odd, sweet moments in you.' Giving her a mock leer, he added, 'And Katherine is also a wanton woman, filled with fire and mystery.' He growled sexily and Katie laughed, reminding herself, lest she get carried away, that Jonathan was Irish on his father's side and clearly more than capable of a little blarney himself. But she didn't mind in the least. 'She sounds fascinating.'

'You are, my darling.'

It had grown light outside the window as Jonathan and Katie sat together in the bed drinking the coffee Jonathan had prepared, and talking. Katie had begun absent-mindedly to stroke the blanket covering them, scarlet against black, she noticed now, the two colors woven to form a bold, intricate pattern of z's.

'This is lovely,' Katie commented. 'Your mother's work?'

'My grandmother's. I fell heir to those things precious to my mother, and in turn, to me. Lona was never very much interested in her Indian heritage.'

Hearing Lona's name spoken so casually by Jonathan, so unexpectedly in this intimate setting, with Katie still aglow from their recent lovemaking, punctured her new-found serenity, her confidence. 'Lona's Indian?' she said, unable to look at him, her stomach knotting.

'Half, like me.' There was mischief in his eyes. 'Lona's my sister.'

Katie could only stare at him. Then, a slow anger beginning to build in her, she repeated, 'Your sister.'

'My kid sister, actually.'

'Why didn't you tell me that before, Jonathan Shea? Why did you let me go on thinking — a modern, open relationship. Really. You let me make a complete fool of myself.'

He set his coffee mug down on the night table to run a hand slowly down her arm. 'Never for a minute. When Lona telephoned your house that night, I thought I detected just a hint of jealousy from you — but I was afraid to hope. After all, I was operating under the belief that Drake was still in the picture. So I told myself it was more probable you were just annoyed at having your phone number given out so freely, which was understandable, particularly under the circumstances.'

'Even so, you could still have told me yesterday.'

The mischief was back in his eyes. 'Yes,' he said, grinning, 'I suppose I could have.'

'I hate you.'

'Do you?'

'No.'

'Good.' He kissed her.

When they parted, Katie asked him if Lona was unhappy, and it was wonderful to be able to say the name without feeling the old pangs of jealousy. 'You said she stayed with you between plays — and lovers.'

Jonathan was thoughtful. 'Unhappy? Yes, she has her moments. Lona lives life at fever pitch. She's only really happy, or perhaps euphoric is a better word, when she's on the threshold of a new romance, or a new play. Which fortunately,' he added, his smile one of deep fondness, 'is more often than not.'

He told her with modest pride that Lona was a wonderful actress while admitting he might be slightly biased. 'But she does get great reviews,' he said, 'and audiences seem to love her.'

'It's a life riddled with insecurities, though, isn't it?'

'Anything safer would bore Lona to death. She likes to live on the edge, scaling mountain peaks, occasionally dipping into valleys of darkness, just to see if she can climb back up again.'

'I'd like to meet her sometime. She sounds interesting.'

'She is. A bit overwhelming at times, but I think you'd like her. I know she'd be crazy about you. Our mother used to worry constantly over Lona. She . . . ' He stopped abruptly, a haunted expression coming into his eyes He seemed to slip away from her. She'd seen the expression before, but now, whatever was carving away at his insides was working much closer to the surface.

'What is it, Jonathan?'

He was staring out the window where trees swayed lightly as if to music only they could hear. 'Nothing,' he said.

Katie rose on one elbow and set her coffee cup on the night table alongside Jonathan's. Turning to him, she said quietly, 'Please don't shut me out. This has something to do with the dream, doesn't it? You — called out to your mother in the dream.' She traced his arm, felt the fine mat of dark hair beneath her fingers, felt his muscle tighten. His withdrawal from her became more total, his eyes more distant. Then Katie was above him, her breasts flattened against his chest. She tried to will him with her eyes. 'Tell me, Jonathan — please.'

He came back to her. He smiled, but she saw the falseness there. 'Yes, I want to tell you everything,' he said, reaching up and playfully winding his fingers in her hair. 'And someday I will — I promise. But I want to know about you. I want to know about the sort of things that made you cry when you were a little girl — that made you laugh. I want to feel jealous of all the people who were in your life when I wasn't.'

'Tell me, Jonathan.'

His hand dropped from her hair. Anger flashed in his blue eyes. 'You just keep tapping away, don't you? Delicate little taps with your trusty feminine chisel.' The hard tone of his voice was like a cut and Katie winced visibly.

The anger fled from his eyes, and he pulled her fiercely to him. 'I'm sorry.'

'It's not just idle curiosity, you know,' she said, her face buried in the hollow of his neck, feeling the pulse there beat soft and warm against her mouth.

'Yes, I do know that, I do,' he murmured. Though Katie didn't hear the sigh, she felt it throughout his body — a sigh of resignation, of defeat. 'I thought I'd dealt with all of it,' he said. ' 'Come to terms' as they say in the wacky world of psychiatry.'

She smiled and waited, sensing him needing only the gentle push of love she offered. This was agonizing for him, she knew, and she was suddenly taken with a sense of responsibility that almost frightened her. She mustn't let him down. 'Jonathan,' she prodded gently.

'It's a long and, I'm sure, very boring story,' he said, trying to smile and failing miserably.

'Not to me. And I've got all the time in the world.'

He gazed at her a moment longer, then shifted his eyes to the ceiling, to the square, acoustic tiles above them. Abruptly, his eyes snapped shut, as if in response to something he was seeing — something too painful to look at. They opened slowly, continued to stare at the ceiling. Katie had moved off him, now lay quietly at his side.

'It all happened such a long time ago,' he began haltingly. 'I was twelve years old. My father was a big, outgoing Irishman. He taught school on the Indian reserve where my mother lived.' He glanced at Katie. 'I told you she was Indian.'

'Yes, but I would have guessed from looking at you that one of your parents were.' She regretted her lightness of tone at once, and prayed it didn't put him off. She felt a moment's tenseness. To her relief, the remark brought a genuine smile.

'Lona looks more like her. Dad often talked to Lona about mother — in the beginning. Lona never wanted to hear, though. She said it was depressing. But I hung on his every word. I wanted to know everything about her.'

Katie nodded, sensing that something bad had happened to his mother.

'Anyway, they met and my father fell madly in love with her. She was just seventeen. He said she was lovely, like a rare and fragile flower. Apparently, too fragile,' he said more to himself than to Katie. 'She was tiny, with large brown eyes that often darted about like a frightened fawn.'

He sees her now, Katie thought. He sees her and it's killing him. 'Why was she afraid?' she asked quietly.

Jonathan shifted his weight in the bed, and when he spoke again his voice was oddly wooden and empty, and she understood that he'd needed to detach himself emotionally in order to get the words out.

'The fear came later. But I'm getting ahead of my story. As I said, these things I'm telling you were related to me by my father.' He cleared his throat. 'Except for her eyes — oh, yes, I do remember her eyes. I remember . . . he took her from the reservation and married her, and her people turned their backs on her; she was no longer one of them.'

'Oh, Jonathan, how terrible.'

'My father said she grieved every moment of her short life for her family, her friends. She was an outcast in our neighborhood. She made no friends. There were prejudices, as there are now, only then they were more deeply embedded, more overt.'

'Did you feel the prejudices too?'

A pause. 'Often.'

Katie understood now why he made his little ethnic jokes. It was a defense mechanism. You make the joke before someone else gets the chance to.

'Go on.'

'I never really saw her depression until I was much older,' he said. 'She always had a smile for me and Lona, a touch. Sometimes she sang to us at night — sweet, soft lullabies that I never understood the words

339

to, though it didn't matter. I can still hear them.' He smiled at the memory. Waited, went on. 'I remember the way she smelled when she hugged me close, of some delicate wild flower I never knew, and don't now. Anyway, my father — he said if she left him, she might be accepted back into the tribe. I think they talked about it. He couldn't bear her unhappiness, and naturally he blamed himself. But she loved him — loved us, and she wouldn't leave.'

Jonathan plucked at a loose thread in the blanket, and Katie ached for him, for the terrible pain that was in him, and a part of her wanted to halt the flow of words, to chase back the memories, yet she felt that he needed to look at his past, to delve into it, and perhaps in this way to rid it forever of the power to torment him with such savagery. She waited.

'And — and then one day . . . ' He began, faltered, stared harder at the ceiling, began again. 'It was in the summer toward the end of the school term. I'd run all the way home from school to plead to be allowed to go swimming. Lona was five then, and being the gregarious one, was off playing with her friends. I can't be sure, of course, it was such a long time ago, but I think she was. Even before I burst into the house, I heard my mother's screams. In my rush, I'd paid little attention to the ambulance parked outside the house, thinking, if I thought of it at all, that it didn't have anything to do with us.

'Two men in green hospital coats, and a tall woman wearing glasses shaped like cat's eyes — were in our living room. My mother was caught between the grim, red-faced men who were attempting to drag her by her arms toward the door where I stood, watching. She just kept screaming and screaming, bucking and kicking like a trapped animal, trying to free herself, while my father stood by like a grey statue, silent tears rolling down his face.'

Katie's heart wrenched at the scene Jonathan described — a scene so traumatic it would etch itself forever in a child's mind and follow him like some demon throughout his adult life.

'And suddenly she was looking straight at me. Her screams stopped and her body went limp. The biggest of the two men picked her up in his arms as easily as if she were a child. I will never forget her eyes then — big, empty velvet eyes that saw nothing. Or perhaps some long ago memory. She didn't know me, that much I understood.'

'I flew at them, flailing out with my fists, commanding the man to let her go, but it was like beating a wall, like commanding the wind. When I could do nothing, I ran after them into the street, chasing the ambulance that was taking her from me even after it was long out of sight, and the wailing siren only an echo in my mind. I ran until I could run no more . . . '

Again, Jonathan shifted his weight in the bed, and his pain was almost visible in the movement. 'At last my father came and took me home. I never saw her again. It was just three weeks later that Dad told us she was dead. He didn't explain why or how, just that she was dead. It was only much later that I found out that one night she slipped out of bed in the darkness of her room in that mental hospital where they'd taken her. Her mind must have surfaced from the shadows for that brief moment — I've often imagined how frightened, how alone she must have felt, then. Some attendant or careless nurse had left a glass in the room. My mother found it, smashed it, and slashed her wrists. They didn't find her until the next morning.'

'My God,' Katie whispered, her hand going out to cover his. Neither of them spoke for a long time.

At last, Jonathan said, 'See, I told you it was a long story.'

Ignoring his feeble attempt at lightness, she asked, 'What — what about your father?'

Jonathan shrugged. 'He nursed his grief with alcohol. His suicide took a little longer to accomplish — about ten years.

'Anyway, I had this idea I wanted to help people with emotional — mental illness. I couldn't do anything for my parents — I thought I might — I might be able to do something for . . . ' He swallowed hard.

'And you have. It's a noble calling, Jonathan, and with good motivation.'

'I don't know,' he said, his voice weary now. He laced his hands behind his head. 'Maybe I was only trying to help myself to understand it all. I — uh, lost a young patient recently.' A bewildered frown creased his forehead. 'A girl — sixteen . . . ' His voice failed.

'Yes, I know.'

He looked at her in mild surprise. 'Linda Ring, no doubt. A first rate nurse, but she can't bear confidences.' Another sigh. 'It doesn't matter. Anyway, I found myself wondering for the first time if what I was doing had any real worth. You talk — you apply years of accumulated knowledge — you try. And then . . . '

Katie, anxious to still his self-doubts, said, 'You know better than anyone, Jonathan, that psychiatry isn't an exact science. And you do help people. I know from my stay in the hospital that you have a fine reputation.

'You said you try — and that's all any of us can do. That girl wasn't your failure. Maybe she was society's — or her own . . . '

'Maybe.'

'Does Lona remember her mother?'

'She says she doesn't, but I suspect she's blocked it out. Maybe that's part of the reason the acting profession has such an appeal for her. She can pretend.'

'You blame yourself for your mother's suicide, don't you?' she said softly, having deliberately returned to the subject, going only on her instincts.

Jonathan didn't answer.

'Did you cry when your father told you she was dead?'

'No.'

'Did you ever let yourself cry?'

'Katherine.' A plea. A warning.

Katie began to stroke his arm. 'Did you?'

He shook his head, releasing them from behind. 'I — I couldn't.'

She had no thought as to where her questions were leading, only that they came from her heart, from the love she had for this man beside her, and that the words, finally, felt right.

She reached for his hand. 'Then why don't you cry for her now. Let it all come out once and for all.'

'Katherine,' he protested, trying to laugh and not succeeding. 'I'm a grown man. I'm no longer that twelve year old boy. All of that — it happened a long time ago.'

'No, it didn't, darling,' she whispered. 'It happened yesterday.' She kissed his face, his hair, and she held him close against her. And she rocked him, ever so gently, she rocked him.

And at last, she felt something break within him, heard the harsh, wracking sobs that shook his body, sobs that seemed to tear up from the very depths of his soul.

25

It was coming on to darkness when they finally left Stoneybrook for Black Lake. The smell of more snow was in the air. As Katie drove down Belleville's Main Street, she glanced in her rearview mirror, warming at the sight of Jonathan following in his car, waving to him, honking her horn like a happy schoolgirl, grinning when he honked back.

Damn, he was sexy. No, he was far more than just sexy; he was downright beautiful, inside and out, and he was hers, she thought in glad possessiveness, and would have hugged herself right there had her hands not been on the wheel.

At first, he'd been embarrassed by his tears, barely able to look at her, making feeble jokes about her sending him a bill for analysis, uncomfortable that she had witnessed his terrible vulnerability. But it had only made her love him all the more, and she'd been quick to reassure him that tears were not a sign of weakness, only of feeling. He sure didn't know much for a psychiatrist, she thought. Not when it came to himself.

It seemed no time at all until she was making the turn onto Black Lake Road, feeling the car, as always, beginning to jump and bounce over the washboard road. Soon, the road narrowed, the trees closing them in. Minutes later, the brown house loomed into view. Katie eased up on the gas, wiping her hands alternately on her coat. They were perspiring. She turned off the ignition. Sat in silence. I don't want to be here, she thought. I want to turn around and go back. Behind her, Jonathan's door opened and closed.

She had a right to happiness. She did. She would not allow negative thoughts to rob her of her good feelings. Maybe Jason really did just slip and fall in the lake, after all. A tragic accident, but an accident all the same.

The police would have accepted it as that, too, if not for 'the strawmen,' which could, she tried to convince herself, have been merely the work of a prankster. And then she remembered her photograph clutched in Jason's hand — and the tire tracks down by the lake — and the phone calls, and the gladness in her heart began to fade, eclipsed by a dark foreboding. She got out of the car just as Jonathan came up to her. As they stood looking up at the house, Katie's chest grew heavy. She shivered involuntarily.

Why couldn't she and Jonathan just have

stayed forever in that fairy-tale house in the woods? she thought in childlike petulance.

Inside, the air was cold and dank and musty. No surprise.

'I used to love this house so much,' Katie said, feeling a welling of sadness as they walked through to the studio. 'Now it looks as cold as it feels.' All the charm and warmth Aunt Katherine's presence had given the house had somehow vanished, been replaced with something else — something frightening. There is evil here now, she thought. I can feel it all around me, emitting from the very walls, filling the air. She told herself she was being melodramatic, but the fact remained that she could not go upstairs to her room without seeing that effigy of Todd. Nor could she bring herself to go down to the cellar again, which, of course, she would have to do if she stayed on here. She would just have to — deal with it. And then there was the lake where she loved to swim in the summer. She sighed heavily as Jonathan's arms went around her.

'Maybe that cop's suggestion that you move wasn't such a bad one at that. Maybe you should consider selling this house. Would you really mind?'

'No,' she said at once, and knew it was true. This house was no longer her home.

Something else, some dark and malevolent presence had taken it over. 'I'll list it tomorrow,' she said. 'And I won't mind one bit.'

'You're sure.'

'I'm very sure.'

'Good.' He smiled. 'I know I'll be a lot happier not having to think of you being way out here.'

'Do you think it'll bring much of a price without electricity or heating?'

'It won't matter. I've got enough money for both of us.'

'Oh, I see,' she teased. 'I've got me a rich man as well as a handsome one.'

'Flattery, my dear,' he said, draping the afghan over her shoulders and sitting her down in the chair in front of the fireplace, 'will get you anywhere. Now, don't go 'way. I'll get some wood, and as soon as I get a fire going, I'll make some tea. Hungry?'

'You must be kidding. After that feast you prepared?'

Grinning, he said, 'I always knew I'd make someone a good wife. Comfortable?'

'Like a 'bug-in-a-rug,' as they say. You'll spoil me, Jonathan.'

His eyes swept over her. 'Every chance I get.' Then he laughed. 'I love it. A woman who knows how to blush.'

'You're terrible. I hate to tell you, but I think I used up the last of the wood you stacked in the pantry.'

'Then I'll get it from the cellar. Won't take me but a minute.' As he turned, his gaze stopped on the nearly completed portrait of Hattie Holloway. Katie felt a rush of pleasure at the unmistakable gleam of admiration in his eyes.

'Katherine, this is wonderful,' he said, moving to get a closer look. 'The likeness — the detail . . . '

'You really like it?'

He turned to her, smiling. 'Darling, you must stop sounding like an insecure little girl. You're a truly gifted artist, and there's no reason whatever for you not to be very, very pleased with what you've done.'

'Thank you. It's for her husband. An anniversary gift.'

'He'll be crazy about it. And she'll recommend you to all her friends.'

Katie glowed under his praise. 'Will she?'

'Of course. Soon you'll be famous and independently wealthy,' he said, tousling her hair, 'and I'll have to make an appointment to see you.'

'You're making fun of me.' She gave him a mock pout.

The teasing left his eyes. 'No, it really will

happen for you, Katherine. I have absolutely no doubt of that.'

When he was gone, Katie played happily with the idea, indulging in the fantasy of being a rich and famous artist, and after a little of this, laughed at herself. Getting paid for work she'd gladly done for no pay for years, (and maybe just a little recognition) would suit her just fine. She didn't need more than that. Except for Jonathan, of course. She very definitely needed Jonathan.

As she snuggled deeper into the afghan he'd wrapped so tenderly around her, she thought with a smile of utter contentment, I could get used to this.

She looked around the room — this room she had once so loved. It held nothing for her now. All the pleasure she had known here had faded under the terrible things that had happened. She would finish the portrait of Hattie Holloway, and then she would never work in this room again.

Jonathan had talked about building a studio for her at the house in Stoneybrook. He had also hinted at his desire for a child. Was it possible? Dare she hope? It all seemed too good to be true.

Perhaps it was.

No! Why did that thought keep coming back? She mustn't let it. Mustn't think that way. She and Jonathan were good and decent people. They deserved a chance at happiness. Yes, they would have a good life together, one filled with love and sharing. No guarantees, of course, but she now knew that without the risk of pain, of disappointment, no joy was possible.

Katie looked at her watch, frowning, it suddenly occurring to her that Jonathan should be back by now. It had been nearly twenty minutes since he had gone down for the wood. What was keeping him? Maybe he was checking locks — or had found something. After several more minutes of sitting, of fidgeting, she rose and opened the drapes and stood looking out through the glass doors.

The moon floated in and out of dark boiling clouds, a scene the lake mirrored perfectly. As Katie stared down into it, she had the uncanny sensation that if she jumped she would just float down and down for all eternity, like falling through space. She made herself look away. At the same time she heard a loud thud that made her jerk the edge of the drape she still held in her hand. What was that? It had seemed to come from outside. But she couldn't be sure of that.

Sliding the doors open, Katie shivered against the cold and drew the afghan more tightly about her shoulders as she stepped onto the tiny balcony.

A stirring of uneasiness in the hollow of her stomach.

Behind her, the telephone began to ring.

It surprised her to hear Clayton Jackson's softly modulated voice on the line. She couldn't remember her art teacher ever phoning her before. It must be important, she thought, especially to call so late.

'I've been trying to track you down most of the day,' he was saying. 'I called The Coffee Shop, but they said you no longer were employed there.'

'No, Mr. Jackson, I don't. We — uh, decided to part company.'

'Well, no matter, Katie . . . '

Did she detect a note of excitement in the unexcitable Mr. Jackson? She pressed the receiver closer to her ear.

' . . . I just wanted to give you the good news, Katie,' he said, and she heard the rattling of paper. 'I only received the word by mail this morning. Your painting took second prize in the state art competition, dear, and I wanted to be the first to congratulate you.'

Mr. Jackson chuckled. 'Well, believe it, my dear, because it's true. I'm so very pleased for you, Katie. And since you're no longer working at The Coffee Shop, I've a proposition for you. I was wondering if you'd be interested in teaching a beginner's class, part-time. We could start the first of the year. There's been a fair amount of interest locally, and I've been wanting for some time now to open the school to less advanced students.'

Katie accepted without hesitation. 'And thank you — for everything, Mr. Jackson,' she said.

'It's I who thank you, Katie. I'm not so without ego that I'm not extremely proud to have two of my students walk off with the two top honors.'

'Two of your . . . ' There had been the faintest hint of sadness in his voice as he'd said it. In the space of a breath, Katie understood. 'Jason,' she half-whispered, her eyes filling.

'Yes, his painting CITY AT NIGHT won first prize. And I can't think of anyone Jason would rather have accepting the award for him than you, Katie.'

After hanging up the phone, Katie just stood there trying to digest her instructor's words, playing them again and again in her mind like a favorite song. Finally, desperate to share her good news, she took off through the house — through the dining room, the parlor, past the front door in the hallway and on into the kitchen.

The door leading down into the cellar was partly open.

'Jonathan?' she called out.

Through narrowed eyes, Katie strained to see into the thick darkness. (There should be some light from his flashlight.) The dank cellar smell rose up to her like the smell of the grave and sent the faintest trickling of fear along her spine.

Too good to be true, an inner voice taunted. There was a sense of déjà vu. She had run this scene before, only days ago when she had received the phone call from Hattie Holloway. Then, too, she had felt an eagerness to share her good news. Then, too, she had raced through the house, gone down to the cellar.

There was a lamp on the kitchen counter. Katie lit it, turned up the wick a little. She checked the time. A half hour now since Jonathan had gone down to get the wood. Far too long. She stepped down one, two — hesitated — three steps, called out his name again, heard the tremor in her voice, listened hard for some sign that he was safe (maybe he'd found something down there, she thought again, some old artifact, something that had caught his interest, and the time had simply gotten away from him), but heard only the dull beating of her heart.

'Jonathan, are you down there?' Her fear was in her voice. 'Please answer me.' She stepped down onto the fifth step, closer now to the din of silence and darkness below. The lamp was slippery in her hand as she played the light slowly over each step below her, crouching low to allow the light to reach as far as possible.

Panic gripped her all of a sudden, and she screamed Jonathan's name. Easy, easy, she told herself, fighting back a wave of dizziness that threatened to send her tumbling down the rest of the stairs. She gripped the railing. She must remain calm. Getting hysterical would help no one — not Jonathan, not her.

He'd been there for her all along. Now it was her turn. She must be strong — and clever. She had to think what to do. She took a deep breath, let it out slowly. And again.

Something — someone was down there — waiting. Jonathan was hurt or gagged or — NO! Don't even think it. He's fine — just fine. You just have to figure out what to do, that's all. Whoever is down there with Jonathan expects you to come rushing to the rescue, is counting on it. But she wouldn't do that. No, she would do the sensible, logical thing. She would go back upstairs and call the police.

A rush of air behind her — a footstep. Before Katie could turn around, or even complete the thought, the door above her slammed shut. The metal bolt clunked home.

She'd taken too long in making her decision, and now, as she stared up at the locked door, a terrible sinking sensation was in her. She thought of trying the knob anyway, but knew it would be futile. She turned away. Holding the lamp, with its tiny, yellow flame, before her, Katie stared down into the black void below.

And waited.

26

Down below, the outside cellar door creaked open slowly on rusted hinges, letting in light that cut a pale blue swath across the cement floor, swallowing it up again as the door closed.

And suddenly he was standing on the bottom step smiling up at her. Katie's breath seemed to clot in her throat. She couldn't move or scream, only stand there in numb disbelief, taking in the baggy overalls, the faded army jacket, the mud-caked boots with their top laces undone.

'You,' she said at last.

'Surprised?'

There was amusement in his voice, and a terrible coldness. She'd heard hints of the coldness before. She remembered now — now that it was too late.

'What have you done with Jonathan?'

'All in due time. Surely you've heard that patience is a virtue. I'm an expert on patience. Oh, yes. You're a long way from Lennoxville, Katie. I've been looking for you for a very long time.'

'Why?' she asked, and it was as if her voice

belonged to someone else.

'Revenge.' His smile widened, a death-smile, lifting the hairs on the nape of Katie's neck.

He watched her fear, enjoyed it. Too bad about her falling for the shrink. It would have been far more interesting to have her rely on him for awhile, trust him. He'd meant to terrorize her to the point where she would be driven to reach out, to cling — well, the plan had worked well enough, he had to admit that. Except that she'd found another hero. Well, no matter . . .

The flame in Katie's lamp flickered precariously as her hand shook. But her voice was firm as she asked again, 'Where's Jonathan, Drake? What have you done with him?'

'Back to that, are we? Well, Jonathan's waiting for you, too, Katie. We're going to have a little party. A sort of farewell party — just the three of us.'

'Jason,' she whispered, as it came to her. 'You killed him.'

'I didn't need a boyfriend on the scene. And then I heard about the letter they found on his body when they pulled him out of the lake. A queer, for Christ's sake.' He laughed, an ugly sound. 'It didn't matter. He could have identified me.'

'He saw you leaving this house.' How could she ever have thought Drake Devlin was even remotely attractive? And yet nothing about him had altered. He had that same clean-cut, masculine face, the same smattering of freckles across his nose and cheeks, the faintly clefted, jutting chin. Only the eyes are different, she thought. Or was it simply that she had not looked closely enough before? She again recalled Sergeant Miller's remarking how easy his job would be if killers always looked like killers.

'He might have gotten away if he'd stayed in his car,' Drake was saying matter-of-factly. 'But he wanted to be a hero — everybody wants to be a hero. I chased him down in the truck; there was no place left for him to go but the lake — or under my wheels.'

'He couldn't swim,' she muttered foolishly.

'Just wasn't his day, was it?' He threw back his head and laughed, that same chilling laugh she'd heard on the telephone. He was crazy — crazy. His laughing cut off as quickly as it began. His eyes slithered over her. 'I have to admit, Raynes had great taste in women. Raynes . . . ' He cocked his head like a dog listening for some alien sound. 'He wanted to be a hero, too.'

This last sentence came out thin and hollow, and it took a moment for it to

360

register in Katie's mind. Then, 'You knew — Todd?'

'I was a little worried you might recognize me from the picture.'

'Picture? What picture?' What was he talking about? Jonathan, please, please be all right. Please, God, let him be all right.

'There were four or five of us in one of the snapshots Raynes sent you. I was the one leaning on the rifle.'

Drake was in a picture Todd had sent her? She remembered then Drake telling her he'd been in Vietnam. 'You were in Todd's regiment,' she said, a statement, not a question. 'No, I don't remember you from any picture Todd sent me.' Drake wanted her to remember, she could tell. His vanity wanted her to remember. It was almost funny, except that she didn't feel like laughing.

'I would only have been looking at Todd,' she said deliberately.

'Not very flattering.'

Something about Jason came to her then — something Drake told her that didn't add up. 'You said the only time you saw Jason was the night you were leaving this house — I mean, the clothes on that — Jason's clothes . . . '

He smiled easily, smoothed his hair in that

361

way he had, with his left hand, the one not clutching the knife. 'I'd already broken into his apartment days before and taken the clothes.'

Drake started up the stairs toward her.

Katie backed up until she was standing with her back pressed against the locked door. There was nowhere to go.

Drake knew it, too. He stopped, in no particular hurry. 'Katie, don't you see? I've known all about you for some time now — where you worked, what you did, who your friends were. I made it my business.' He put out a hand to her.

Fingers reaching out for her — fingers of a man without heart or soul. She remembered her dream, and the hand of 'the strawman' touching her face.

'Come, Katie. It's time.'

She cringed at his touch.

'By the way, I don't really care for the suit. Much too conservative. I have something far more interesting for you to wear. I bought it especially for you. You'll remember when you see it.'

Suddenly aware of the heft of the lamp in her hand, her grip on it tightened. But her intention to bring it down on Drake's head must have registered in her face, in the tensing of her muscles, for Drake's hand clamped down hard on her wrist, nearly knocking the lamp from her grasp, making her cry out with the pain.

'Not smart,' he said quietly, and took the lamp from her.

Close to him now, Katie could smell the damp sour earth blending with the musky odor of stale sweat coming off him. 'Come,' he said, smiling his death-smile.

The instant Katie stepped off the bottom step into the cellar, she saw Jonathan. He was lying in a crumpled heap on the floor. She tried to wrench herself free of Drake's hold on her to go to him, but his grip on her wrist tightened, a powerful hand, like steel. Then she felt a sharp sting of the knife-point breaking her skin, felt the warm trickling of blood down her side, erasing any further thought of escape.

'You want to be with your boyfriend, don't you?' Drake crooned in feigned sympathy. 'Well, don't worry. You will be. Soon. Very soon.' He was eyeing Jonathan curiously, with something like begrudged respect. 'Funny, it never occurred to me this guy was anything other than your doctor. Always room for human error, isn't there?'

You're not human, she thought. You're not . . . he was taking something from beneath his jacket. He tossed it to her.

'Put it on,' he said softly.

She made no move to obey.

She felt the sharp nudge of the knife. Hesitantly, she bent and picked up the filmy negligee off the floor. She recognized it as one of those he'd given her in the hospital, one of the gifts she'd returned. Briefly turning her frightened gaze on Jonathan, she saw now that his hands and feet were bound. He was so still, so awfully still.

'I'll freeze in this,' she said, turning back to Drake.

'Put it on.' His voice left no room for argument. Nor did the knife in his hand.

Her hands shaking, she undid the tiny gold buttons of her jacket, slid it off her shoulders. Next her skirt, pulling it down over her slender hips, painfully aware every agonizing second of Drake's eyes on her. Do what he says. Don't antagonize him. Just wait your chance. Oh, God, what chance? What possible chance was there with Jonathan . . . Why was this happening? Why? She slipped the negligee over her head.

'No!' The word snapped like a whip. 'Everything. Take off everything.' Slowly, deliberately, he began to caress the knife blade, sliding the flat of it back and forth between his thumb and forefinger.

A moment later she stood naked before

him, writhing inwardly beneath his scalding, vile scrutiny. The pores of her skin tightened against the penetrating cold of the cellar — against him. Her fingers clumsy, she quickly put on the negligee, sliding the flimsy straps over her shoulders, feeling the skirt like spider webbing against her bare legs.

'Now, get down on the floor.'

She did as he said. The cement was rough and needle-cold against her flesh.

His eyes moved over her. He smiled — a slow smile. 'Nice,' he said. 'Very nice.'

Was he going to rape her now? Was it all part of some sick ritual he'd planned for revenge? Revenge for what? Please, God, help me. She hated the tears that blinded her eyes. She hated her helplessness.

He knelt down, but other than to tie her hands and feet, he made no attempt to touch her. A reprieve? She allowed herself a faint ray of hope. Jonathan was tied up, too. There would have been no need for Drake to tie him up if he were already dead.

Maybe if she started Drake talking, stalled for time, she would think of something — something to do. It worked in the movies. God, she was so cold. She ached with it. Why don't the police come? Aren't they supposed to be watching the house? Maybe Jonathan

365

will come to. And do what, Katie? His hands and feet are bound.

'You said you wanted revenge,' she said, trying to keep her voice steady. 'Why, Drake? Was it because I couldn't love you?' She knew, of course, it was something far more complex than that. Hadn't Drake said he'd been searching for her for a long time? He'd known all about her — even that she'd once lived in Lennoxville. And he was in the war with Todd. But it was the only thing she could think of to get him talking.

He grunted as he gave the rope about her right wrist an extra turn. She winced, feeling it cut into her flesh. 'Don't flatter yourself,' he spat out. His pale eyes bored into hers. It was all she could do not to look away. 'It's Raynes I want revenge against. You're nothing more than the means.'

'But Todd — Todd's dead.' Wasn't he?

'I know that,' he said, standing now to appraise his work. He looked pleased with himself. 'I took your picture off his body. It was in his wallet along with your address.'

His tone was so matter-of-fact that for a moment Katie couldn't comprehend the words. She did understand that Drake put that picture in Jason's hand, which of course was the sole reason he'd gone to the funeral parlor. But why? Why did he take that picture from Todd? And why was Todd's body never found?

Keep him talking. That's your only hope now. Jonathan's only hope. Fortunately, he seemed to need little prodding. She could sense him wanting to talk — wanting to spew out all the deep, dark secrets worming around inside of him. But not from any feelings of guilt. Oh, no, not guilt. Never guilt. Rage was what she felt from him. That, and a need to brag.

'Tell me, Drake,' she said in the way of a sympathetic friend. 'Tell me what happened.'

He gave her a long, hard look, as though deciding something about her. Then, when her gaze didn't waver, his eyes shifted to a spot just above her head, becoming gradually veiled as if he were seeing something in the distance — something from some other time and place. He began suddenly to pace the brief expanse of cement floor, his movements, jerky, erratic.

His words began falteringly. 'We — uh, were on our bellies crawling through the hot, stinking jungle. Everything was quiet — quiet, like death. There was just me and Raynes by that time. The rest of them — gone — blown away.' He caught her in the grip of his stare. Katie wasn't sure he saw her. She didn't move her head.

He turned from her, bent and picked up the lamp from the floor and positioned it on the sawhorse near the small, dirt-smeared window.

In the lamplight, his face was an evil mask.

'Only me and Raynes left,' he mumbled, almost to himself. His eyes darted back to her, seeing her now. No doubt of that. 'I itched,' he blurted, and chuckled low in his throat. 'Now, isn't that the damnedest thing to remember? Just between my shoulder blades, I itched. It was making me crazy. My hair under my cap felt like one giant, squirming insect. I was filthy and sweating, and it was so damned hot — and the bugs — the sweat running into my eyes, half-blinding me. But I didn't dare move a muscle — not one hair — and then I heard something.

'Beside me, Raynes whispered, 'It's okay, Devlin, they're on our side'. Now, how could he be sure of that? They all looked alike.' He sneered, and Katie saw the terrible cruelty of his mouth. 'We'd come upon a small village,' he went on. 'I could see an old man working the paddy field just a ways off.' Drake wiped his forehead with the back of his hand, though there was no warmth in the cellar.

368

'A woman — not a real woman — not like you, Katie . . . ' He crouched down beside her, then, and brushed her cheek with his fingertips. Katie remained very still. 'A hank of hair, and bones was all she was; she was standing in front of this shack calling out to the old man.' Drake's face was dangerously close to hers now, his breath warm and moist and vile. His eyes moved from her, fixing on the space of cellar where Jason's effigy had hung — swaying — creaking — she remembered the feel of a warm breath on her cheek in the darkness, then.

Drake straightened, went on. 'Naturally, her speaking in that turkey-talk, I didn't know what the hell she was saying. And then, suddenly, like a shot, this kid comes running and yelling out of nowhere.' Drake's eyes took on a glitter of excitement. 'Coming right at us. I cocked my rifle — ' He mimed the action. 'Aimed . . . '

'Don't,' she whispered, unable to stop herself, wanting to shut her eyes and mind to the terrible images. She couldn't bear to hear more of this horror story, yet she knew she needed to, needed to hear all of it.

'Yeah,' he said, and smiled. 'That's what Raynes said. Only he screamed it. Goddamn bleeding-heart, Raynes. 'Hold your fire', he yelled, but it was too late. I didn't hear him.

I'd already squeezed the trigger.'

And something squeezed Katie's heart.

Drake's voice lowered. 'Or maybe I did hear. And maybe I just said 'the hell with you, Raynes; I ain't takin' no chance on dying for some gook kid.' ' He gave a harsh laugh. 'Well, you don't ask for an identity card, do you? You by any chance armed?' His fingers dug into Katie's bare shoulder with savagery. 'Do you know what I'm telling you?'

'Yes,' she managed past the taste of bile rising in her throat.

Todd's face came to her clearly, then, as it had not done in many months, each dear feature of his face, his sensitive brown eyes, his easy grin. Todd would have loathed the sort of man Drake was. Even in the midst of war, Katie had no doubt that Todd would have bled in his soul for the murdered boy.

'You shoot, goddammit! You shoot!' Eyes wild, he reminded Katie of a killer dog on a frayed leash.

'How old was the boy?' she asked, a dangerous, futile question, but she was remembering the vision she'd had in the hospital, and it seemed, for some reason, important to know.

Drake didn't answer right away, then quietly, 'Like I said, I didn't ask. What's the difference? Six — eight — they weren't kids. They were goddamned midgets carrying guns and grenades.'

'Was he — the boy . . . ?'

Fury leapt into Drake's eyes, and for a horrifying instant Katie feared she had gone too far. 'No, he wasn't armed. But how the hell could I know that?' He thrust his face close to hers, his fingers digging ever deeper into her shoulder. 'Answer me! How the hell could I know the little bastard wasn't armed?' His voice was edged with madness, and she sensed the twisted threads of his mind were as precarious as fine wires in a time bomb.

'You c — couldn't,' she stammered, knowing it wouldn't have mattered. There was no remorse, no regret in Drake. Only hatred — and blood-lust. Blood-lust as he relived the moment of impact when his bullet struck the boy down.

The phrase 'the thrill of the hunt' came to mind, and Katie knew it was that that had made Drake so tenacious, so tireless in his efforts to track her down. But more than that, Drake enjoyed killing. There was no question in her mind about that. None at all. As he stood up, Katie's hand went involuntarily to soothe her bruised, throbbing shoulder.

'Raynes came at me like a madman,'

Drake was saying, 'and he kept coming at me until I . . . '

At the abrupt distortion of Drake's features, Katie's thoughts swept back across time to when she was in the sixth grade. She even remembered the boy's name — Greg Coombs. He was the school bully. He'd picked on little Billy Miller the entire year, but on that one day in early June, something snapped in Billy, and he turned on him, beat him until Greg begged him to stop and all the kids were cheering Billy on. She remembered the look on Greg's face — it was the same expression Drake wore now, and Katie understood more clearly what had happened.

Todd kept coming at you until you begged him to stop, didn't he, Drake? She was glad, but as on that day in the sixth grade, not brave enough to cheer aloud.

'They watched — women, old men, kids — watched while Raynes made me wrap the kid in an army blanket and dig a grave. He stood over me, arms folded across his chest like some goddamned sentinel while I lifted shovelful after shovelful of stinking, heavy mud — I lifted, while they all watched, wailing the whole time like Christless banshees. Even Raynes — snivelling, wiping his eyes, while I wiped sweat from mine.'

Drake was calmer now, his voice dropping, becoming monotone, almost hypnotic. 'After I buried the kid, Raynes turned and walked away — turned his back on me like the fool he was. I picked up the rifle — let him hear me cock it, saw his back stiffen. Someone screamed a warning, but too late. I pumped the life out of that bleeding-heart, left him sprawled right there on that stinking swampland in a pool of his own bleeding-heart blood. And then I buried him.' He smiled. 'Do you know what day that was, Katie?'

Katie could only look at him. My God! Todd had been murdered. Murdered by one of his own men.

'It was November fifth.'

He was waiting for her response, congratulating himself for the touch of irony. But the date meant nothing to her. She didn't receive word of Todd being missing in action until the third of December. Despite her fear, anger boiled in her. Todd might have made it back home.

'There were witnesses,' she said carelessly. Maybe one could be found, and Drake would be made to pay for his crime — if she and Jonathan ever got out of here.

'Not when I left that village.' He grinned at her. 'Even if any of them could have spoken anything but that damned turkey-talk.'

He was watching her face, clearly enjoying the impact of his words. At last, in a voice void of emotion, Katie said, 'Then you have your revenge.'

'Oh no. It didn't mean anything. A lot of people died in Nam. It wasn't special.' As he picked up the lamp from the sawhorse, his face went eerily in and out of shadow. 'There are a few finishing touches I have to take care of,' he said. 'I'll be back.'

And then he was gone, and the wooden bar on the outside cellar door thumped into place. Katie struggled at once to a sitting position. 'Jonathan?' she whispered into the darkness.

Nothing.

The window was low, and Katie began inching her way toward it.

She could make out Drake's silhouette easily in the moonlight. He was standing about forty yards off to her right, among the trees. The lamp was on the ground beside him.

As Katie watched the shovel lift — drop — then lift again, each time imagining the soft thud of upturned earth plopping on the hard ground, her mouth went dry. It was a scene out of a horror film.

Drake was digging a grave.

He turned suddenly, as though sensing her watching him, and leaned on his shovel. Katie could not see his face, but she felt the heat of his stare burning into her, and tore her own eyes away, the heart-stopping knowledge that Drake meant to bury them alive coming to her. Why else would they still be breathing? My God! And all because Todd had humiliated him all those years ago.

Gripped with panic, Katie began working her way along the floor toward where Jonathan lay, her movements agonizingly slow, the cold cement rubbing her flesh raw, Hurry! she commanded herself, terrified that any moment the door would open, and Drake would be standing there. Hurry!

At last she reached Jonathan's still form. 'Wake up, darling.' How badly is he hurt? she wondered. Was it possible . . . ? No, she would not even allow herself to think it. Yet, there was no sound from him, no stirring of life to reassure her. Tears of fear and helplessness welled, and she couldn't even wipe them away. 'He's outside now, Jonathan,' she said. 'He's digging a grave to bury us in.' When Jonathan gave no response, Katie lay her cheek in near despair against his hair and at once felt the sticky wetness there, matted in the strands. Please, no! She moved her face lower, pressed an ear to his chest to listen. Only when she heard the strong, steady beat of his heart did she let out her own breath.

'Jonathan, please hear me. I need you. We're both going to die if you don't help me. We are both going to die horribly.'

There was the softest moan from Jonathan, enough to send a surge of hope through Katie. 'Katherine?' his voice was weak and thready.

'Yes, Jonathan, it's me.' She could barely see him in the pale light from the window. 'Are you all right?'

Moaning, he struggled to get up, falling back again before Katie remembered to tell him that his hands and feet were bound, as were her own. 'Christ, my head,' he groaned. 'What happened?'

Briefly, prodded by a powerful sense of urgency, Katie quickly explained their perilous situation, relaying as well all that Drake had told her. 'Both exits are locked,' she finished. 'I don't know how we're going to get out of here, but we don't have much time.' She paused, becoming aware that Jonathan did not seem at all surprised. 'You knew all along that it was Drake, didn't you?'

'No, not really,' he said, keeping his own

voice to a near whisper, 'but I did get a sense of — I don't know — the uncanny, I suppose, when we ran into him at the funeral parlor. There was something in his eyes — like hearing a sour note on the piano. I put my aversion to him down to jealousy, though I found myself remembering something my mother told me years ago — that dried wheat stems make excellent straw, and Devlin had said that he and his father grew wheat on their land. But that bit of trivia isn't going to help us now — 'too little, too late', as they say. Our first job is to get out of these ropes. We need something to cut them with.'

Katie wracked her brain, then, in a flash of recall, saw herself dropping the flashlight down here the other night, heard the splintering of glass. She told Jonathan. 'I dropped it when I saw — anyway, if the police didn't clean it up, the glass is still here.'

Face down on the floor, Katie began working her way toward the woodpile where she'd been when she dropped the flashlight.

'Be careful,' Jonathan said behind her. 'Don't cut yourself.'

After only a moment's searching, an excitement rippled through Katie at the touch of something smooth and cool against her cheek. 'I've got it,' she said. Seizing the

377

fair-sized sliver of glass between her teeth, she made her way back to Jonathan and maneuvered the glass into his hand.

Backs pressed together, Jonathan worked feverishly at the ropes binding her wrists. Their combined breathing seemed deafening in the quiet of the cellar. The seconds crept by with nerve-screaming slowness. Katie was about to despair that their plan would fail, when, suddenly, the rope snapped. Her hands were free. Briskly, she rubbed the circulation back into them, then quickly undid the rope around her ankles.

'Listen!' Jonathan whispered.

Katie froze. 'I don't hear anything.' And then she did, a soft rustling just outside the door. Oh, God, she had to untie Jonathan.

'No!' he whispered, as she turned to him. 'No time. Get away from me. He has to believe I'm still out. It's our only chance. Go!'

Katie barely managed to put a few feet between them when the door swung open. Drake's silhouetted form seemed to fill the doorway. The knife was in his hand, its blade gleaming in the moonlight. He came inside, slowly, warily, the knife poised now, leaving the door open behind him to let in light. His eyes went from Katie to Jonathan who lay perfectly still and in the same position as

Drake had left him. After a moment, Katie saw the tension leave Drake's shoulders, and the wild look go out of his eyes. 'So you've managed to free yourself,' he drawled, moving toward her, reaching out a hand to stroke her breast beneath the tissue-thin fabric, while Katie's skin recoiled at his touch. 'Nice,' he murmured.

At once, an almost uncontrollable hatred for Drake Devlin washed over Katie, and she had to fight the compulsion to ignore the knife, and just fly into him, hands, feet, everything. But in the rational part of her mind, she knew she would be no match for a madman wielding a knife. He would kill her. And then he would kill Jonathan.

'I've got something I want to show you,' he said, his hot, greedy eyes raking her body, 'then you and I will take a little trip upstairs. No sense in our not being comfortable, is there? By the way, you do look ravishing in that negligee. A nice touch, don't you think?' He shifted his gaze to Jonathan again. 'Did you try to wake your boyfriend?' He sauntered over to where Jonathan lay, not seeming even to breathe, and nudged his ribs with the toe of his boot.

Katie's own breath stopped.

'I thought you'd try,' he said, coming back to her. 'But I made sure he wouldn't be waking up for a long, long time.'

As he reached to take her hand, Katie flattened herself against the wall. 'No. You're crazy, Drake. You'll never get away with this. They'll find you. Jonathan will . . . '

'What they'll find,' he cut in softly, 'is the good doctor here slumped over your grave with his wrists slashed. Murder and suicide. A crime of passion; happens all the time.' He gave a hard laugh.

'No one will believe . . . '

'Oh, of course they will. A psychiatrist who'd just lost a patient — blames himself, poor man. He takes a year off. A mental breakdown, they'll say. Poor Dr. Shea had a mental breakdown.'

She felt herself beginning to hyperventilate, tried to control it. 'You — you said you didn't know that Jonathan and I were . . . '

'I didn't. Until I saw you together. Then all it took was a little phone call to Belleville General to collect a bit of information. What I got was a bonus, of course. You'd be surprised how cooperative some women can be — how they love to divulge secrets. But after all, what could be so threatening about a guy who just landed into town and wants to look up his old college buddy?' Closing his hand around Katie's wrist, he pulled her roughly to her feet and toward the door.

'Enough talk. Come. Your bridal bed is ready.'

Twisting her arm painfully behind her back, Drake marched her ahead of him, the knife point prodding her forward in a near run over the hard, frosty ground that burned her bare feet.

And then she was standing amidst a semicircle of shadowy trees and staring down in horror at the black water that glistened like oil at the bottom of the grave Drake had dug, while above her the moon slipped in and out of darkness, and the cold night air bit into her near nakedness with cruel and savage teeth.

Drake's hands were gripping her shoulders and he was pushing her forward, closer and closer to the edge of the deep, rectangular hole in the earth, teasing her. Katie screamed, kept screaming, her hands flailing wildly at empty air, finally managing to clutch onto the rough fabric of his jacket. He drew her back, then, held her gently against his chest, murmured soothing words while she sobbed in terror.

★ ★ ★

Her screams tore the silence, echoed horribly, accusingly inside Jonathan's mind. The dream he'd had rushed back to him, the dream of her falling — falling, tumbling over and over like a rag doll spinning through space, lost to him forever. Tears and sweat blinded him, burned his eyes as he worked frantically at the ropes binding his wrists. You can't fail again, a voice screamed within him. You can't.

And then another scream from Katie, and the tiny shard of glass slipped from his grasp, shattered on the cement floor. There was a moment of utter disbelief, and then nausea gripped him as he felt, like a blind man tracing a stranger's features, along the floor. At last, he touched a sliver of glass, tried to trap it between his fingers, but it was too fragile and crushed like salt, embedding itself in his skin, leaving the tips of his fingers wet with blood.

He began to weep.

As Drake tried to pull her to him again, Katie's hand shot out, found flesh, and she raked his face with her nails as hard as she could, and felt an immense satisfaction when some of his skin came away beneath her fingernails.

He let out a yelp, his hand leaping to his face, and Katie seized the moment to drop to her knees on the ground, just inches from the open grave, and scramble away from him.

And then she was on her feet, running as fast as her legs could carry her, in the direction of the house.

Close, too close, his boots thumped the ground behind her, his raspy breathing seeming amplified in the crisp night air. Oblivious now to stones and twigs that cut into the soles of her feet, and even to the cold, Katie ran with every ounce that was in her.

And then she was taking the back steps by twos — was inside the house. Her fingers were clumsy and numb with cold and terror, refusing to obey, but at last she'd managed to lock the doors behind her and draw the drapes. Crossing the floor in the darkness, she picked up the receiver and dialed zero.

'Operator,' came the sing-song voice over the line. 'What number, plee-eze?' the voice repeated in maddening monotone.

Feet pounding up the back steps, the door rattling violently, then, suddenly, an explosion of glass.

At the sight of his hand worming through the hole in the glass, Katie dropped the phone. His fingers were groping for the lock. Could she get out the front door and make it down to the car? Was there time? Even if there was, he would immediately kill Jonathan in his rage. Why hadn't she looked for the gun, learned how to use it? She would have shot him without hesitation. But it was too late now — too late. All this ran through her mind in a matter of seconds, until she heard the door-lock click into release.

Grabbing up the stove poker, Katie slipped behind the cot, crouching low, trying to still her tortured breathing.

The door opened slowly, sending a draft of icy air to swirl about Katie's legs. She tightened her grip on the poker and made herself as small as possible. The cot was kitty-cornered, and she could see through the space between it and the wall, Drake's boots, then the knife, leap into view. So close she could have reached out and touched him. He closed the door behind him, shutting out all light.

Silence.

Katie's heart was pounding so hard she was sure he must be able to hear it.

Then, softly, 'I know you're here, Katie. We were coming up here, anyway, remember? I told you that. Oh, Katie, I'm so pleased you're as eager for me as I am for you,' he mocked.

She heard him begin to move about the room, heard the desk slide out from the wall.

'Not he-ere,' he sang, as though playing a

child's game. 'Now let me see — where could she be hiding?' He crossed the floor heavily. 'Not under the table. Oh, Katie, I like this game. I'm so glad you thought of it.'

For several minutes there was only the sound of his breathing, and then he was walking again — but away from her. She heard the French doors open, and his footsteps become muffled, and she knew he'd stepped into the carpeted dining room. She waited a few more minutes to be sure he was really gone, and then, having remembered there was a pair of scissors in the desk drawer, she rose and crept from her hiding place, moving quickly but cautiously, afraid of knocking against something in the darkness. But the room was her own and familiar, and in seconds she was easing the desk drawer open. She would slip down the back stairs and cut Jonathan free with the scissors. Drake had forgotten to lock the cellar door when he forced her outside. Or perhaps, believing that Jonathan was unconscious, felt there was no need.

Katie sifted hurriedly through sheets of paper, found a ball of twine, a bunch of elastics, paperclips — but no scissors. She must have put them somewhere else. A sense of hopelessness threatened to overwhelm her.

Sudden light danced on the wall in front

of her. Her heart constricted, her body momentarily paralyzed. Then, slowly, she turned. Drake was standing before her, a benign smile on his face, holding the lamp in one hand, the knife in the other. 'It's over, Katie. All over. I found you. I won the game.'

In her moment of blind terror, Katie had forgotten about the poker in her hand; now, remembering, fight returned as she raised it and struck out at Drake; but she was too close to get any real leverage, and the poker glanced off his shoulder. Drake let out a curse and twisted it from her grasp, tossed it on the floor behind him. His eyes riveted on Katie's face, he set the lamp on the desk.

As he made a move toward her, Katie tried to duck past him, get to the door, but his hand caught in her hair, closed and forced her back, and then he was dragging her down on the floor, straddling her, pinning her solidly beneath his weight.

'No,' she whimpered, 'no, please don't . . . '

His face moved close to hers, his breath hot and sour. As his wet, open mouth sought hers, Katie twisted her head wildly from side to side trying to escape it, but he only gripped her hair more savagely until Katie was sure she would pass out from the pain.

But she mustn't let herself. She mustn't.

Time held little meaning for her. It might have been hours or mere minutes that they struggled there on the floor. From time to time, weakness swept over her, exhaustion threatened to betray her. Drake was so strong, yet her own renewed bursts of energy, born of desperation, allowed her to hold him off. But for how long? she wondered.

Near collapse, she saw the knife. It seemed to have come out of nowhere. She had almost forgotten about it. Now, like a snake, it hovered above her, poised to strike. He lowered the cold steel, his labored breathing matching her own, until the point of the blade was touching the hollow of her throat.

Her mouth went dust-dry.

'I don't want to make you ugly, Katie. Don't make me.'

She prayed for a miracle, knowing the pleasure he would take in carving her up. Even if she did give in to Drake, she knew he would kill her afterward. She was certain of that. Raping her would not be enough. He had not dug that grave with a view to letting her live. Hadn't he already told her this plan?

But right now — right this minute she was still alive. Katie forced herself to go limp.

'That's a good girl,' he crooned, praising

her as one might an obedient child. 'I won't cut you unless you fight me. You won't fight me anymore, will you?'

'No,' she choked out between parched lips. 'No, I won't fight you anymore. Please, don't hurt me.'

He weighed her promise in his mind, then, seeming satisfied, set the knife on the floor beside him. He shifted his weight so that he was on his knees in front of her. 'I might even let you live,' he said, but they both knew he wouldn't.

He was working at his belt buckle. His tongue flicked obscenely over his lower lip as if already tasting victory. He'd stalked his prey and now he was going to collect the spoils.

And this is the miracle, Katie told herself. This is all the miracle you're going to get. NOW! And in that split second, while Drake was preoccupied with unbuckling his pants, Katie drew her knees up tight to her body, and with every ounce of strength that was left in her, slammed both feet into his chest.

The impact drove him backward, and Katie heard him grunt as his head hit the floor with a sickening thud.

She waited, almost surprised that it had worked, her body heaving with each labored breath.

No sound from him.

She sat up slowly, at the same time sliding backward, toward the door, away from him. His boots, with their mud-caked soles, were splayed in front of her. Her eyes travelled warily over his still form, not yet trusting. His eyes were open, staring blankly at her. Was he dead? Or was it just another game?

Katie stood on rubbery legs. Was it over? Tears slid down her face. Please let it be over. Unable to take her eyes from him, she reached behind her, felt for the door knob, found it. Spotting the knife on the floor, she hesitated, thinking she should take it to cut Jonathan free. But it was too close to him, nearly touching his leg, and she couldn't bring herself to go closer to pick it up. Even in death, he terrified her.

At last, she opened the door and slipped outside. Holding tightly to the handrail for support, Katie started down the stairs. She was no longer able to run, barely able to walk — but she was free. The monster was dead. Her tears came faster now, mingling with the perspiration that bathed her face, becoming quickly chilled in the cold air.

'Jonathan,' she whimpered. 'Jonathan.'

Just as she stepped off the bottom step, a hand closed around the back of her neck.

27

Half-carrying, half-dragging Katie toward the tall, shadowy trees, his voice shook with rage and pain. 'You've ruined everything. You've ruined the plan.'

She'd hurt him, she knew. But he hadn't struck his head as she'd first thought. Perhaps a knee or an elbow, but not hard enough. Never hard enough. She was going to die, after all.

She saw with a wave of fresh terror that they were at the edge of the grave. There was no hint of playfulness in Drake now, and without a moment's warning, he gave her a powerful shove that sent her tumbling into the black, murky grave.

Her body struck hard, knocking the wind from her, leaving her momentarily stunned. And then she was sobbing, struggling to get to her feet as the icy dark water bubbled up over her ankles.

She lifted pleading eyes to Drake. 'Please, not like this. Kill me first.'

Above her, his face was that of a crazed animal — eyes wild, his mouth an evil slit in his grinning face — a face devoid of mercy.

She clawed at the wall of moist earth, but it was no use. Again, she begged Drake to let her up, promising to do whatever he wanted, but his expression now reflected disinterest, even boredom. He raised the shovel, and would have brought it viciously down on Katie's hands had she not jerked them out of the way. As she did, she fell to her hands and knees.

Something squiggled against the flat of her palm, and she cried out.

The first mound of earth came down on her. She breathed it, tasted its black sourness. Gagging, she tried again to stand, but it was no use. Another shovelful slamming into the back of her head, knocking her face-down in the foul-smelling water where she crawled about like a frenzied thing, one hand pulling at the hair now plastered against her face.

As more earth fell on top of her, she began to pray — a prayer she had said many times as a child. It came back to her now like an old and trusted friend, to comfort her. 'Now I lay me down to sleep . . . '

The earth rose rapidly, the water fast disappearing, becoming hard mud casts trapping her feet and legs. She raised her eyes to the upturned bowl of sky, to the moon that exploded into fragments of itself through her blurred vision, and knew it was the last of life that she would see . . . 'If I die before I wake . . . ' Words said through trembling lips, faint and desperate, but as she prayed a strange calm began to descend upon her.

Drake Devlin stopped working to lean on his shovel. He looked down at her. Fight bitch! Fight to your last damn breath. Can you see, Raynes? Can you see what I'm doing to your sweet, precious Katie?

His work took on a more fevered pace.

★ ★ ★

Wood clattered to the floor as Jonathan, fingers outstretched behind him as far as they would go, felt along the pile for an axe. His hands and feet still bound, he'd managed to stand by backing against a wall and sliding up it. Then he'd hopped to the woodpile, driven by this new inspiration. There had to be an axe, didn't there? You had to have an axe to chop wood. Unless Charlie Black brought his own axe with him, a favorite axe.

Jonathan's arms ached with the strain, and he was forced to relax them. He let himself sag against the woodpile. His breathing was labored, his clothes drenched with perspiration. He had to think. Not panic again. After he'd dropped the glass, and then the smaller fragment had crushed between his fingers, he'd lost control completely, and it was only by telling himself over and over that Drake Devlin wouldn't overtake Katherine easily, that she was a fighter, that he'd finally managed to calm himself. And her screams, however much they tore at his mind and soul, meant that she was still alive.

He'd listened to their footsteps overhead, and to the sounds of scuffling that seemed to go on and on until he thought he would go out of his mind.

That last time he'd heard her scream, she'd been outside the house and not terribly far from him. But that was at least ten minutes ago. There'd been nothing since.

Battling the terror that was in him, that threatened to overpower him and bring him down, Jonathan thought for the hundredth time: there has to be something in this cellar, something I can cut these ropes with. But it was too dark to see. It came to him suddenly that when Devlin took Katherine away, he hadn't remembered to bar the door after him. He could be wrong about that, of course; it wasn't the most rational moment he'd ever known, but he was pretty sure he hadn't heard the bar thud into place.

Would Devlin be so careless? Why not, if

he didn't expect him to regain consciousness.

Guided by the meager light from the window, Jonathan hopped across the floor toward the door. Once there, he nudged it as hard as he could with his shoulder, nearly stumbling and falling headlong on the ground as it swung easily open.

Off to his right, a point of light quivered among the trees. He could see Drake in silhouette. He could see the rise and fall of the shovel in his hand — and his heart lurched painfully. Hysteria gripped him momentarily, and he nearly screamed out at Devlin. Easy, Shea, he told himself. Easy.

Back in the cellar, he scanned the now faintly visible objects.

In the corner by the window, a mop, with little left of it but the handle, stood uselessly. Beneath the mop were several cans of paint, a galvanized pail, a broken window frame. Further on, a folded lawn chair, its flowered fabric torn and hanging, stood against the wall. Nothing of any use.

His frustration mounted, but he tried to ignore it, tried not to think of what was going on outside, as he continued to search among the objects for something sharp with which to cut himself free. And then he found himself studying the sawhorse in front of him, remembering idly that it was where Devlin had set the lamp. He stared at the sawhorse for several seconds, then thought, and wondered why the thought was so long in coming, that if there was a sawhorse, maybe . . . he raised his eyes intuitively, almost afraid to hope.

But there it was. A partly rusted hand-saw hanging from a spike in the wall.

Triumph soared in him, to be replaced in the very next instant by a feeling of near despair. For the saw was far beyond his reach. And then the answer came to him. Alternating between a hop and a shuffle, Jonathan moved along the wall, past the window, toward where the mop stood in the corner, not quite so useless now. Not useless at all.

★ ★ ★

Only her shoulders and head were free now; she could not feel her arms or legs. A few more lifts of the shovel and it would be all over. She remembered hearing somewhere that people buried alive took a long time to die, and when exhumed, were found in tortured positions, faces contorted in agony, dirt caked beneath fingernails, fingers bent into claws.

The thought broke through the calm her prayers had brought, and she cried out — unaware that she had made no sound.

Why did unconsciousness evade her now when she so begged for it? What great knowledge was to be gained that she must experience these final moments without some blessed anesthetic to ease the horror — the pain of a death of suffocation?

Her eyes shut instinctively against a sudden, glaring light.

'Katherine!'

Someone calling her name — an anguished sound. Jonathan? No, not Jonathan. The voice must be inside her head, a miracle she'd conjured up when all else had failed. She supposed she was quite mad by now, hoping where there was no hope, praying when there was no one to listen.

She felt gentle hands pushing the wet, filthy hair from her face. As if in a dream, she saw him.

'Jonathan,' she whispered. And then, as though his face were being swept backward through a long, dark tunnel, it drifted from her, and there was only darkness.

When she came to, she was in Jonathan's arms. Her confused gaze travelled to Drake who was lying on the ground, his arms pinned beneath him. Blood trickled darkly from the corner of his mouth. His pale eyes locked onto hers.

She stiffened, whimpered like a child.

'It's all right, honey,' Jonathan said, his own voice breaking on a sob. 'It's all right now. He can't hurt you anymore. Where he's going, he won't be hurting anyone for a long, long time.'

But she barely heard his words of reassurance as she watched Drake's lips curl into a slow, icy smile.

28

After treating her for superficial wounds, bruises, and a mild case of hyperthermia, the hospital kept her under observation for twenty-four hours, then released her in Jonathan's care. He'd put her directly to bed, dressing her in the now familiar pajamas, and she fell back to sleep at once, sleeping (she calculated by the clock on his bedside table) twelve hours straight.

With a little moan, she turned on her side. The sun coming through the window lay a bronze path across the polished wood floor.

'Damn, you look good, Katherine Summers.'

She turned to see Jonathan standing in the doorway, tall and lean and sexy in faded jeans and a white tee-shirt, and despite everything, felt a stirring of her blood. Some things are worth opening your eyes for, she thought lustily, and felt a welling up of gratitude for the life she came so very close to losing.

As he came nearer, she could see the lines surrounding his eyes, the deep creases tracking his hollowed cheeks, evidence of the nightmare they'd both come through.

'Did you know,' he said, 'that in a certain angle of sunlight, your hair is the color of spun gold?'

'Do I detect a bit of the old Irish blarney spillin' from me darlin's lips?' she teased. 'And if I do, could I be hearin' a dash more, just to get the old blood circulatin'?'

He grinned, the lines and creases seeming to vanish magically from his face. 'My, you do have remarkable recuperative powers.'

'Like you said, it's over. Besides, I've always thought of myself as fairly resilient.'

He lifted her hand from the blanket, kissed her palm. 'Yes, you are that, to say the very least, and I thank God for it.' He sat down on the side of the bed. The mattress sagged a little with his weight. 'And how does me darlin' like her eggs?'

'In the refrigerator in their shells.'

'Cute.'

'But the coffee smells wonderful.'

'You've got it.'

How could she have been so taken in? she wondered. Drake had never attended university as he'd told her, nor did he work on his father's farm. Oh, he'd worked on a farm, all right, but as a hired hand for a woman named Rose Nickerson over in Deacon's Hill, about thirty miles or so out of Belleville. Just as he'd lied to

Katie about being a lawyer, he'd told Mrs. Nickerson he was a struggling writer. When she began to suspect some darker side of Drake she became uncomfortable and asked him to leave. She was, of course, still terribly traumatized at finding her decapitated pet in the mailbox, but Katie couldn't help thinking, as tragically horrible as that must have been, the woman was very lucky to have escaped with her own life.

'He was such a good actor,' Katie said to Jonathan, who had returned with their coffee and was slipping into bed beside her, a pleasant ritual begun and one they would enjoy for many years to come.

'Killers often are. Do you remember my telling you I saw something in Devlin's eyes that triggered an immediate negative response in me?'

'Yes. You said it was the reason you phoned Captain Peterson right after I fell asleep — with a little help from your specially brewed tea.'

He grinned, then his face grew serious again. 'Well, now that I think about it, it was more a lack of something. Several years ago,' he said, 'a young man was sent to me for analysis. A good-looking kid, blond, blue-eyed — he might have been a choir boy.

'He'd just murdered his entire family,

including a three year old sister asleep upstairs in her crib. Just walked into the house one afternoon, and killed them all with a shotgun.'

'My God!'

Jonathan set his coffee on the bedside table, made a careful pyramid of his fingers. When he spoke again, his voice was very soft. 'He was absolutely — normal looking. In every way — save one. Nothing you could pin a name to, not merely cold or empty, nothing so obvious. But deep down in those eyes, where you should glimpse something of a man's humanity, of his soul — there was a void.'

Katie saw that slow, evil smile again as Drake lay on the ground looking up at her, and shivered inwardly. 'Let's not talk about it anymore, okay?' she said, setting her cup with Jonathan's on the table. She wanted him to hold her, to chase back the chill that had begun to creep back into her bones. The trees looked so beautiful outside the window, the sun so bright. Surely a good omen of the days ahead of them.

He held her tightly against him, drawing away for a moment to cup her chin in his hand. 'You're good for me. You know that?'

'Of course I do,' she said, eager to bring

401

back the lightness she'd felt upon waking. 'I'll be so damned good you won't be able to stand it.'

She was rewarded with a soft laugh. 'I'll try to bear up.'

Cuddled against him, she caressed the warm, smooth planes of his back beneath the tee-shirt, once more revelling in the clean, male scent of him, the taste. She would never be able to get enough. They kissed, a long and tender kiss that gradually grew more passionate, more demanding as her mouth moved hungrily under his.

He was undoing the buttons of her pajama top, parting the fabric as though he were unveiling a precious painting. 'Katherine, you're beautiful,' he murmured, his head moving downward, his lips tracing the softness of her breasts. He whispered to her, sweet, maddening words as his fingers worked at the string of her pajama bottoms.

And then she heard him mutter, 'What kind of a damned knot did I put in these, anyway?'

And they both laughed like children.

Epilogue

Two hundred miles from Stoneybrook, inside the grey walls of Wellington Mental Institution, a man and a woman sat across from one another, a large, cluttered desk between them, speaking softly, faces solemn, thoughtful.

'Then you have absolutely no reservations at all, Laura, about setting the patient free?' The man who spoke was Dr. David Thurston, Chief of Psychiatry at the institution, a tall, bony man with thinning hair. He had intelligent blue eyes and a soft, almost hypnotic way of speaking. He tapped his long fingers lightly on the desk top.

'Absolutely none at all, David,' Dr. Laura Rankin said, laying a hand gently, almost protectively, on the thick file in front of her. The name on the file said DEVLIN, DRAKE EDWARD. She'd been his therapist since he arrived at Wellington.

Dr. Rankin was an attractive woman with silver-blonde hair coiled around her head. She wore a pin-striped suit, and a white, simply styled blouse. Her only adornment was an expensive sapphire ring on the third finger of her left hand.

She picked up the file. 'If you'd studied this as carefully as I have, you'd see that Drake Devlin is really guilty of little more than harassment, about which he has no recollection. David, he passed every test we have. Yes, I do think he's ready to make his way again in the outside world.'

'What about the man who drowned?'

'Jason Belding. I see you did read the file.'

'Yes,' he said with a hint of impatience. 'I also read the papers.'

'I'm sorry.' Her eyes on him were respectful, without taking anything away from herself. 'There was no concrete evidence Drake had anything to do with the drowning. He denies it adamantly, and I believe him.'

'An accident, then.'

'I'm sure of it.'

'What about his plot to murder Dr. Jonathan Shea and his fiancee. Have you forgotten about that, Laura? We can't discount that,' he said calmly.

'No, and I don't. But he's been here five years now. Surely, his debt to society is paid.' She leaned forward in the chair. 'He came back from the war under tremendous stress. He should have had treatment then. Drake Devlin is as much a victim as anyone.'

Dr. Thurston took the file from her hand, scanned the pages. He sighed. 'He's supposed to have shot one of his own men.'

'Guilt, David. He took the responsibility for his friend's death upon his own shoulders. You know how common that sort of transference of blame is. Especially when you consider that Drake Devlin was the sole survivor of his company.'

Sun slanted through the long, narrow window behind Dr. Thurston's chair and lay a path across the wine-colored carpet. Outside, Laura could see some of the patients walking about in the yard — shuffling, moving aimlessly, like zombies. Grey, bowed men. She took a cigarette from her pack, lit it, and dragged deeply, her eyes narrowing against the curling ribbon of smoke. Drake Devlin didn't belong here; he wasn't one of the lost souls.

'Dr. Shea thinks there is no cure for Drake Devlin's problem,' Dr. Thurston said. 'He believes the man is evil.'

Laura suppressed a smile. 'Well, I'm well aware of Dr. Shea's reputation as a noted psychiatrist, of course, but surely, David, you can see that its quite unreasonable to expect him to be objective in this case. As I said, I don't deny that he and his wife were victimized by my patient, but Drake is better now. As sane as you or I. And evil, David? Not a terribly scientific diagnosis, wouldn't you agree?'

Dr. David Thurston stood up then, his long frame seeming to unfold. 'Well, we'll see. There's a meeting of the board in . . . ' He glanced at his watch. ' . . . in five minutes.'

★ ★ ★

One hour later, the young woman behind the ticket counter of Wellington Bus Terminal looked up from the stubs she was sorting.

'May I help you?' she said to the sandy-haired man whose smattering of freckles seemed to leap out from the paleness of his skin. Evelyn Rider fancied herself skilled at guessing other people's jobs, and figured this one for a bookkeeper. He obviously spent a lot of time indoors. Not bad looking, though.

He fingered the tiny square of yellowing newspaper in his pocket. A daughter. They'd called her Joanna.

He smiled. A slow smile that did not reach his eyes. 'I'd like a ticket to Belleville, please,' he said.

THE WORLD AT NIGHT

Alan Furst

Jean Casson, a well-dressed, well-bred Parisian film producer, spends his days in the finest cafes and bistros, his evenings at elegant dinner parties and nights in the apartments of numerous women friends — until his agreeable lifestyle is changed for ever by the German invasion. As he struggles to put his world back together and to come to terms with the uncomfortable realities of life under German occupation, he becomes caught up — reluctantly — in the early activities of what was to become the French Resistance, and is faced with the first of many impossible choices.